I'LL
NEVER GET
OUT OF
THIS WORLD
ALIVE

Also by Steve Earle

Doghouse Roses

Allan,

I'LL
NEVER GET
OUT OF
THIS WORLD
ALIVE

Steve Earle

[signature]

Harvill Secker
LONDON

Published by Harvill Secker 2011

2 4 6 8 10 9 7 5 3

First published in Great Britain in 2011 by
HARVILL SECKER
Random House
20 Vauxhall Bridge Road
London SW1V 2SA

www.randomhouse.co.uk

Addresses for companies within The Random House Group Limited can be
found at: www.randomhouse.co.uk/offices.htm

The Random House Group Limited Reg. No. 954009

A CIP catalogue record for this book is available from the British Library

ISBN 9781846555084

The Random House Group Limited supports The Forest Stewardship
Council (FSC®), the leading international forest certification organisation.
Our books carrying the FSC label are printed on FSC® certified paper.
FSC is the only forest certification scheme endorsed by the leading environmental
organisations, including Greenpeace. Our paper procurement policy can be found at
www.randomhouse.co.uk/environment

Printed and bound in Great Britain by
Clays Ltd, St Ives PLC

In memory of my father, Jack Dublin Earle

I'LL
NEVER GET
OUT OF
THIS WORLD
ALIVE

I

Doc woke up sick, every cell in his body screaming for morphine — head pounding — eyes, nose, and throat burning. His back and legs ached deep down inside and when he tried to sit up he immediately doubled over, racked with abdominal cramps. He barely managed to make it to the toilet down the hall before his guts turned inside out.

Just like every day. Day in, day out. No pardon, no parole. Until he got a shot of dope in him, it wasn't going to get any better. Doc knew well that the physical withdrawal symptoms were nothing compared with the deeper demons, the mind-numbing fear and heart-crushing despair that awaited him if he didn't get his ass moving and out on the street. The worst part was that three quarters of a mile of semi-molten asphalt and humiliation lay between him and his first fix, and every inch would be an insistent reminder of just how far he had fallen in the last ten years.

In the old days, back in Bossier City, all Doc had to do was sit up and swing his needle-ravaged legs over the edge of the bed and his wake-up shot was always right there on the nightstand, loaded up and ready to go.

Well, almost always. Sometimes he would wake in the middle of the night swearing that someone was calling his name. When morning came he was never sure that it wasn't a dream until he reached for his rig and found it was empty. Even then, he had only to make his way to the medication cabinet in his office downstairs to get what he needed – pure, sterile morphine sulfate measured out in precise doses in row after tidy row of little glass bottles. And he was a physician, after all, and there was always more where that came from.

"But that was then," sighed Doc. The sad truth was that, these days, he had to hustle like any other hophead on the street, trading his services for milk-sugar– and quinine-contaminated heroin that may very well have made its way across the border up somebody's ass.

San Antonio, Texas, was less than a day's drive from New Orleans but Doc had come there via the long, hard route, slipping and sliding downhill every inch of the way. Consequences of his own lack of discretion and intemperance had driven him from his rightful place in Crescent City society before his thirtieth birthday. In one desperate attempt after another to escape his not-so-distant past he had completed a circuit of the Gulf Coast in a little over a decade, taking in the seamier sides of Mobile, Gulfport, and Baton Rouge. But when he landed in Bossier City, Shreveport's black-sheep sister across the Red River, he reckoned that he had finally hit bottom.

But he was wrong.

The South Presa Strip on the south side of San Antonio was a shadow world, even in broad daylight. Squares drove up and down it every day, never noticing this transaction taking place in that doorway or even wondering what the girls down on the corner were up to. The pimps and the pushers were just as invisible to the solid citizens of San Antonio as the undercover cops who parked in the side streets and alleyways and watched it all come down more or less the same way, day after day, were.

Doc stepped out into the street. The block and a half between the Yellow Rose Guest Home and the nearest shot of dope was an obstacle course, and every step was excruciating; nothing but paper-thin shoe leather separating broken pavement and raw nerve. The sun seemed to focus on the point on the back of his neck that was unprotected by the narrow brim of his Panama hat and burn through his brain to the roof of his mouth. He spat every few feet but could not expel the taste of decay as he ran the gauntlet of junkies and working girls out early or up all night and every bit as sick as he was.

There was a rumor on the street that Doc had a quantity of good pharmaceutical dope secreted away somewhere in the dilapidated boarding house. The other residents had torn the place apart several times, even prying up the floorboards, and found nothing. Of course, that didn't stop some of the more gullible among the girls from trying to charm the location out of him from time to time.

Doc never emphatically denied the stories, especially when he was lonely.

He turned left at the liquor store, slipping around to the parking lot in back where Big Manny the Dope Man lounged against the fender of his car every morning serving the wake-up trade.

"Manny, my friend, can you carry me until about lunchtime? Just a taste so I can get straight."

Big Manny was his handle, but in fact, *big* was simply too small a word to do the six-foot-five, two-hundred-and-eighty-odd-pound Mexican justice. *Gargantuan* would have been more accurate if anybody on South Presa besides Doc could have pronounced it, but everyone just called Manny Castro Big Manny. Doc shivered in the pusher's immense shadow but Manny was shaking his head before Doc got the first word out.

"I don' know, Doc. You still ain't paid me for yesterday. *¡Me lleva la chingada!* Fuckin' Hugo!" He snatched a small paper sack from beneath the bumper of his car and lateraled it to a rangy youth loitering nearby. *"¡Vamanos!"* Manny coughed, and the kid took off like a shot across the parking lot and vanished over the fence.

The portly plainclothes cop never broke his stride, barely acknowledging the runner and producing no ID or warrant as he crossed the lot in a more or less direct line to where Manny, Doc, and a handful of loiterers were already turning around and placing their hands on the hood of Manny's car.

Detective Hugo Ackerman rarely hurried even when attempting to catch a fleeing offender. He had worked narcotics for over a decade, and in his experience neither the junkies nor the pushers were going far. He caught up with everybody eventually.

"That's right, gentlemen, you know how the dance goes. Hands flat, legs spread. Anybody got any needles or knives, best you tell me now!"

He started with Manny, haphazardly frisking him from just below his knees up, about as far as Hugo could comfortably bend over. His three-hundred-pound mass was all the authority he needed to hold even a big man like Manny in place, leaving his chubby hands free to roam at will.

"How's business, Manny. You know, I just come from Junior Trevino's spot. He looked like he was doing pretty good to me."

"Junior!" Manny snorted. *"¡Pendejo!* That shit he sells wouldn't get a fly high, he steps on it so hard! Anybody that gets their dope from Junior's either a *baboso* or they owe me money. Hey! You see Bobby Menchaca down there? I want to talk to that *maricón.*" When Hugo shoved his hand down the back of Manny's slacks, the big man winced.

"Chingada madre, Hugo! Careful down there. My pistol's in the glove box if that's what you're lookin' for. Your envelope's where it always is."

"That's Detective Ackerman to you, asshole!" Hugo continued to grope around, emptying Manny's pockets onto the hood of the Ford and intentionally saving the inside of his sport coat for last and then pocketing the envelope he found there.

"Ain't you heard? Bobby's in the county. Been there since last Saturday. Fell through the roof of an auto-parts store he was breakin' into over on the east side. I guess the doors were in better shape than the roof was 'cause he was still inside jackin' with the latch when the radio car rolled up." He patted the envelope he'd put into the breast pocket of his own sport coat.

"It all here?"

"Every fuckin' dime."

Doc was next.

"How about you, Doc? Got anything for me?"

Doc half grinned. "As a matter of fact, Detective Ackerman, I regret that you catch me temporarily financially embarrassed. You usually don't come around to see me until Sunday so I reckoned I had a day or two. Fact is I'm flat broke. Hell, I haven't even had my wake-up yet."

"He ain't lyin', Detective." Manny intervened. "I was just getting ready to send his broke ass down to Bobby."

"Relax, relax, Doc. Just thought I'd ask while I had you, so to speak. I'll see you Sunday, but damn, Manny! That's cold! I reckoned Doc's credit was better than that around here!" He patted Doc on the butt and turned and ambled back toward the street. "All right, then." Halfway there, he turned around.

"Was that the Reyes kid? The one that took off with the pack?" Manny shrugged. "Maybe."

"Well, I'd count it twice when it comes back. He was showin' tracks the last time I rousted him."

"Yeah, right," Manny muttered, but he made a mental note to check the kid's arms when he got back. He and the others replaced their effects in their pockets, and as soon as Hugo was out of sight Manny stuck two fingers in his mouth and whistled loud enough that there could be no doubt that the runner would hear him.

"*Pinche* Hugo! *¡Cabrón!*" Manny grumbled. "He leaves me alone 'cause I pay him but then he sits across the street in an unmarked car and picks off half my customers when they leave the spot. That shit's bad for business!" He spat on the ground and threw in an extra *¡cabrón!* for good measure.

"Yeah," Doc agreed. "The fat son of a bitch takes a fair bite out of my ass every week as well, not to mention the odd course of penicillin on the cuff. Then again, I guess he needs to make it look good . . . Hey, speakin' of on the cuff, Manny, I know I owe you but . . ."

At that moment the kid rounded the corner, huffing and puffing, and handed off the pack. Manny didn't even look inside before grabbing the kid by the wrist and peeling his shirtsleeve back, up above his elbow, to reveal that Hugo hadn't been lying. "*¡Maricón!*" he snarled as he backhanded the kid across the face with such ferocity that blood spurted instantly from both his nose and his mouth and he tumbled backward in an awkward somersault. He skidded on the seat of his pants but he hadn't even come to a full stop before he was up and gone.

"Don't come back, Ramón!" Manny shouted after him. "And I'm gonna tell your mama!" He turned back to Doc, shaking his head. "I told you, Doc. I can't carry every junkie on the south side that comes up short . . ."

"Oh, ferchrissake, Manny. Tell me, have I ever let you down? When did I ever fail to pay a debt, to you or anybody you know! I can't work in this condition. Besides, amigo, I wasn't worryin' about money when I was diggin' that twenty-two slug out of your ass last year, now was I?"

"Oh, so that's how it is, huh, Doc? All right, then. See how you do . . ."

The bickering continued until the ritual was completed with an unintelligible grunt and a secret handshake, Manny pressing the little red balloon into the palm of Doc's hand. Manny had known he was good for it all along. All the hemming and hawing was just for show, an oft-repeated performance for the benefit of any deadbeats standing within earshot. A businessman had his reputation to consider, after all.

The hardest part of the whole ordeal was the long haul back up the block, retracing the same steps on even heavier, shakier legs. He never carried his wake-up shot back to the boarding house in his pocket or his hatband anymore. Instead, he cupped the dope in the hollow of a clenched fist as if it were some magical winged creature that would vanish into thin air if allowed to escape. He could feel the balloon against his sweaty palm and sometimes he swore that he could taste the dope inside. By the time he got back to his room and cooked it up he had to fight back a wave of nausea, a Pavlovian response to the smell of sulfur and heated morphine. Tie the tourniquet, find the vein, pull the trigger . . .

Burnt sugar on the back of the tongue, tingling scalp, aches and pains evaporate, leaving only a whisper behind:
  "Say, hey there, Doc, my old back's actin' up somethin' awful . . ."

"Not now, Hank," Doc said out loud and the sound of his own voice was all that was needed to weigh him back down to earth and the business at hand.

Oh, well. It was only a taste to get him straight enough to work. The beer joint was dark, if not cool, inside, and this time of day it was quiet because only the most hard-core alcoholics came in this early and they never wasted their money on the jukebox or the pool table in the back. Doc ordered a draft, and Teresa, the barmaid, dutifully drew it and took his money, though they both knew good and well he couldn't choke it down on a bet, at least not until he got a little more dope in his system. The two bits was more like a rental fee on the little table in the back of the joint where everybody on South Presa knew Doc could be found every day between eleven and five.

Business had been slow lately and there were days that Doc resorted to petty theft and short-change scams to support his habit, vocations that he considered beneath him and that he was never very good at. By noon that day he was beginning to get more than a little discouraged. No one had so much as looked in his direction all morning long and it was only Tuesday; the week ahead loomed like a long, dark tunnel. Then the screen door creaked open, announcing a new arrival, a stranger, and things started looking up.

The tough-looking *pachuco* clicked and clacked noisily across the room, the metal taps on his brilliantly polished tangerine shoes announcing that he was a big man in his barrio and not afraid of anyone in this one. A sad-eyed young girl followed a few tentative steps behind. He ordered a bottle of Falstaff, and when Teresa reached for the dollar bill he laid on the bar, he covered it with a cross-tattooed hand and leaned over to whisper in her ear. She nodded in Doc's direction, and the youth clattered across the room to stand threateningly over Doc, a dark little cloud ringed in fluorescent light. The girl waited by the bar.

"This girl" — the boy motioned behind him with a cock of his head — "is in trouble."

Up close the *chico* didn't look so tough. All the hair grease and attitude couldn't hide the fact that he was just a kid, at most nineteen or twenty. Doc gripped the edge of the table to steady himself and leaned sideways to peer around him at the girl, who was even younger.

"You the daddy?"

The boy only stared coldly back.

"Well, Slick, where I come from a gentleman never leaves a lady who's in the family way standing around on a hard concrete floor." Doc waved at the girl. "Honey, why don't you come on over here and take a load off your feet?"

The kid's fierce features instantly darkened but he still said nothing, and the girl didn't move.

"Okay, Slick, it's up to you. But if you want me to help you, then I need to ask your gal some questions, or maybe you can tell me what I need to know. When did she have her last menstrual period?"

That did it. The boy motioned the girl over to the table. Doc pulled out a chair for her and began talking directly to the girl in low, reassuring tones, though he knew she couldn't understand

9

a word. He eyeballed the boy, who grudgingly interpreted the girl's obvious terror into impatient, condescending English. A big tear that suddenly escaped her eye, trailing down one cheek, confirmed Doc's suspicions that his bedside manner was being lost in the translation.

Doc stood up, and the boy suddenly shrank beside him as Doc threw a surprisingly strong arm around him and escorted him toward the door.

"Tell you what, Slick. First things first. If you cross the street out here you'll be standin' right in front of a liquor store. Walk on around to the parking lot in the back, where you will be immediately set upon by jackals — son, I'm talkin' dope fiends of the lowest order — who will insist on trying to sell you inferior narcotics at exorbitant prices."

"*Chiva?* I don't fuck with that shit, man."

"Of course you don't, son. Of course you don't. It's obvious that you're a pillar of the community. The dope's for me. Listen. You walk right past those charlatans to the back of the lot, where you'll find a black 1950-model Ford occupied by a heavyset gentleman that answers to the name of Manny. Give the man twenty dollars and tell him that Doc sent you. Bring what he gives you straight back here to me."

"Twenty bucks? You must be crazy, *cabrón.* My friend told me you were a *médico,* not a *pinche* junkie."

"I was a physician, once upon a time, but if I were still licensed to practice I would not be sitting here in this, uh, establishment engaged in this tedious conversation. The service that you and your lady friend here require is highly illegal and very expensive. Your friend no doubt informed you what my fee would be."

"He said a hundred and fifty. I paid him fifty up front."

"Your friend is a very enterprising young man. The price is a hundred. Twenty, in cash, to the gentleman across the street and the remainder to me *before* I perform the procedure. You'll have to take up the matter of your friend's commission with him personally. Now run along, son. I'll take good care of her until you get back."

He motioned to the barmaid to come over.

"Teresa, will you help me out, hon? My Spanish leaves a lot to be desired."

The boy stood there seething for a moment, his hand straying to the small-caliber pistol tucked into the waistband of his pants, but then he thought better of it. He was alone there, far from the west side, with no one to back him, so he resigned himself, turned, and slunk out the door. By the time the kid returned from his errand Doc had learned all he needed to know from the girl but he was getting sick again so he held out his hand for the dope and excused himself.

"Boarding house just up the street there. One hour from now and bring the rest of the money.

"Now we're cooking with gas!" Doc rubbed his hands together and none of the regular customers even looked up from their beers as he muttered through his preprocedure checklist on his way to the door.

He made one stop, at the liquor store across the street for a fifth of pure grain alcohol. Most of the liquor store's patrons actually drank the stuff, but Doc bought it only for its antiseptic properties; the owner was an occasional patient, so Doc's credit was good. He was reasonably sure that he had everything else he needed on hand in his room.

Doc couldn't help feeling bad for the girl. The people that Doc usually treated were like him, outcasts of various persuasions, marginalized largely through actions and choices of their own.

Granted, almost none of them came from as privileged a background as Doc's, but Doc knew that poverty alone could never account for the complete lack of compassion for one's fellow man in evidence on any South Presa Saturday night. They lied and they cheated and they turned one another in to the police. They cut and they shot and they pounded their neighbors' faces into bloody pulp and strangled their own best drinking buddies with their bare hands, but Doc tried not to judge. Being in the unique position of having lived on both sides of the tracks, he knew first-hand that there was, truly, no more or less honor among patricians than among thieves.

The whores were Doc's most regular patrons. For the most part he treated them for infections of their "moneymakers," which were invariably remedied by large intramuscular doses of black-market penicillin. Over Doc's halfhearted objections, most girls were back at work in less than a week, but he always recited his litany of dos and don'ts for the working girl anyway, if only to make himself feel better.

By far the most debilitating of all the hazards of the world's oldest profession was pregnancy. The girls were all junkies. Most supported their own habits as well as their boyfriends' and could ill afford an enforced nine-month sabbatical. A few were simply careless and came to Doc for help again and again, and he wondered that they were still able to conceive after so many years of abusing themselves. Nevertheless, he took their money and performed the procedure.

And he'd take the *pachuco*'s money but only after an intense internal dialogue on his way down the street and up the stairs to his room.

Normally Doc had no compunction about performing the procedure that had long been his stock-in-trade and the primary

12

means of supporting his habit, and he wasn't sure why he was having trouble with this one. Maybe it was the girl herself. Doc didn't need more than one look to know she didn't belong there. She was Mexican and obviously only recently arrived on this side of the border and therefore undoubtedly Catholic. She was also not much more than a child. Doc knew that to someone like her, the very idea of terminating a pregnancy had to be at once deeply shameful and utterly terrifying. Doc had performed well over a hundred abortions since setting up shop on the South Presa Strip, but not a single Mexican girl had sought his services until now. They sat out their pregnancies and then, against Doc's advice, went straight back to work, some taking turns caring for one another's children in shifts. It was the gringo girls, the lost daughters of Baptists, Methodists, and Pentecostals, who came to Doc when they were in trouble. After taking into account the complete lack of character exhibited by the father of the Mexican girl's baby, Doc finally succeeded in convincing himself that it was all for the best.

Marge was a big-boned, snuff-dipping, fifty-something red-head who ran the Yellow Rose Guest Home with an iron hand. Doc knew that if Marge's door was closed before dark, then Dallas, the blonde who ostensibly rented the room next to his, was in there with her, so he didn't knock.

Marge had lived in the ground-floor apartment all of her life, having inherited the property and little else when her father died, when she was barely out of her teens. She understood the secret language of every creaking board in the place and she knew all of her tenants by their footfalls, so when she heard Doc mount the staircase, taking the steps two at a time, she hollered through the closed door like a field hand, her usual mode of communication.

"Doc, you all right up there? Anything I can do?"

Doc was already cooking up the dime bag of dope. "Well, if you ain't too busy you could boil some water for me and . . . you hadn't got any more old towels that you were going to get rid of, do you, hon?"

Downstairs, the bedroom door opened and Marge emerged holding her battered terry-cloth robe together with one hand.

"Oh, hell, who's knocked up?"

"Nobody you know. Just a kid. A civilian."

"Civilian? Now wait just a minute, Doc. I don't need no pain-in-the-ass regular citizen down here looking for his slut-of-a-knocked-up-cheerleader daughter!"

"She ain't that kind of civilian, Marge. This one's a Mexican girl. Wetback, fresh up from the interior. Hell, she's just a baby herself. She'll be along directly, her and a sawed-off little west-side punk. Holler before you send them up. And try not to scare the hell out of her, if you don't mind."

Marge got a smile out of that one but she took full advantage of the fact that Doc couldn't see it.

"Scare her? Well, I'm sure I don't know what you mean, Doc."

Dallas emerged from the door behind Marge brushing her long platinum-blond-shot-with-silver hair; it cascaded over one shoulder in a shimmering curtain.

"You know, Marge. Like that little colored gal that Harelip Jimmy brought around. She probably kept runnin' down the river to the Gulf of Mexico you scared her so bad!"

"Well, that's different. She was a nigger and Jimmy should have known better than to bring her up in my house without he gets permission first. Besides, they scare easy when they ain't travelin' in a crowd, niggers do, everybody knows that. Dallas, darlin', if you could put the water on I'll just run out to the laundry room and see about those towels. Scare her! The very goddamn idea!"

Manny had charged the *pachuco* twenty dollars for a dime

bag, that is, ten dollars' worth of dope in a red balloon. The one-hundred-percent markup was his usual premium for selling to someone that he didn't know based on Doc's word alone. A South Presa dime bag was a serious shot of dope. Novices usually split one into two shots and did well not to throw up. Doc had been known to bang as many as three at once, but right now he needed to keep his wits about him. Actually, he'd been operating at a deficit for most of the day and the dime bag felt pretty good; he tasted the taste, the tingle, and, for a fleeting instant, his chin dropped down on his chest.

The voice starts out low like it always does but it isn't soft. Subliminally irritating, like a fine grade of sandpaper.
   "Come on, Doc. Can't you help me out? My back's killin' me!"
   "You're already dead!" Doc barks. "Now leave me alone!"

"Wha's that, Doc?" Marge bellowed.
   But the spell was broken and the voice faded away into a vague ringing in Doc's ears along with any trace of a buzz.

"Nothin'. Nothin' at all. Just thinkin' out loud."
   There was a sharp rap on the screen door downstairs.
   "Hey, Doc! You got company down here!"
   "All right, all right, already! I ain't deaf! Quit your caterwaulin' and send 'em on up!"
   Normally, Doc would have completed his business with the young couple in a little over an hour and sent them on their way with a handful of penicillin capsules, but this time there were problems. The girl bled profusely and it didn't want to stop. It was touch and go for a while but Doc's hands were rock steady as long as he had enough dope in him, and his fingers remem-

bered what to do even though morphine had long shrouded his brain in perpetual mist. Without any conscious deliberation, his focus shifted, allowing him to concentrate on the crisis at hand and to forget about anything and everything that haunted him, be it whispering voices or the discarded remains of the fetus in the washbasin on the dresser.

Without a hospital's facilities at his disposal, Doc had to improvise. A transfusion was obviously out of the question, so it was imperative that he stop the bleeding immediately. He knew better than to expect any helping hand from the girls. Marge couldn't be bothered, and Dallas instantly lost consciousness at the sight of blood. He scrambled to rip narrow strips from the sheets, dropping them into the boiling water in hopes of killing any organism that had taken up residence there, and, when they cooled a little, he packed the birth canal full of the makeshift bandages and applied constant pressure with the heel of his hand until the bleeding finally stopped.

The girl had lost a lot of blood and couldn't be moved and so far the boy had only been underfoot, so Doc sent him home, assuring him that she would be strong enough to go in the morning. Doc noted that the little bastard didn't hesitate for a second, leaving without so much as a nod to the girl. The bleeding came back in fits and starts, and the dressing had to be changed every couple of hours, so for Doc it was a long, anxious afternoon.

But by four o'clock, the bleeding had finally stopped for good and the girl was resting comfortably enough that Doc felt safe asking Dallas to keep an eye on her while he slipped out to Manny's spot to cop.

The afternoon's windfall allowed the purchase of a *quarta* – two and a half grams of dope for fifty dollars – and Doc still had a few bucks left over for a week's rent, some groceries, and a carton of smokes. He looked in on the girl, shot another lick of dope, and by four thirty he was back at his table in the beer joint nursing a beer and chain-smoking Camels in hopes that lightning would strike twice in one day.

The happy-hour crowd began to filter in. Unlike the daytime patrons, these folks were mostly squares who busted their backs all day long building houses that they could never afford to live in or repaving perfectly serviceable roads in neighborhoods way across town. They arrived in groups of three or four, drank a pitcher of beer among them, and maybe shot a game of pool before hurrying home in time for supper. It was always one of them who dropped the first nickel in the jukebox.

The Mexicans usually played records by the local *conjuntos*, like Santiago Jimenez or Trio de San Antonio, or maybe one of the big mariachi bands from Mexico, with blaring trumpets and a singer with a voice to match. Songs about the black-eyed girl they left behind and the beautiful mountains they would never see again.

Fine. Sad songs in a language that he barely understood were easy enough for Doc to tune out. He knew some of the melodies by heart and hummed along when he was in the mood.

But when one of the redneck boys lurched toward the box, fishing in his Wranglers for a nickel, the hair stood up on the back of Doc's neck. He knew it was only a matter of time before one of these peckerwoods bellied up to the Wurlitzer and punched in N26.

Now you're lookin' at a man that's gettin' kinda mad
I've had a lot of luck but it's all been bad.

17

"Fuck me," Doc grumbled under his breath. He'd spent a lot of his life in bars all over the South, and it never fucking failed. If you sat there long enough, some asshole would play a Hank Williams record. Ol' Hank dead and buried beneath six feet of rusty red Alabama dirt for the better part of a decade now, still taking their nickels and making them cry. Doc looked around the room. There were construction workers, warehouse hands, soldiers from Fort Sam, and layabouts on disability. They ranged in age from their early twenties to seventy-something but they all loved Hank. They loved him when he was alive and now that he was dead they loved him even more. Even the Mexicans loved the son of a bitch, even though most of them couldn't understand what he was singing about. Hank's songs were their very own trials and tribulations set to a rock-steady beat that they could dance to. Each and every one believed that Ol' Hank was singing to him individually, or at least exclusively to people like him. Regular folks with kids to raise and bills to pay, most of them overdue. They had no way of knowing that at this very moment somewhere across town, in solid, old-money Victorian houses in Olmos Park and Alamo Heights, doctors, lawyers, and politicians were mixing themselves highballs and cranking up Hank on their hi-fis. Oh, they had plenty of Frank Sinatra and Nat King Cole records on their automatic changers, but when they were drinking, only Hank would do, and there wasn't one of them who would pay a dime to hear any other hillbilly singer in the world.

Doc didn't wonder why they all insisted on doing this to themselves. He knew what was getting ready to happen. When one of Hank's records dropped into place on an automated turntable, even the initial rumble of the needle in the well-worn grooves sounded lonesome. The crying steel guitar was the bait but it was

18

the beat that set the hook, and by the time Hank's voice crackled from the speaker it was too late. There was no escaping now.

No matter how I struggle and strive
I'll never get out of this world alive.

Jesus Christ! That voice. That gut-wrenching, heart-rending wail that got down in your bones like a cold wet day. The keening of a hillbilly banshee, heralding imminent doom.

"That's enough, goddamn it!" Doc shouted out loud – but only a handful of patrons paid any attention and none of the regulars even looked up from their beers. They'd all witnessed outbursts from "that crazy old man who sits at the table in the back of the joint," but they could never make heads or tails of what he was going on about. "He just does that," they'd whisper. "He talks to himself sometimes."

Doc pried his fingers loose from the edge of the table and propelled himself through the door and out into the street.

It was hot and dark and quiet. The streetlights cast elongated shadows on the empty street, out-of-kilter trapezoidal ghosts of simple one- and two-story structures that had housed respectable businesses. The pawnshop was a barbershop once, a place where people gathered to trade neighborhood gossip and tell tall tales. The abandoned building across the street was a family-owned hardware store, bins filled with shiny new fasteners and fittings of every description: wing nuts and carriage bolts and ten-penny nails.

But, like Doc, the buildings were derelict. Has-beens; shadows of their former selves waiting around for time to take its slow but steady toll.

• • •

The familiar fall of faltering footsteps follows behind him. The shuffling echo ceases abruptly each time Doc breaks his stride, but he knows from experience that if he turns around he'll see only his own shadow stretching from sidewalk to sidewalk like a black chasm opening in the middle of the street. So he just keeps on walking and the ghost follows him all the way home.

The Mexican girl was still sleeping soundly so Doc excused Dallas; he sprinkled a good lick of dope on a Juicy Fruit wrapper, which she accepted gratefully before hurrying away. He had intended the *quarta* to last for a while. At least a couple of days. It would have been like taking a little vacation, a rare reprieve from the daily grind. Just sit up, reach for his outfit, and get straight without having to leave his room, just like the old days. Maybe put a pot of coffee on the hot plate and read the morning paper like a citizen.

Maybe next time. He needed to get high. Mindful not to disturb the girl, he located his outfit by feel, carefully fishing around between the mattress and the box spring for the blue velvet bag. It had once dressed an elegantly shaped bottle of Canadian whiskey. Now it held all Doc's paraphernalia: bent-handled spoon, rubber tourniquet, and gleaming glass-and-stainless-steel syringe.

Most junkies had to settle for homemade contraptions contrived from eyedroppers and rubber bands, but not Doc. His rig was a family heirloom, part of a fine old set of German-made instruments that his grandfather had given his father when he graduated from medical school. Dr. Ebersole the second had kept them unused in a glass case in his office until the proud day they were handed down to Doc. Only the syringe had survived, and at times he'd been tempted to toss it into the nearest trash can, but the truth was that Doc hadn't carried it around all these years for sentimental reasons.

In a half cc of water (the capacity of the average rig on the street), three bags of Mexican brown cooked down to the consistency of a good milk shake. Granddaddy's giant-size German behemoth held three times that amount, so Doc could load up without fear of a clogged needle and a wasted thirty-dollar shot.

Yeah, Doc liked the big shots, the kind that would kill most junkies, the kind that rattled his teeth and made him sweat and drool as he rocked back and forth on the edge of his chair. But he never fell out. He always came back at the last possible instant, blinking and sighing in resignation as he found himself back in his shit-hole room. And the ghost was always there watching him.

"You got to help me, Doc, I'm in pretty rough shape."

Doc always tries to tell himself that it's just the dope talking but that never stops him from talking back.

"I can't do nothin' for you, Hank. I told you. I'm not a doctor anymore."

"Now, Doc," the ghost admonishes in a stage whisper too thin to conceal his contempt, "we both know you weren't no doctor when I first laid eyes on you. Just another snake-oil salesman hangin' around after the show as far I knew. But I took all them potions and powders you was hawkin'. And you took my cash money, make no mistake there. But let's forget all that. That's business. Why, we're old fishin' buddies, you and me!"

Doc opens his eyes and finds the apparition perched on the edge of the spare chair in the corner, narrow shoulders hunched over as if he were racked by pain or cold. Impossibly thin, Hank is, and the straw-colored western-cut suit he's wearing hangs flat and limp on his frame as if there is nothing substantial inside to fill it out, and there's not. His silverbelly Stetson hat casts a diagonal shadow across his face, which is as pale and drawn as it was in life, and his one visible eye is hungry, expectant, one of a pair of frightened-animal eyes frozen in a perpetual, silent scream, and Doc knows better than to allow himself to look in there. He focuses his gaze a little lower and shudders as he realizes that he can easily read the house rules posted on the door through the visitor's transparent torso. There are some things about being haunted that Doc will never get used to.

"The way I remember it, Hank, you called me whenever your back hurt, you or your mama, God rest her, and I came running. Maybe I got a line wet at some point in the process but that was small consolation when it was all said and done!"

"You were always paid for the shots, Doc. In advance. Hell, I've shelled out a small fortune to quacks like you for one remedy or another. Some helped. Some didn't. You said it yourself, Doc, that you never in all your life seen nobody walkin' around with such a bad case of the spinal-whatever-it-was you called that bump on my back."

"Spina bifida, Hank. It's Latin. Means 'divided spine.' And I have no doubt that it hurt like hell when you were alive —"

"That's another thing!" the ghost hisses. "I've been thinkin', Doc. Maybe I ain't dead!"

"Oh, you're dead all right."

"Well, what if you got it wrong? I mean, I'm sittin' here talkin' to you, ain't I? Maybe this is all just a bad dream and any minute now I'm gonna wake up —"

Doc's patience collapses.

"Well, wake the fuck up then, Hank! It's about goddamn time, *being that it's the summer of nineteen-sixty-fucking-three. That's ten years! Ten fucking years and God only knows how many miles and it would appear that you have, indeed, expired somewhere along the way, amigo, seeing as how you've taken to walking through walls and exhibiting all manner of other unnatural fucking behavior. Actually, it is my own personal belief as well as my professional opinion that you are merely a figment of my fucking imagination but that hasn't deterred you from dogging my every step from Louisiana to hell and back to here, now, has it? But you're dead all right, Hank! That is, if you are who you say you are and I must say that if you ain't Hank Williams then you're his spittin' image and one thing I know for certain is that Hank Williams is dead. Deader than the proverbial doornail, don't you know, and if you're him then there ain't no fucking way that you're in any kind of physical pain, not anymore, anyway, and even if you were I'm still not sure I could bring myself to feel sorry for you. Hell, to tell you the truth there are times that I wish I had the luxury of an incurable, chronic infirmity to cry about every time I get a hankering for a shot of dope!"*

The ghost stands up or maybe he simply grows like the afternoon shadow of a ramshackle church spreading across a graveyard until he looms over Doc, wagging a skeletal finger in his face.

"Now, you just hold your horses there, Doc! Maybe I'm dead and maybe I ain't, but one thing for goddamn certain is I ain't no hophead. I never took nothin' that a doctor didn't order. Never give myself a shot neither, and I always took mine in the pants pocket, not straight in the mainline like a goddamn nigger!"

Suddenly conscious of the tourniquet that still encircles his upper arm, Doc unwinds it and puts it away. As he rolls down his sleeve he rests his hand palm-down on one quivering knee, shield-

ing tiny telltale flecks of dried blood from the phantom's view . . .
or maybe not. If Doc can see through Hank, maybe Hank can see
through him as well. He stands up and pulls on his coat.

"How many of those other doctors told you to stop drinking,
Hank?"

"Oh, here we go . . ."

"How many times did I tell you the same goddamn thing? You
weren't listening to them back then. And you're not listening to me
now."

"Okay, so I drink."

"No. Actually, Hank, you don't," Doc parries.

"Maybe, sometimes I drink a lot. It ain't like I got nothin' goin'
on in my life that wouldn't drive a man to drink, Doc."

"You can't drink, Hank. And you've got no life because you're
dead, goddamn it!"

Hank continues to whine. "People buzzin' all around like skee-
ters on a hog!"

Doc sidesteps to the dresser, uncaps the bottle of pure grain alcohol there, pours two fingers into a dusty tumbler, and slams it
down on the table next to Hank.

"Here you go, Hank."

The spirit begins to quiver, or maybe shimmer is a better word.
Doc persists.

"What you waitin' for?"

The ghost recoils into the corner, flattening into two dimen-
sions, twisting and writhing like a ribbon in the wind.

"Go on, Hank, have a goddamn drink!" Doc barks, and he emp-
ties the contents of the glass in the phantasm's face, but both the
alcohol and the ghost instantly vaporize, leaving a sickly-sweet
fume hanging in the air.

. . .

"Asshole." Doc exhaled.

When he opened his eyes the Mexican girl was sitting straight up in bed watching him, wide-eyed but surprisingly calm. He hurriedly scooped up his paraphernalia and hid it away in his coat pocket and then dragged the rickety chair to the side of the bed.

"Shh! There, now," he whispered. "I must have scared you to death."

Up close, her eyes were darker and even sadder.

"Christ, child. How old are you? Sixteen? Seventeen?"

She was eighteen, but her last birthday had passed nearly unobserved while her family crossed the border as cargo in the back of a twelve-foot-box-back truck. Her father had spent his life shuttling back and forth from Mexico in search of a better living than he could hammer out making tin boxes for the tourists in tiny Dolores Hidalgo. She carried only the vaguest memory of him, and it grew dimmer with every day, like a fading photograph. For most of her life the only connections between them were her mother's assurance that he would return one day soon and a pasteboard box containing every gift he had ever brought back from his wanderings in the north: cheap plastic dolls with slightly off-kilter red lips, and games that she couldn't comprehend. The box and its contents were long gone now, culled and jettisoned as nonessential when the family followed him to San Antonio.

Her father had finally found a more or less permanent job with an outfit contracted to build housing on the military bases that encircled the city. He saved enough money to pay the coyote to bring his family north, and then less than a year later he suffered a massive heart attack, collapsed on the job site, and died.

Now her mother and her older sisters had to ride the bus up to the north side to clean rich gringos' houses; she was left at home with the younger children, and her days were long and hot and humid and punctuated by lapses into longing for the cool high-desert nights of her home in Mexico.

She had never met anyone like Armando before. He was a second-generation Tejano, dark and dangerous and sure of himself in this strange land, and she was lonely and homesick and easy prey. She barely remembered giving herself to him in the back seat of his car; he had fed her sloe gin mixed with 7-Up, and the encounter was brief. More vividly she recalled that he'd slapped her so hard that her ears rang for an hour because she threw up on his new black-and-white tuck-and-roll upholstery.

She was sick to her stomach again six weeks later, and again the next morning, and then, for the second month, her period failed to arrive.

She couldn't bear to face her mother. Her mother was a pious woman hardened by misfortune who had assured her children that if they didn't behave, La Llorona would come and carry them away. According to legend, the Weeping Woman was the spirit of a young widow who had drowned her three children in hopes of enhancing her eligibility to marry a rich nobleman. When her horrified suitor turned her away, she threw herself in the river after them. Now she wandered the banks in search of her children's souls. The tale was told so convincingly that there was no doubt in Graciela's mind that her mother believed every word was true.

So Graciela went to Armando, bursting into tears as she told him the news. He only shrugged and allowed that he might know a guy who knew a guy who could take care of her "little problem" and that he would foot the bill on the condition that she keep her mouth shut.

She was heartbroken. Not that she loved Armando, but she had assumed that he would do the right thing like her cousin Rosa's husband had done. Diego and Rosa were never in love but they both worked hard and they had three children now and seemed happy enough.

Armando only laughed and informed her in no uncertain terms that when it came time for him to settle down he would find a good girl from his own barrio, a Tejana who would make him fat flour tortillas like his mama made instead of thin, coarse corn.

Now he had abandoned her here in this awful place with this old gringo, and she knew he would never be back.

She awoke several times during the night to find the gringo there beside her, cooling her with a wet rag or gently lifting her head so that she could sip water from a thick, bone-colored coffee cup. Once she thought for a moment that her mother had found her and forgiven her of her great sin, but then the gringo spoke to her in a soft, low rumble and she was disappointed but she wasn't afraid. There was something oddly familiar about this perfect stranger. An appearance of calmness she'd witnessed before.

Her grandfather had chosen to stay behind in Dolores, where he'd buried his wife and two of his sons. He was kinder and in-finitely more patient than her father and the other men in the prime of their lives that she had known. He wasted no motion but he was by no means feeble and he still gathered firewood to sell every day. He hauled his wares to the market on the back of an ancient burro called El Piedro, whom he drove with constant flicks of a creosote switch. There and back he bypassed the can-tinas and the domino parlor and he was always home before dark bearing the fruits of his labor, a bundle containing an assortment of unrecognizable roots and oddly scented herbs and a stalk of sugar cane for each of his seven grandchildren.

But the girl shared some special connection with the old man and for as long as she could remember she had followed him wherever she could. Her brothers and sisters grew to know that their father's father was a man who commanded no small amount of respect in their barrio. Everyone in Dolores called him Don Tomas, and it was whispered that he was a *curandero*, a healer, and even her mother, who spent half of her life in church and crossed herself when anyone appeared at her door inquiring after the old man, overcame her trepidation when one of her children fell ill.

But Graciela alone had actually witnessed her grandfather's handiwork, breathed in the aroma of the manzanilla and agave leaves steeping in the cauldron, seen the steam rising in waves and fashioning itself into shapes that moved and changed. Perhaps this gringo wasn't talking to himself after all. Perhaps he invoked something older and darker on her behalf. Something akin to the spirits her grandfather sometimes enlisted in his battles against disease and malaise. Was there something cat-shaped there in the corner? Perhaps her new benefactor had summoned it to watch over her while she slept? She only knew that for some reason beyond her understanding she felt safer in the care of a stranger in a forgotten part of a foreign city than in all the time since she'd left Mexico.

She had always admired her grandfather's constancy, which she perceived as the badge of wisdom and strength gleaned from years of experience. To her eye this gringo was cut from the same solid fabric. He moved slowly and deliberately, as if he could make time stand still and had no more pressing business than to watch over her until, little by little, she began to recover her strength.

She had no way of knowing that in their youth, both her grandfather and the gringo were every bit as restless as her father, and that what she mistook for stability was merely resignation.

II

Hank's cold. A sharp, dry kind of cold, deep down where the marrow in his bones used to be, but he doesn't shiver and he doesn't shake. In fact, he hardly notices at all. Hank's been cold for as long as he can remember now, and it's only when some errant echo of human warmth accidentally strays into his colorless domain that he even bothers to give it a name.

It's the girl.

Hank hates the girl. He doesn't know why. For some reason that he doesn't understand it really gets his goat when Doc makes over her the way he does. Watching over her. Waiting on her. Spoon-feeding her like a goddamn baby.

What's so special about this girl anyway? Okay, so she's young and she's not half bad-looking if you like them skinny (and Hank doesn't), but if it's dark meat you hanker after, Hank reckons you might as well go all the way. On top of all that she doesn't understand a single word of American! What's an educated man like Doc want with a woman like that?

Ask Doc, and he'll tell you it's not about that. This girl's like all

*the others. In trouble. Nowhere to turn. That's what Doc does. He
helps them out if they got the money.*

Well, sometimes even when they don't.

*But something's different this time. Hank's been haunting Doc
for a while now, and Doc's never looked at or talked to or touched
anybody the way he does this Mexican girl. Oh, he's always gentle
enough in his manner, if a little gruff in his words now and then,
but with this girl he's downright . . . tender . . . yeah, that's the
word,* tender. *The way you treat a tiny baby or a brand-new lover.*

*If Hank didn't know any better, he'd swear Doc's sweet on the
Mexican girl.*

*And if anybody else in the world besides Doc could hear or see
Hank, they'd swear Hank's jealous.*

*But that's crazy! Just because Hank wants to yank the little
bitch out of the bed by her hair and slap the beans out of her
doesn't make him jealous, because that would make him some
kind of a queer, wouldn't it? Besides, it don't matter anyway because he can't touch her, her or anybody else. Otherwise, he'd send
the dusky little whore running like a scalded dog back to wherever
the hell it was she came from, after he told her a thing or two, that
is, but then there it is again, the fly in the ointment. Only Doc can
hear Hank. And Doc rarely listens. And he never answers except
when he's got him an armful of dope.*

*Why is that? Why Doc? Why not somebody else? There are folks
he was closer to in life, folks he loved, who loved him back even
though loving him wasn't easy sometimes. Surely he has more un-
finished business elsewhere in the world, isn't that what a haunting is all about? But for what seems like an eternity now . . . perish
the thought . . . Hank's followed Doc wherever he traveled. Bossier,
Mobile, Houston, one shit hole after another. Sometimes days or*

even weeks pass by in a new town before Hank's aware he and Doc have moved on.

So, how come they're still hanging around this particular corner of hell? Hank's tried steering Doc by sheer will back east toward Montgomery. That's where Hank's bones are buried; maybe he can rest there. Or what about Nashville, or even Shreveport, someplace Hank has people, old friends and ex-lovers who either love him or hate him, no matter, just as long they don't walk right through him and then shiver like he's nothing but a draft coming up from underneath the door.

But for whatever reason, Doc's in the driver's seat now. And to be sure, he's a strange one, wandering from pillar to post all these years, and of all places to finally settle down, why here? What's so great about this shit-hole room, in this shit-hole town? Hell, what's so great about his whole shit-hole world?

Seems to Hank that Doc'd get tired of all this hustling around from one shot of dope to the next. Like he'd be good and ready for a nice long rest about now. How come Doc's not sick and tired of being sick and tired and lonesome?

Not lonely. Lonesome.

Lonely's a temporary condition, a cloud that blocks out the sun for a spell and then makes the sunshine seem even brighter after it travels along. Like when you're far away from home and you miss the people you love and it seems like you're never going to see them again. But you will, and you do, and then you're not lonely anymore.

Lonesome's a whole other thing. Incurable. Terminal. A hole in your heart you could drive a semi truck through. So big and so deep that no amount of money or whiskey or pussy or dope in the whole goddamn world can fill it up because you dug it yourself

31

and you're digging it still, one lie, one disappointment, one broken promise at a time.

Both Doc and Hank crossed over that line between lonely and lonesome a long time ago. One fateful step, way back up the road. Hank doesn't know where, but he sure enough knows lonesome when he sees it. As a matter of fact, Hank's a goddamn leading authority on lonesome. Just ask anybody in any honky-tonk anywhere in the world. And Hank reckons that Doc's got about the worst case of lonesome that he's ever seen and it's just a matter of time until Doc comes to a bend in the road he can't negotiate and then, alone in the middle of nowhere, he'll surrender to complete and utter despair. And Hank will be waiting.

Then it'll be just like old times. Ol' Hank and Doc, rolling down the highway, going nowhere, but going in style. And then, Hank reckons, it'll be Doc's turn to follow Hank even to the very gates of hell. Or Alabama.

III

"What's your name, child? Uh . . . *¿Cómo se llama usted?*"

For an awful instant Doc was afraid that the girl would laugh out loud at his lousy Spanish, but instead she only smiled and slowly and carefully pronounced her given name.

"Graciela."

"Grass-see-el-uh," Doc ventured, and this time the girl couldn't help but laugh but there wasn't a hint of reproach in her voice and it was impossible for Doc to take offense.

"Hey, tell you what. How 'bout I just call you Grace for short. How'd that be?" He pointed at her and repeated, "Grace."

Without warning her dark eyes smoldered and her lips pressed together in a thin, determined line.

"Uh-oh," said Doc. "That went over like a lead balloon, didn't it? Listen, child, I didn't mean to hurt your feelings. It's just that I've always had kind of a hard time with foreign languages. I mean, even back in medical school I had to take Latin over again three times. Grace is a whole lot easier for me—"

The girl suddenly sat up in bed, one hand gathering the sheet under her chin to keep herself covered. "No!" she complained. "No *Gress!*" She reached out with her free hand to touch Doc's lips with two fingers, gently, with almost no perceptible pressure, stopping Doc in midexcuse.

It was the first time that he realized how beautiful she was, her finely chiseled features more Indian than mestiza, glossy black hair contrasting against her bare shoulders, the color of caramel in the surprisingly flattering light that filtered through the dirty window behind her.

"*Grah-see-ay-lah,*" she intoned.

Even her name was beautiful, strangely musical, like soft rain on a tin roof, and because she was fully aware of just how beautiful it was it became exquisite when she pronounced it herself. It was her name, hers and hers alone. The only one of the many names her mother had given her that she shared with no one else in her family, and she would not stand to hear it profaned.

Doc tried again and then again, each time with better results. Finally he managed a rendition acceptable to Graciela and she settled back into her pillow. Still she lay there, her eyes wide open and expectant, and Doc realized that he had been remiss.

"Oh! Me? *Me llamo* Doc. Call me Doc, child. Everybody else does."

Graciela looked confused, so Doc resorted to the Tarzan-and-Jane routine once again, pointing to Graciela and repeating her name accurately enough to make his own monosyllabic moniker sound hopelessly guttural in comparison when he then indicated himself and croaked, "Doc."

Graciela's first attempts came out more like *Duck,* but after a few tries, she mastered it. Even then there was still a look of puzzlement about her, an unanswered question that began as tiny lines in her forehead and spread quickly to her eyes and then to the corners of her mouth.

"*¿Es todo?*" she queried, and for once, Doc understood her perfectly well. The phrase was one of a handful that came up frequently in various contexts in the course of tense transactions and desperate procedures in the middle of the night.

"*Sí, es todo.*" Yes, that's all.

He was Doc. Just plain Doc. With the exception of a few isolated incidents involving the local constabulary, it was the only name he had answered to in years. Nobody on South Presa knew him by any other name.

Somewhere back in the Orleans Parish courthouse there was a fading piece of bond paper with an official-looking seal attached that said his name was Joseph Alexander Ebersole III and that he'd been born alive at 10:37 on the morning of January 17, 1910. The same name appeared elsewhere in the state archives as Dr. Joseph A. Ebersole, but there was an ugly red stamp across the face of the document declaring that his license to practice medicine in the State of Louisiana had been permanently revoked. He did possess a valid driver's license, for what it was worth, but as far as Doc knew his old Buick was still broken down east of town on the side of the highway. That had happened over two years ago and he'd just walked off and left it behind. He had no legal income, no bank account, and therefore no use for documentation of any kind, and what's more he liked it that way. The fact was that he had been "just plain Doc" for so long now that he no longer identified with that other name previously owned by his father and his grandfather, both of whom had practiced medicine and were at that moment, Doc was certain, simultaneously rolling over in their adjacent marble crypts. And Doc didn't blame them.

So he was Doc now. Not Doctor. Not Dr. Ebersole. Just plain old Doc and that was that.

Graciela, obviously dissatisfied with the exchange but unable to keep her eyes open any longer, finally fell asleep. Doc couldn't blame her for feeling shortchanged but it couldn't be helped. He simply saw no need to squander more than a single syllable on a miserable life such as his own.

Doc spent that night propped up in the corner catching only occasional catnaps. The next morning Dallas produced an old folding cot that had been gathering dust beneath her bed, and Doc accepted it gratefully and set it up against the wall opposite the bed. All that week he left Graciela's side for only an hour each morning to get straight. Dallas kept watch in his stead, over no small amount of grumbling from Marge, who constantly wondered out loud when "that goddamn beaner" was coming back for his girlfriend. By Friday morning even Doc had to admit that it was unlikely that they would ever see Armando again, and as the weekend approached Graciela's continuing convalescence became increasingly problematic.

The moon would be full that night, and Doc's quarters saw a fair amount of traffic whenever the natives were restless. Even if Marge had been disposed to help, the fact remained that every room in the Yellow Rose was currently occupied. All the big corner rooms on the first and second floors were rented to more or less permanent tenants like Doc. At the other end of the range were the "chicken coops": eight windowless cubicles formed by subdividing the attic and accessed by the rumbling steel stairs out back. They were dark and cramped, each not much larger than the twin-size bed that was its only appointment, but the rooms saw a brisk turnover on the weekends at an hourly rate. In between were the smaller rooms, like the one that Marge's special friend Dallas kept for the sake of appearances and to see specialty clients who were more interested in the fulfillment of bizarre fantasies than in the sexual act itself. Marge, more than a little jealous of "the creeps," as she called them, grudgingly agreed that Graciela could stay when Dallas volunteered to take a little time off, which meant that she wouldn't need her room. It was settled then: Doc would see patients in Dallas's room while Graciela recovered in Doc's.

By sunup on Sunday, Doc had performed another abortion procedure, treated a half a dozen cases of gonorrhea, and removed an ice pick embedded deep in the left latissimus dorsi of a truck driver, dangerously close to his spine.

"Another inch to the right, hoss, and you'd have been fucked," Doc assured the patient as he wrapped his torso in tape to ease the collateral pain of at least two broken ribs. The action had reached a crescendo in the wee hours of Saturday: two gunshot victims, both shot with small-caliber Saturday night specials fired at close range and badly aimed.

The two young bucks had evidently squared off in the middle of the dance floor down at the beer joint and emptied their pistols into each other at fewer than ten paces. Only one of the sixteen rounds discharged penetrated any vital area, collapsing the unlucky combatant's left lung. Doc left the bullet where it was, thoracic surgery being a little out of his league, but he did manage to stop the bleeding. Doc kept up an optimistic front for the victim. "That's why you have two lungs, son," he observed, "in case something happens to one." But in the other room, he advised the boy's *compadres* that they needed to get him to a real hospital if he was to survive the infection that would certainly ensue.

All of Doc's nonpregnant patients had good reasons to avoid a visit to the emergency room at Robert B. Green Memorial Hospital and the subsequent obligatory police report. Some were in the country illegally and were simply eager to steer clear of any contact whatsoever with the authorities. Others had been wounded by police or property owners while committing crimes or had outstanding warrants for their arrests. Some sought the anonymity of Doc's practice for more personal reasons.

Old Santo from the pawnshop showed up late on Sunday afternoon with a nasty gash from a carpet knife above his left eye. The assailant was Maria, his wife of forty-five years, who sat by the bed and sobbed during the entire procedure, all the while holding an ice pack to her face to bring down the swelling of an ugly red welt on her left cheek, as Doc stitched up the old man, not for the first time. Then Doc watched, bemused, from the window above as the couple walked down the street arm in arm on their way back home. "It'll be a while before he hits her again," he predicted.

Back in his own room just after sunrise, Doc half collapsed in his chair and lit up a Camel, only his second smoke of the day. Graciela was sleeping soundly. Dallas marked her place in the romance novel she'd been reading and excused herself, but Doc gently caught her wrist as she reached out to open the door and proffered two neatly folded twenty-dollar bills. Tobacco wasn't the only habit of Doc's that had been neglected in all of the rush.

"Dallas, honey, would you mind finding Manny and bringing us back a good piece of dope?"

One bag for Dallas, which she tucked away in her brassiere for later. Three for Doc, which he dumped in the spoon all at once.

Doc was only just able to lay his rig on the table before the rush reached his extremities, and his arms hung limp at his sides.

This was it. The precipice. Doc balanced precariously on the edge of a tiny flat world, one foot on the ground and one poised to step off into the abyss. Nothing to it. Hard-core dope fiends like Doc sought a destination just this side of death every time they got off. But Doc's curse was that it was in that place that Hank's voice grew loudest and clearest.

"She sure is a pretty thing, Doc."

Doc's out of his chair in an instant but it takes him a second or two to bring the ghost into focus. Hank's on the foot of the bed, one bony leg crossed over the other and a spiderlike hand reaching toward Graciela's thigh. Doc lunges on unsteady legs.

"Get away from her, goddamn you to hell! She's just a child, for chrissake!"

Whoosh! Did Hank leap across the bed or simply collapse out of his grasp like smoke and rematerialize on the other side? Doc isn't certain. He rounds the foot of the bed in an attempt to shield Graciela, but the ghost stretches himself like a rubber band, elongating his already impossibly angular frame and leering over Doc's shoulder.

"Yeah, like you wouldn't fuck her."

Still a little wobbly from the dope, Doc drops back down on the edge of the bed, and Graciela stirs but, mercifully, doesn't wake. The ghost shrinks to life-size or perhaps a little smaller and settles in a chair by the door.

"You ain't got nothin' to worry about, Doc. I can't touch her no how. You know that." The ghost takes off his Stetson and hangs his balding, transparent head and sighs. "I just wanted to talk is all. Seems like here lately you been too busy to bother with Ol' Hank."

Doc sighs, checks to make sure that Graciela's still sleeping, and then picks up his chair, lifts and carries it as quietly as he can manage across the room, and sets it down opposite Hank's.

"Okay, Hank. You want to talk? Let's talk. But quietly, and

with a minimum of, uh, theatrics, if that's possible. You're going to wake the whole goddamn house up."

The ghost leans forward and cranes his neck until his face is only inches from Doc's and whispers, his breath cold and vaguely foul, like a deep freeze full of out-of-date meat.

"Them dykes can't hear me neither, Doc. You know that. They just hear you when you holler back at me and they think that you're losin' your mind."

"Who says that I'm not?" Doc shrugs. "Who says I'm even talking to you right now? I mean, at the moment I am high enough to hunt ducks with a rake."

"You don't believe that, Doc." Hank pouts, pivoting noiselessly in his chair and very nearly disappearing altogether as he presents an almost one-dimensional profile, head back with his nose in the air like a wounded schoolgirl.

"What I don't believe," Doc qualifies, feeling a little guilty for hurting Hank's feelings, "is that there's any such thing as ghosts. Hell, Hank, I'm an educated man. A medical doctor."

"Ex-doctor!" Hank challenges. "You said so yourself."

"All right, ex-doctor, but my legal difficulties with the State of Louisiana notwithstanding, I simply don't believe that you exist, and what's more, I never have! If I were ignorant enough to believe that the spirits of the dead walked the earth seeking revenge or whatever, I'd be shaking in my boots about now, and I'm not, and there's the proof right there, Hank. I'm not scared of you and I never have been. Not since the first time I thought I heard you calling my name, back in Louisiana. So either I am crazy, or you're just as pitiful an excuse for a ghost as you were for a human being."

Doc knows immediately that he's gone too far and braces for some sort of paranormal conniption, but instead the ghost stands *up, head bowed, lower lip protruding like a dejected child's, and dissolves through the wall.*

With each passing day Graciela grew a little stronger and soon it was all her unlikely caregivers could do to keep her lying down. Doc tried to convince her that she still needed rest but the truth was that he put off issuing her a clean bill of health only because he knew that she had nowhere to go. Marge had never been thrilled with Graciela's presence under her roof in the first place. Though she had found it financially expedient in recent years to abandon her father's "No Meskins" policy, she was slow to trust anyone whose complexion was darker than her own, and Negroes were still not allowed past the porch. Doc knew that it was only a matter of time before Graciela's room and board became a bone of contention between the landlady and himself.

Then one morning Doc looked in on Graciela to find that she was not only out of bed but dressed and cooking huevos con chorizo on the hot plate over in the corner.

She wore a simple cotton shift that Dallas had scared up somewhere, and the room had been swept and dusted, the bed made, and the windows propped open on sawed-off broomsticks to let in a little fresh air. Doc protested, in English and in vain, while he racked his brain for the Spanish for *bed*. *"¡La cama!"* he finally blurted out. *"¡Postrado en cama!"* but to no avail. Graciela continued fussing over the eggs and shrugged in the direction of the little table by the window, which she had set for two as best she could with what she had to work with. In the end, defeated, Doc plopped down in the chair, and Graciela served up the eggs and sausage, a large helping for Doc, only a spoonful or two for herself, and they were delicious. When they were finished eating,

Graciela bussed the table, and the morning paper almost magically appeared with Doc's second cup of coffee. It was as if he had dropped into a dream. Some sort of vision of what could have been if only he'd never taken that first shot of dope. A part of him wanted to bolt, but he was in no hurry. He'd had a little lick of dope to hold him over and he had to admit that this wasn't bad, this little anomalous episode of normalcy or whatever it was.

Doc finished his coffee and thanked Graciela, and in spite of the nagging ache in his legs and the rumble in his guts, he made his way to Manny's spot with an uncustomary spring in his step. After getting straight in the beer joint men's room, Doc took his seat in the back and finished his paper.

Manny's morning package usually ran out about the middle of the day, and sometimes he'd stop by for a beer and a game of dominoes before he drove over to the west side to replenish his supply. On this particular day, more than once Doc glanced up from his hand and caught his friend regarding him quizzically, but he let it slide. By happy hour, Doc had dispensed a couple of courses of antibiotics and lined up another pregnancy termination for later on that evening, so he was flush, and he stopped by Manny's spot to spend his advance. The big man gave him yet another sideways glance when he allowed that he couldn't hang around as was his custom.

"What's your hurry, Doc?" Manny wondered. "It ain't like you got nothin' to go home to." He got a big laugh from his boys out of that one. Doc just kept on walking.

That night Graciela insisted on repatriating Doc to his own bed, and she slept on the cot across the room. There were freshly laundered sheets on Doc's bed when he turned in, and he was conscious of the rasp of his own breathing and worried that he was keeping Graciela awake. Graciela was listening but she was reminded of home, her family, all of them together in a single room. They were both soon asleep.

Graciela made breakfast again the next morning, and the morning after that, and the morning after that.

On one of those mornings, weeks later, Doc unfolded his paper and half-mumbled, "I'll be damned," as he skimmed the story beneath an unusually bold headline. "'President Coming to San Antonio,'" he read. Realizing that Graciela didn't understand, Doc folded back the front page and held it up so that Graciela could see the picture of the young president. *"¡El presidente!"* he translated. *"¡Aquí, en* San Antonio!" Graciela peered over Doc's shoulder at the confusing jumble of characters. She could barely read a Spanish newspaper, but she recognized the picture well enough.

Everyone back in Dolores Hidalgo knew the face of the first Catholic president of the Estados Unidos, as well as those of his beautiful wife and their two small children. The Mexican tabloids followed their daily lives with a level of interest normally reserved for movie stars and unheard-of for the First Family of a foreign country. Graciela and her mother had even lit a candle for them in the parish church when they heard that the First Lady had suffered a miscarriage; they could imagine no greater tragedy that could befall a family than losing a child, especially a boy. Graciela pointed to the picture at the bottom of the page: Jacqueline Bouvier Kennedy, resplendent in her beautiful gown at a recent state dinner. She pronounced her name the way everyone in Dolores had.

"Yah-kee!" She beamed.

Doc chuckled. "No, child. That's *Jack*ie." He pointed at the paper and enunciated as clearly and slowly as he could. "The president's wife's name is Jackie. It's like Jack—well, no, he's Jack, but . . . oh, hell!" It was obvious that the little pantomime wasn't getting him anywhere, so he finally gave up. "Never mind, child. It doesn't matter anyhow. Any coffee left in that pot?"

IV

Sometimes Hank doesn't know what to make of Doc. Just the sort of yahoo that a feller meets on his way down. There's Hank, fired from the Grand Ole Opry, back down in Shreveport playing the Louisiana Hayride every Saturday night, just like the bad old days. He's down on his back after the show one night, and some wannabe hillbilly singer shows up backstage with this tall feller in tow. Introduces him as Doc. He looks the part, all right: forty, forty-five, wire-frame glasses. Got on a nice suit, if a little on the threadbare side. Gives Hank a shot of morphine, fixes his back right up, and then asks him for his autograph. Oh, yeah, he's a fan, but not like all those kids that holler for "Lovesick Blues" all night. Knows every record Hank's ever made but his favorites are Hank's songs, the ones he wrote himself: "I Can't Help It," "Cold, Cold, Heart," "I'm So Lonesome I Could Cry." Doc's even a fair hand with a spinning rig, and over the summer, the pair catch their weight in bass and crappie together during long afternoons out on the lake. Then, for no good reason that Hank can figure, Doc has to go and spoil it all.

Cure for alcoholism, my ass. What's that Doc calls them horse pills of his? Chloral somethin'-or-other, or some goddamn thing? Horseshit, in concentrated form, if you ask Hank. Oh, they help with the shimmies and the shakes and all, but they don't do a damn thing for what's really ailing Hank, and besides, who ever asked Doc to cure anybody of anything in the first goddamn place? Hank don't need a sheepskin from some fancy college to know what he needs and when he needs it! Just give him steak and taters when he's hungry, whiskey when he's dry, pussy when he's lonely, and maybe a little old-time religion when he dies.

See, Hank reckons that when his time comes, he'll see it coming. Some kind of a sign, so he'll know it's time to get right with God.

But Death's not playing fair that night, nine New Year's Eves ago. Sneaks up on Ol' Hank like an Injun while he's sleeping in the back seat of his own Cadillac somewhere in West Virginia. Or is it Tennessee?

Even Hank doesn't know.

He's booked to play two shows that weekend, one on New Year's Eve in Charleston, West Virginia, and one the next day in Canton, Ohio. He hires a kid to drive him up from Montgomery, but by the time they make Chattanooga it's snowing like a son of a bitch. Takes more than four hours to make the hundred and ten miles from there to Knoxville and now his only shot at making the Charleston show is the three o'clock plane. The weather goes from bad to worse, and the pilot has to turn the little puddle jumper around and lands Hank right back in Knoxville where he started.

They check into the Andrew Johnson Hotel and ol' Doc's waitin' there and Hank's never been so glad to see anybody in his life. Doc says it was Hank's mama sent him. That she rang him up in Shreveport and told him that her boy was ailing and he'd better get his tail to Knoxville. Doc gives him a good shot of morphine and insists on him choking down one of those pills of his. There's a knock on the door and the kid says he just got off the phone with the promoter and the Charleston show's canceled but he'll see them in Canton for sure, so Hank drifts away to a place nearer to death than to sleep.

Then somebody's pulling and shaking and slapping Hank around, hollering, "Wake up, Hank, it's time to roll!" and then big powerful black arms, a hotel porter, maybe, scoop him up and carry him downstairs like a baby, gently but firmly, cradling him and loading him into the back seat of the car.

Then the kid's behind the wheel and Doc's riding shotgun and they're rolling and the big Caddy takes every bump and pothole in stride. Hank doesn't mind riding when his back doesn't hurt. Big tires thumping, windshield wipers slapping. That was where the best songs came from, that rhythm of the road.

"You think he's gonna be all right?" he hears somebody ask. They're talking about him like he's not even there, and he's only a foot and a half away! He mumbles back, "Ain't nothin' gonna be all right, no how."

Or maybe he only dreamed that he said it.

Or maybe nobody said anything at all.

The morphine talks to Hank sometimes, the way that ghosts talk, in low, rattling whispers that dare him to listen and catch every single word.

"You been headed down this road all your miserable life, Hank."

Sheer terror grips Hank; icy fingers close around that cele-brated throat of his, squeezing him, choking him, but he manages to muster a barely audible moan that sputters and sharpens and then explodes upon contact with the night air into a whine, not a complaint, but an insistent resonant frequency that bypasses all of the sensory intermediaries and travels directly to the heart . . .

A sound that can be made by no creature on this earth except for Hank.

"He-e-e-y! No-o-o-o! Hell, no! Who the hell are you? Where you takin' me to?"

"Canton, Hank." But it's Doc's voice this time, deep and soothing and familiar. "You got a show to do in Canton, Ohio." A little penlight shines in Hank's eyes, blinding him, but Hank doesn't need to see Doc's face to know that everything will be just fine in a minute or two.

"Better pull this thing over the next chance you get," says Doc to the kid, and when they stop he gives Hank another shot and another pill.

And then the tires are singing again, and more miles slip by, and Ernest Tubb and Webb Pierce and even Ol' Hank himself are on the radio cutting through the static like a brand-new Barlow knife. Up front Doc and the kid talk baseball and they must think Hank's sleeping but they're wrong and they damn sure don't know he's got a pint of whiskey hid out in the crack of the seat. Between the shot and the pill and a pull or two on the secret pint, Hank's back doesn't hurt and his hands don't shake and he's floating, drifting along like a flatbottom boat on a lazy Alabama river, and . . . wait a minute . . .

Now it's Christmastime and Hank's back home in Nashville and Audrey's there and she's not mad anymore and there's little Bocephus bouncing on his knee and Audrey says, "Hank, honey, go easy on that whiskey now, 'cause you got to play the Opry tonight," and Hank says, "Yes'm, Miss Audrey, don't you worry none. I'll be fine!" And the gang's all there and they're laughing and singing "Silent Night" and the tree's all lit up and you can see it shining through the big picture window a half a mile down

Franklin road . . . but then the lights go all fuzzy and fade and flicker and one by one . . . they blink out . . .

Hank's all by himself in the middle of the loneliest stretch of highway in the universe. He stands there for a minute and he looks all around, or maybe it's an hour, a week, or even a month.

He could be anywhere. There are no landmarks; there's no recognizable terrain he can use to fix his position. He only knows that he has to find Doc somehow but he has no earthly idea where to start. There are no signs. No white lines to follow, only black asphalt threading through the shadows of unnamed mountains and disappearing into a starless sky.

And the only visible light is the faint red glow of the taillights of his own goddamn Cadillac melting into the darkness.

V

Graciela was adamant.

"Yah-kee," she intoned again and again as she pursued Doc around the tiny room. Doc did his level best to pretend that he didn't understand a word she was saying and continued to go through the motions of ransacking the room, all the while muttering under his breath. "Where the hell did that bag of mine get to? Manny's got himself one hell of a dose of the clap. If I've told him once I've told him a thousand times to put a rubber on that thing when he goes with those east-side girls."

The game continued until Graciela finally resorted to ducking under Doc's arm as he reached for his hat. Standing on her tiptoes on the tops of Doc's shoes afforded her just enough reach to shove that morning's edition of *La Noticia* into Doc's face, where he could no longer ignore the photo on the front page or Graciela's determination.

"Yah-kee!" she repeated. *"¡Yah-kee en el aeropuerto!"*

"That's Jackie. *Jack*-ie, child. At the airport. I know. Everybody knows. But you don't understand. The airport is way north of town and I don't have a car. How would we get way the hell out there? And it'll be a madhouse and . . . there will be cops everywhere and not just the local boys either. I'm talkin' *federales! Migra!* And you illegal and all."

The laundry list of excuses went on for another half an hour but Graciela continued to press her case, alternately pleading and pouting and occasionally stamping her tiny bare feet on the linoleum floor. Mercifully, Doc finally managed to locate his bag and, pointing at an imaginary wristwatch, somehow slipped out the door.

But there was no escape. Manny was sitting at Doc's table in the back of the beer joint reading the *Express-News,* which featured the same wire-service photo of the First Lady as its Spanish-language counterpart. As Doc approached the table, Manny tapped the paper with a short thick forefinger.

"Yah-kee!" He grinned.

"Yeah, yeah, I've seen it already. Just drop your pants and lean over the table there and shut the fuck up."

Manny complied and it was all over in an instant. The ritual had been repeated countless times, and Doc, as usual, had preloaded the syringe with an adult dose of penicillin. Manny hauled his suspenders back over his shoulders and walked off the cramp, cursing under his breath. Doc dropped the empty syringe in his bag and snapped it shut for emphasis.

"Oh, did that hurt? Well, good! Maybe next time you'll use your head before you go stickin' your dick where half of the Fourth Army's already been. Those Nigra gals on the east side all got the clap and everybody seems to know it but you, Manny. Hell, they work right outside the back gate of Fort Sam Houston, and for the life of me, I do not understand why you think you need to go all the way over there when there's plenty of girls right here on the south side who would gladly shine your knob for a dollar's worth of dope."

Manny gingerly sat down and retreated behind a shield of newsprint.

"I told you, Doc. I don't shit in my own backyard. It's bad for business. Next thing you know every *puta* on South Presa's lined up at my spot with their hands out and their skirts up."

"Point taken. But at least put a bag on it, son. There are some maladies that a man can contract with his pants down that are beyond my limited abilities to cure."

Manny shrugged and kept right on reading. "It says that the president's comin' here to talk about space medicine. What's space medicine, Doc?"

"That's aerospace medicine. He's coming to dedicate some new buildings at the Brooks Aerospace Medical Center. It's a place where they study the effects of space flight on the human body, I suppose. A research facility. It's out at Brooks Field."

Manny finally dropped the paper. "Brooks Field? That's right down the road, Doc. Maybe five, six miles at the most."

"So what."

"Think about it, Doc. *Yah-kee!* Right here on the south side!"

Doc lost it. *"Yah-kee, Yah-kee, Yah-kee!* I swear to God if one more fool so much as mentions the name Yah-kee, I'll go screamin' down the road to the state hospital and turn myself in . . . and would you listen to me? Now I'm startin' to say it! It's Jackie, goddamn it. *Jacqueline!* Christ! Graciela can't talk about anything else and just exactly what is it that you people find so fucking fascinating about the First Lady? The president's coming. The president of the United fucking States of America. He's a war hero, a great man, and all you people want to talk about is his wife. I mean, she's a lovely woman and all but, well, what the hell is that, anyway? Some kind of Mexican thing?"

"It's a Catholic thing," suggested Teresa, the barmaid, as she made her way across the room, sweeping and setting down chairs as she came.

"A wh-what?" Doc stammered, taken by surprise.

"He's a Catholic, this president. A Catholic man. He may think he runs the world but men ain't nothin' without women. Animals. Beasts."

"Now wait just a goddamn minute!" began Doc. "There's no need to – "

"Oh, no offense, Doc. I know you don't mean no harm. You can't help it. God made you that way. You got to get dirty, to root around in the dirt like pigs. Oh, you go to Mass and give confession when you're children, but once you're grown you go to work and then you don't never set a filthy foot inside a church again unless it's for a wedding or a christening or a funeral Mass and then . . . maybe. But that's okay. Praying is a woman's work. Men would only mess it up. It is a woman's job to keep the shrines and light the candles and pray for the soul of her man so that he can do what a man's got to do in this fucked-up world. Maybe it will be different in the next one, maybe it'll all begin and end with men up there, but here, it's women who give 'em life and it's women who clean up the shit and the blood. Rich man. Poor man. President. Priest. No matter. The bigger the man, the bigger the mess. She's a saint, our Yah-kee."

Doc was speechless. In eight years of his seeing Teresa every day, no more than a mouthful of words had ever passed between them. Suddenly, freed from her fixed position behind the bar, the usually placid matron was not only formidable but downright intimidating. Doc looked to Manny for moral support but found that none was forthcoming. The big man only squirmed in his chair, and his downcast eyes suggested to Doc that he didn't disagree.

In a feeble defense of his gender, Doc asked Teresa, "Just for the record, hon, how long's it been since you've been to church?"

Teresa stood five foot four at best but Doc was seated, and, standing less than a foot away, she seemed to loom over him.

"I have no man to pray for."

Only when Teresa had withdrawn to her usual place behind the bar did the men feel it was safe to resume their conversation, in quieter tones.

"I'm going," resolved Manny.

"Going where?"

"To Brooks Field. To see Yah-kee."

"Oh, for chrissake, Manny, Brooks is an air force base. A military installation. You can't just walk in there, especially when the president of the United States is in town. It'll be open to military personnel and invited guests only, the working press and the like. Hell, they ain't about to let a couple of broke dicks like us get anywhere near that place, president or no president."

Manny frowned for an instant, but he recovered quickly and began rustling through the paper once again. "It says right here that 'hundreds are expected to be on hand when the president's plane arrives at San Antonio International Airport.' What about the airport? They can't keep us out of the airport, can they, Doc? That's a public place, ain't it?"

Teresa re-approached the table slowly and deliberately, wiping her hands on her apron, and Doc could have sworn that she and Manny wore precisely the same determined expression.

Doc could see it coming now but it was too late. It was like witnessing a train wreck. He sat paralyzed as two powerful forces completely and totally out of his control converged on a course destined for certain catastrophe before his very eyes; there was nothing he could do, but being no stranger to hopeless causes, he had to try.

"Now see here, Manny, do you even know where the airport is? It's a long damn way up there — "

"I got a car," volunteered Manny.

Teresa suggested that if they got an early start, "say, seven thirty or eight, we can get a good spot right up front where we can see."

"But it's on the north side, Manny," Doc pleaded. "Have either of you two ever even been up to the north side? You don't see many Mexicans up there, not unless they're diggin' a ditch or cleanin' somebody's house. Cops on the north side pull over carloads of Mexicans just because they're Mexicans. Aw, hell, go ahead then. Haul your asses up there and make fools of yourselves and see if I care. But I'm not going. No sirree. Not me. I'm staying right here on the raggedy-ass end of South Presa where I belong."

Doc snatched up his bag, intent on a dramatic exit, but before he could reach the door it suddenly opened and Graciela stood in his path bathed in intense yellow sunlight, a tiny avenging angel, still brandishing her newspaper like a tablet of Scripture. Before Graciela could rejoin her assault on Doc, Teresa enthused, "Graciela! We are going to see Yah-kee!"

"Oh, ferchrissake," grumbled Doc.

By the next morning, the South Presa delegation to the United States had swollen to six in number due to the addition of Marge and Dallas. Dallas had overheard Doc's last-ditch effort to dissuade Graciela and simply invited herself. Marge didn't give a

55

damn about the Kennedys one way or the other and found it more than a little irritating that Graciela had the whole house jumping through hoops, but she wasn't about to let Dallas out of her sight.

Word had reached the pawnshop around a quarter to nine, just as old Santo arrived to open up for the day, and he phoned Maria and told her to drop whatever she was doing and get her *culo grande* down to Marge's. Normally, such a dictatorial tone would have cost Santo another trip up to Doc's makeshift surgery for a dozen or so fresh stitches, but he had only to invoke the magical name Yah-kee, and Maria was dressed in her Sunday best and out the door.

And then they were eight.

Manny was behind the wheel, Teresa in the middle, and Doc rode shotgun. In the back, Marge and Dallas barely managed to squeeze into the third of the seat that wasn't already occupied by Santo and Maria. By the time Graciela came running down the back stairs, Manny's old Ford was fairly groaning under the load, and the only seat available was in Doc's lap. She climbed in without hesitating, twisting Manny's rearview mirror around to blot her lipstick on a scrap of toilet paper.

Doc marveled at how tiny Graciela was. She seemed to weigh next to nothing, but when the big V-8 lurched forward, the press of her body against his was profound. Her hair whispered of chamomile and Ivory soap, and Doc shuddered when she leaned across him to roll the passenger-side window up.

He was reminded, against his will, of another young girl a long time ago, back in New Orleans. A beautiful girl from a good family whose expensive, store-bought perfume made promises she had no intention of keeping. Her name was Cynthia. Not Cindy; he had made that mistake once and she had corrected him in a cultured drawl as icy as the first week of February. Other voices

56

out of his carefully suppressed past intruded now, like his mother's, thick and sweet as cane syrup, cooing her assurance of his superior bloodline and upbringing, ever reminding him of who he was and what was expected of him . . . in sharp contrast to his father's insistence that he would never amount to anything at all.

Maybe it was the change of scenery that awakened those ghosts as Doc and the delegates rolled out Broadway and past Brackenridge Park; warm yellow light filtered through the lush canopy of live oak and pecan trees that shaded the neat rows of stately Victorian houses they passed on their way uptown. Quiet, orderly streets, not unlike the one Doc grew up on. Nothing like the bleached-out monochrome of South Presa. Years of living in the back alleys of Louisiana and Texas, not to mention a boatload of dope, had hardened Doc against most memories: the disappointments, the betrayals, the humiliations of his youth. He had cultivated his heartbreaks in the shadows, nurturing them with anger and remorse until they crystallized into a seemingly impervious shield around him. Now, as Manny's Ford dragged him out into the light, he didn't kick or scream but he wanted to and he could feel his carefully crafted veneer beginning to crack; he felt naked and vulnerable.

The delegates watched the big houses go by and oohed and aahed like sightseers on a guided tour of polite society. They had only a vague idea of Doc's past but they reckoned that he was infinitely more familiar than they with the alien landscape that unfolded before them, and they bombarded him with an endless barrage of questions. Manny had dabbled in burglary in his youth, and though he'd often heard tales of big scores in fat houses uptown, he always stuck to the south side, knowing that stealing from his own would attract little or no attention from the police. He marveled at how the old Ford glided along on the smoothly paved north-side streets. Santo intimated that he had been to the park for birthday parties when he was a small boy. His father would hang the piñata from a low-hanging limb of a great pecan tree, and his mother would bake the cake, and the family would sing "Las Mañanitas" and feast on homemade tamales around a concrete picnic table. Though he was within sight of the entrance to the world-famous zoo, Santo had never been inside to see what sorts of exotic beasts made all of the strange noises that emanated from beyond the stone gates. The price of admission for a family of nine was simply beyond his father's means. Marge and Dallas hadn't always been whores but they had always been white trash and the north side was every bit as foreign to them as it was to the Mexicans. When she was younger, Dallas had been a telephone girl who worked the high-dollar johns: doctors, lawyers, even a city councilman or two. Some of them probably lived in big white houses like these, but she always met them in rooms rented by the hour in downtown hotels. Marge whistled long and low when they passed one antebellum structure so opulent that Graciela mistook it for a cathedral. Doc gently corrected her. "That's not a church, child. It's a house. *Está la casa*. Somebody lives there. Somebody very rich. *El ricos*." Teresa just wanted to know how they kept everything so neat and clean and green.

Doc did his best to answer all their questions with a minimum of condescendence. He alone had been inside houses like these, and he fully understood the level of contempt in which he and his *compadres* were held by the kind of people who lived in them.

The big houses petered out as they turned northeast across Wetmore Road, and then, suddenly, the grand tour was over and Broadway abruptly ended, dumping the South Presa contingent out at the main entrance of the San Antonio International Airport. As Doc had predicted, there were cops everywhere: city cops, highway patrol, even Texas Rangers in their telltale sil-verbelly Stetsons and shiny black cowboy boots. It was enough to make Doc wish he'd put a little extra something in the spoon that morning just in case he had to spend the night in jail. Even Manny, the founder of the expedition, wasn't all that crazy about the situation now that they were actually there, but he put on his game face as they rolled up to the checkpoint that the cops had set up at the gate.

"You all right, Doc?"

"Hell, no, I'm not all right! In point of fact I'm about to break out in little assholes and shit all over myself but there's fuck-all I can do about it now that we're here. Manny, I want you to swear on your mother and the Blessed Virgin of Guada-fuckin'-lupe that this car is clean."

Maria crossed herself to ward off any ill effects of Doc's blas-phemy. Even Graciela understood well enough to punch him in the arm, hard, raising a good-size knot.

"Clean as a whistle, Doc. Don't you worry 'bout that none."

As it turned out, all of Doc's anxiety was for nothing because the cop at the checkpoint only asked to see Manny's driver's li-cense and then waved him through to the visitors' parking lot.

"I must say, Manny, I'm impressed. You may be the only person of my recent acquaintance who holds a valid license."

Manny shrugged. "I'm a businessman, Doc. Driving around with a glove box full of dope without a license is bad business."

The parking lot was filling up fast. There were all kinds of people there, spilling out of their cars and filing happily if a little chaotically through the aisles toward the terminal building. Most were Anglos, but there were plenty of Mexicans, and a smatter-ing of blacks. Some wore work clothes, khakis and coveralls and hospital whites, and some business suits of varying quality and style. There were soldiers from Fort Sam and airmen from Lackland, Kelly, and Randolph air bases, officers and enlisted men in dress blues and greens and fatigues. The women outnumbered the men two to one. Well-heeled Alamo Heights matrons in pillbox hats clutching their pocketbooks in two-handed death grips rubbed shoulders with middle-class housewives with school-age children in tow. It was a weekday, but they had been kept home from school especially for the occasion, their hair neatly combed and their little faces scrubbed pink. "You're going to see the president," they were told, "and you can't go looking like heathen!"

The crowd was funneled into the breezeway adjoining the terminal building where they could watch through a chainlink fence from a distance of about a hundred yards as Air Force One taxied to a stop in the center of the tarmac. The U.S. Air Force Band of the West stood at parade rest behind the mayor, a contingent of local dignitaries, and military brass from the local bases.

The crowd chattered excitedly, with the exception of a small group of students who pushed and shoved toward the front, shouting slogans and carrying signs emblazoned with cryptic political messages that even Doc didn't fully understand.

Manny wondered, "Where's Vietnam at, Doc?"

"Close to China. A long fucking way from here." Doc made no attempt to conceal his contempt for the demonstrators.

When the steps were rolled into place and the door of the big blue-and-white jet swung open, the band struck up ruffles and flourishes and then "Hail to the Chief," and the crowd, as one, pressed against the fence for a better view. The youthful president emerged and stood alone in the door of the plane for an instant, blinking in the blazing Texas sunlight, waving with one hand while pushing back a windblown shock of auburn hair with the other.

60

One of the housewives in the front of the crowd spotted her first. "There she is! There's Jackie!" and pandemonium ensued. A high-pitched shriek challenged the big jet engines out on the tarmac, rising to a shrill crescendo and sustaining the same piercing frequency as if an unseen hand held the throttle all the way back: *Jack-e-e-e-e-e!*

Maybe, mused Doc, it wasn't just a Mexican thing after all.

It was impressive. Even Marge had to admit it. "Geez Louise!" she shouted over the racket. "You'd think he was Frank Sinatra or somebody!"

"Well, he *is* very handsome," Dallas gushed, and Marge's newfound enthusiasm deflated like a tire with a sixteen-penny nail in it.

But Graciela had eyes only for Jackie. Doc, paralyzed by the crush of the crowd, could only watch helplessly as she ducked beneath his arm and slipped through the crowd and, by virtue of tenacity and her diminutive stature, reached the fence. The First Lady, dressed in an immaculately tailored powder blue suit, smiled and waved the perfect parade wave to the crowd: elbow, elbow, wrist, wrist . . . Graciela waved back as best she could, squeezing one of her tiny hands through one of the ragged diamond-shaped links in the galvanized fence.

"Yah-kee! Hola, Yah-kee!" she shrilled, not even noticing that she had scraped her wrist badly on the rough fencing as she'd forced her hand through. Tiny drops of blood flecked her dress; she paid no attention. It was worth it. Jackie was so beautiful, the most beautiful woman that Graciela had ever seen. Even at a great distance she radiated warmth and grace and charm. While the president greeted one dignitary after another, the First Lady continued to engage the crowd, smiling and waving until she and the president reached the waiting motorcade lined up along the

taxiway. There was even a moment there when Graciela could have sworn that their eyes met and Jackie smiled at her.

And she was right. All of the other women in the crowd witnessed it and each and every one believed that it was intended for her, and all their hearts melted into one. Even Marge and Maria sensed a common bond with the glamorous Jackie as she regally accompanied her husband down the receiving line, a half step behind, as protocol in the man's world of politics dictated. But in fact, Jackie was smiling at Graciela and Graciela alone, and only Graciela saw the sadness in her eyes and that sadness became her own. Her grandfather had a name for such moments, the instant in which people like himself and Graciela saw what others could not see. He called it *la luz*. The light. Something sacred passed between them, from Jackie to Graciela and from Graciela to Jackie.

And then she was gone. She ducked out of sight, and the massive presidential limousine pulled away, preceded by a brace of police motorcycles and followed by another black limo, and then another, and then two more, and then a final pair of motorcycles for good measure. The din of the crowd died down to a clamor and then a murmur, and then they began to disperse, returning to their cars and their everyday lives. Doc finally managed to make his way up front and found Graciela still sitting on the hard concrete watching in the direction that the motorcade had traveled. He knelt down and as he gently helped her to her feet, Graciela winced a little, and he noticed her wrist.

"What have you done to yourself, child?"

She absently nodded toward the fence but she wasn't the least bit distressed about the injury.

"No, es nada."

"Nada, my foot. That's a nasty little abrasion you've got there.

If I had the serum I'd give you a tetanus shot, just to be on the safe side. At the very least that wrist could do with a good cleaning and a proper dressing. Let's get you home and then we'll see what we can do."

The drive home was a lot quieter than the outward journey. Santo and Maria compared notes quietly in Spanish, and Marge snored loudly, her head resting on Dallas's shoulder. Teresa uttered not a single word the entire ride home, though she was wide awake in wonder at her encounter with royalty. Manny had a question or two.

"How much you reckon a limo costs, Doc?"

"I don't know, Manny, four or five thousand, I reckon. A lot more for that big Lincoln that the president was riding in. It's a custom job, bulletproof, you know."

Manny's eyes widened but never left the road.

"No shit? Bulletproof?"

"That's what they say."

"Well, I'll be damned."

VI

All day long, Hank prowls the South Presa Strip from the beer joint to the railroad tracks, covering the distance each way in the space of single malignant thought. Pedestrians he encounters notice only an incongruous chill, it being a typical sunny South Texas November morning, but they shake it off and go on about their business. There are those lost souls with one foot already in the grave who perceive a shadow falling across their paths, but they shrug it off as too much of this or too little of that and stumble along to their doom. Hank can see them, all right, and worse, he can hear them, whining and crying like babies about nothing, but he can't make them hear him no matter how hard he tries. Only Doc can hear Hank, and Doc's nowhere to be found.

Hank's having one hell of a time keeping up with Doc since he's taken to pretending that he doesn't hear him when he calls. Laying off the dope some too, not that he's taken the cure. He's a hophead to the bone, Doc, but lately he's not hitting the old medicine like he used to do. Just dibs and dabs to keep sickness away.

Hank knows that the higher Doc gets, the better he listens, and more than anything else, the dead want to be heard.

So Hank just keeps searching, up and down the street, eaten from the inside out with rage; not the white-hot, short-lived kind that exorcises lesser demons and affords a body some kind of relief, but the slow-burning, festering strain that neither time nor distance can ever heal. He checks all of the traps, over and over again. Doc's not in his room or at his usual table or anywhere in between. When Hank comes to the railroad track and tries to cross over, he discovers, to his horror, that without Doc to hitch on to, the other side's closed to him now.

That's the last straw. Doc's given Hank the slip and gone off somewhere he can't follow. Hank throws back his head and he opens his mouth. And nothing comes out. Nothing at all.

VII

That night Marge, Dallas, Doc, and Graciela gathered around the TV in the boarding-house parlor and watched the coverage of the day's events on the ten o'clock news.

"I thought I saw you for a second there, Marge!" insisted Dallas. "You was way in the back and there was some kind of a shadow across your face but I'd swear it was you. I'd know that big ol' head of yours anywhere!" Marge snorted and Doc chuckled and excused himself.

"I reckon I'll turn in early tonight. We've all had a big day and I could do with a good night's sleep."

It wasn't to be.

Just after midnight somebody banged on his door.

"Who is it?" Doc called. From the other side a female voice answered, soft and hoarse, obviously in distress. "It's me, Doc! Helen-Anne!"

"Coming!" Doc said, but Graciela, whose cot was a step closer to the door, got there first.

When she opened the door, a statuesque redhead stood there. She was speaking, the words interspersed with sniffs and sobs, but Graciela understood only the tears. One arm around the taller woman's waist, she guided her to a chair and offered a handful of tissue, which was gratefully accepted.

Helen-Anne said she was in trouble again and that there was just no way she could have another baby. Her elderly parents were already raising her little boy and they were barely getting by on her daddy's disability and whatever she could manage to wire home. Like most of the girls on South Presa, Helen-Anne had two habits to support, her own and her boyfriend's, but she had managed to scrape together all but about twenty dollars of Doc's fee, which she offered to let him take out in trade. Doc declined and told her not to worry about it.

"You got any dope, honey?"

"Yeah, Doc, I had a pretty good weekend so I bought a *quarta* last night; how much you need?"

"It's not for me!" Doc chuckled. "I'm fine, but you're going to need a good lick. But not too much, now. I don't want you going out on me. Uh, you best get out of that nice dress first. You got a nightgown or something you can put on?"

"I'm sure I can scare up somethin', Doc," offered Dallas, who had suddenly materialized in the open door blinking and yawning, with Marge right behind her looking more than a little put out.

"I'd appreciate that, hon, and while you're up you think you could take Graciela along and bed her down in your room for the night?"

Graciela didn't understand all the words but it was obvious that she got the gist, and Doc, recognizing a now-familiar glint in her eye, nipped the argument in the bud. "No! You don't need to see this, child. *¡Ahora vaya, muchacha!*" Graciela grudgingly complied and followed Dallas out of the room.

Doc kept Helen-Anne talking while he prepped for the procedure, taking care to keep his instruments out of sight and his patter light and impersonal. Helen-Anne fired up a bag of dope and then lay back on Doc's bed. As she drifted there on the edge of consciousness, her features softened somewhat, and she suddenly appeared years younger. Doc suspected that Helen-Anne was showing her actual age rather than the mileage she had accrued on the street. Doc didn't know any more about Helen-Anne than any of the other girls on South Presa, but he reckoned that she couldn't have been more than twenty-three or twenty-four. She more than likely came from good enough people. Poor, honest, hard-working folks that never got ahead but did all right as long as they kept their heads down and didn't study too much on what they didn't have.

That's probably what happened to Helen-Anne: one day she'd looked up and she caught a glimmer of something shiny just beyond her reach. It could have been anything — a fast car, a fancy dress, a pair of high-heeled shoes. It wouldn't have taken much, just enough of a glimpse of another kind of life to awaken a hunger inside her for something that she had never tasted. Now, as she lay there helpless, her life in Doc's hands, the lines in her face vanished as if hard times and bad luck were soluble in morphine.

The way Doc saw things, it was a crapshoot. Where you were born, who your people were — that's all that mattered. Law and morality had nothing to do with it, let alone anything like justice.

It wasn't like good girls from good families didn't get abortions. Doc used to see them all the time back in New Orleans. The family doctor would register the patient under an assumed name and write her up as a D & C, that is, dilation and curettage, an obstetric housekeeping procedure that consisted of scraping the wall of the uterus with a long, thin surgical instrument, resulting in the expulsion of any material contained therein. If there happened to be a fetus present, then it was an abortion by any other name.

That's what pissed Doc off the most. The duplicity. The way that the rules were bent or even broken for the daughters of doctors, lawyers, and bankers because they had so much to look forward to. College, marriage, summers in Europe. A waste and a shame, the patricians would whisper, to lose all that to the impetuousness of youth. So they looked the other way.

But when the child of a carpenter or a truck driver sought the same service, she had no one to turn to but criminals. Criminals like Doc with some semblance of a medical background, if she was lucky. Shady doctors, ex-doctors, nurses, even dentists and vets, but a girl like Helen-Anne could do worse on the street. Much worse.

By the time Helen-Anne had recovered sufficiently to move down the hall to her own bed, it was nearly three o'clock in the morning. Doc stripped the bloody sheets from his bed and collapsed fully clothed on the bare mattress.

He was awakened by the midmorning sun but he pretended that he was still asleep and watched through nearly closed eyes as Graciela came in from Dallas's room and stood before the mirror brushing and plaiting her blue-black hair into one perfect waist-length braid. The sunlight sifted through her cotton nightgown, forming luminous pools the color of butter about her feet, along the way silhouetting her tiny but graceful form: smallish breasts, gently curving waist, and rounded hips. The smell of coffee brewing and the first pangs of withdrawal urged Doc to haul himself

69

up out of bed but he dared not move for fear that the vision before him would evaporate, so he feigned unconsciousness for well over an hour.

Finally satisfied with her hair, Graciela crossed her arms and pulled the nightgown over her head in one motion, then walked naked to the washbasin against the back wall. As she bathed, she occasionally shivered; the ice-cold water that she squeezed from the washcloth ran down her back and across her spine in one glistening rivulet after another. Doc was deeply ashamed that he continued to watch her, but he could not bring himself to close his eyes. He told himself that his years of practicing medicine afforded him at least a semblance of detachment. His feelings toward Graciela had certainly deepened but remained, at least in practice, patently paternal. He knew, after all, that she venerated him as an elder and a healer, and he held that trust sacred. As long as she was a patient under his care, he told himself, he and she were more or less safe from any intrusion of his baser instincts.

But Graciela wasn't Doc's patient anymore. She was strong and vibrant and more beautiful than ever, tightening her jaw and stamping her feet and setting the whole neighborhood in motion by the sheer power of her will and the audacity of her innocence. Graciela had become, in Doc's eyes, far too formidable to be considered childlike ever again. Maybe, reckoned Doc, it was time that she had her own room.

He waited until she was fully dressed before making a big production of yawning and stretching and sitting up on the edge of the bed. Graciela heard him stirring and she poured him a cup of coffee and set it on the table and then started breakfast.

She wore the same simple peasant dress that she had worn the first day Doc had laid eyes on her. When she finished cooking she set the skillet on a hot pad in the center of the table and served Doc before taking her seat and helping herself. It wasn't until Graciela began to clear away the breakfast dishes that Doc was reminded of the dressing he had applied to her injured wrist the night before.

"Let's have a look at that, child."

Graciela surrendered the affected member, wincing ever so slightly as Doc cut away the bandage with the stainless steel scissors from his bag.

"That hurt? I'm sorry, honey. Let's just see what we got goin' on here. Uh-huh. Well, it looks pretty good, no sign of any infection that I can see."

He felt her forehead with the front of his hand and then the side of her neck with the back.

"No fever. That's good. Now, you sit tight right there for a minute."

Doc got up and put the kettle on the hot plate. While the water was boiling he fished around in his bag for Mercurochrome, cotton gauze, and adhesive tape. When the water was ready, he scalded out the washbasin and filled it with clean soapy water, adding the remaining contents of the kettle to warm it up. He gently cleaned the area with the soap and water and then applied a healthy coat of Mercurochrome. The blood-red disinfectant soaked through the fresh dressing and made the abrasions on Graciela's wrist look a lot worse than they were, which suited Doc just fine. Though he was well aware that the injury wasn't serious, fussing over it allowed him to feel better about putting off any disposition of his and Graciela's sleeping arrangements until another day.

Doc packed up his bag, excused himself, and went down the hallway, intending to look in on Helen-Anne on his way out, but the whore blew by him in the hallway, fully dressed and painted up and headed out to catch the lunchtime trade. She preempted Doc's protests by simply talking louder and faster than he did.

"Now, Doc, before you go and get your shorts all in a knot, I heard what you said, and I promise, blowjobs only for at least a week."

"That is *not* what I said, young lady. My orders were to stay in bed for the rest of the day and not to work, at all, for a week to ten days, depending on how you were feeling—"

"Well, I'm feeling just fine, but jiminy cricket, Doc! A week? You gonna keep me straight for a week? Me and Wayman? Yeah, I didn't think so. Look, I promise, I'll keep my drawers on until I heal up some, but I can't lay off for no week, Doc. You ought to know that better than anybody else."

She was out the door and gone before he had a chance to re-group. Doc stomped back down the hall muttering obscenities under his breath, though, in truth, he wasn't sure whether he was cussing Helen-Anne for her obstinacy or her honesty.

She was right. Who was he trying to fool anyway? Obviously, Helen-Anne wasn't going for it. She knew better. She knew that a dope fiend's got to do what a dope fiend's got to do and that if push came to shove, Doc himself would be out behind the beer joint right now with a cock in his mouth.

Slacking off was one thing, but the only cases of a permanent cure for morphine addiction that Doc had ever heard about involved people who went off to live as monks or missionaries somewhere, and he wasn't the evangelical type. Doc knew that when all was said and done, he was right where he belonged and beyond the grace of anyone's God. Sooner or later this little respite Graciela had afforded him would be over and he would continue his descent, and if the Catholics and the Baptists were right, no act of contrition or good works he ever performed would wash the blood of a thousand aborted fetuses from his hands. In the meantime maybe he could spare a frightened girl from being butchered by some quack in a back alley somewhere, and that was worth going to hell.

Doc hollered, "I'll be at the office!" on his way out. *"Hasta la vista,"* Graciela replied, popping out of the bathroom where she was washing the breakfast dishes. Then she frowned and shook her head and said, "No!" and when Doc turned around she was drying her hands on the hem of her dress; she stood up straight and proudly beamed and said, "See you later!" and Doc couldn't help but smile.

"Later! That's good, hon, that's very good." He waved with his fingers, like a child. "Bye now!"

"Bye!" Graciela repeated and waved back.

About halfway up the block it suddenly occurred to Doc that his casualness of language might be confusing to Graciela. He wondered if she believed that the English word for *cantina* was *office*. If that was true, what other misconceptions was she laboring under as she struggled to acclimate herself to a new life in a strange country? More to the point perhaps, exactly what kind of life was she preparing herself for?

Doc looked up and down the block at the sad little ramshackle buildings, the pothole-riddled streets, and the girls filing in and out of Manny's spot behind the liquor store. This was where he belonged, all right. He had been afforded every opportunity to make something of himself; in fact, he had been handed a life on a silver platter that most people would have given anything to earn, and he had single-handedly fucked it up. The same could be said for most of the folks down here. Yeah, maybe they weren't born into privilege, but not everyone who grows up poor becomes a whore or a pimp or a pusher. They had all made some choices along the way that they probably wished they could take back, but now it was too late.

But what did Graciela ever do to wind up down here?

She fell in love. She fell in love, and she believed her punk-ass little *pachuco* boyfriend when he told her that he loved her too. Then when she was in trouble he dragged her down here to this shit hole to get rid of the baby, and then he dumped her. Truth was her mother might have understood the unwanted pregnancy. She would probably have cried a lot and yelled a little and maybe even taken a hairbrush to her, but in the end Graciela would have been allowed to raise her child with her sisters and brothers and be part of a family.

But not now. Graciela had committed, in the eyes of her mother's God, the most unforgivable of all sins, and she could never, ever go home again.

Doc looked down at his hands and found that they were beginning to shake a little. And he was sick. Not the nerve-racking, head-splitting, puking-and-shitting kind of sick he used to wake up to, but he needed a fix, just the same.

Manny was open for business as usual, leaning against the front fender of his car holding forth for whoever would listen about the previous day's events. He retraced every mile of the ride out to the airport, and some of the younger, more ambitious hustlers made mental notes to take a trip out to Alamo Heights and have a look around. Doc arrived just in time to vouch for Manny's veracity when he got to the part about the president's limo.

"Hey, Doc, tell 'em that it's bulletproof, ain't it?"

"That's right, Manny. Says so in the *Express*. It's a custom-built 1963 model Lincoln. It's got a radiotelephone, and it's armored with one-inch-thick steel plate and has a removable bubble top made out of bulletproof glass. And it weighs three and three-quarter tons."

"Tons?" marveled one of the listeners.

"Yep, that's nearly seven thousand pounds."

"Damn!"

Doc slipped Manny a twenty and tucked the proffered balloon into his hatband, leaving the big Mexican to tell the tale about how he had blown in and out of the *federale*-infested airport with a carload of outlaws, and the cops hadn't even looked twice.

"We was so cool," Manny asserted.

Down at the beer joint it was Teresa's turn, and her audience hung on her every word.

"She was *sooo* beautiful. The face of an angel, I tell you! In all of my life I have never seen a more beautiful smile, and she waved at all of the people like a queen. And then Graciela wiggled her way right up to the front of the crowd like a fish and she reached through the fence. Poor Graciela! Her poor little hand! But she didn't even notice that she was bleeding and she pushed her hand through and she waved and she shouted and Jackie waved back! She waved and she smiled right back at our own little Graciela! I swear on our Blessed Lady of Guadalupe that's the truth."

So captivated were the regulars that no one took any notice of Doc as he made his way to the men's room in the back to get straight.

Once alone in the stall, Doc considered dumping the whole bag in the spoon but thought better of it and settled for half, as had become his habit of late. "Child's portion," he muttered under his breath as he shoved it home.

"That don't look like much dope, Doc."

Doc cracks the stall door to peek out and there's Hank sitting on the counter between the two sinks, his weight shifted forward and his feet dangling. Doc stands and flushes out of habit and steps up to the sink and, literally looking through Hank at his own image in the mirror, produces a pocket comb that Hank's never seen before, wets it, and drags it through his hair.

"It's enough, I reckon," Doc assures him.

Hank retaliates by hopping down and walking through Doc.

"Goddamn it, Hank!" Doc shivers. "I hate it when you do that!"

Hank's behind Doc now, his head nearly resting on Doc's shoulder, and two tortured faces stare back from the mirror, reflected side by side, and Doc's hard put to swear that one is more substantial than the other.

Hank hisses between clenched teeth, "Yeah, well, I'd just as soon you didn't try and pretend that I ain't here neither. Where you been, Doc? I looked all over hell for you!"

Doc only grunts and continues in vain to establish a part in his unruly mane. Hank presses the attack.

"Primpin'." Hank spits out the word. "Primpin' like a prom date. It's that little Meskin whore, ain't it, Doc? After all you and me been through. You can't just run off and leave me like that. We're in this together, you and me."

Doc turns to confront him, and Hank, caught off-guard, gives ground, backing up into the stall.

"We're not in anything together, Hank. I'm still alive and stuck in this shit hole, and you're — well, you've gone on, Hank, and if you had any sense you'd just keep on going. Hell, anyplace has got to be better than this."

Doc takes a step toward the door but before he can get there Hank's already indistinct image breaks apart into waves that shimmer like a mirage on a desert highway, rising up and slip-

76

ping over the top of the stall to reassemble themselves in Doc's path.

But there's no menace left in Hank's presence. He's fading, becoming less solid by the second, and he can feel it and in desperation he plays the only card that he has left.

"You're all I got, Doc," the specter admits, the hint of a sob at the back of his throat.

Empathy has always been Doc's downfall.

Hank was never a bad sort in life, the usual foibles of fame and fortune aside. Just a shade intemperate, that's all.

Well, maybe more than a shade, but Doc's certainly in no position to sit in judgment about that, and truth be told, he knows every single song Hank ever sang by heart and had considered it an honor to be a member of his ever-shrinking circle of friends.

Of course, that was before the son of a bitch died and then took it upon himself to come back and haunt him from one end of the Ark-La-Tex region to the other.

Now here's Hank with whatever passes for tears in the great beyond streaming down his face, and he's growing dimmer and fainter until finally there's not enough left of Hank to prevent Doc from walking out the door.

"I'll see you around, Hank. I mean, where else am I going to go?"

It was only a few steps from the door to Doc's table, and he dragged out a chair and sat with his back to the wall watching all the comings and goings in the center of his ever-contracting universe, which at that moment didn't seem like such a bad place to be.

Manny came in on his re-up break about eleven thirty and

plopped down in the chair opposite Doc. Teresa preempted the umpteenth telling of the Jackie and Graciela saga when she realized that it was time for her favorite soap opera and distractedly served the regulars with one eye on the TV above the bar.

"Finally," observed Doc, "things are getting back to normal around here."

Manny opened the domino game with a double-six, slamming the black-on-white Bakelite tile down with a flourish and a loud *crack!* as Doc mulled over a mediocre draw and cussed him for a son of a bitch. Behind the bar Teresa shushed a paying customer who'd had the audacity to order a beer just as the soap-opera organ swelled to a dramatic crescendo in anticipation of a climactic revelation that never came.

"We interrupt this broadcast for a special bulletin . . ."

At first Teresa desperately manipulated the rabbit ears atop the set in an attempt to get her soap opera back.

" . . . shots fired at the presidential motorcade in downtown Dallas, Texas . . ."

There was no face on the screen, only the CBS eye and the legend special news bulletin, but the voice was unmistakably Walter Cronkite's. Doc stood up and strained to make out the details over the din, finally resorting to wielding Manny's beer bottle like a gavel and hammering on the table for order. "Listen up, goddamn it! Something's going on!"

" . . . several unconfirmed reports that the president and others may have been wounded . . ."

As the gravity of the situation slowly began to sink in, the beer joint took on the atmosphere of a hospital waiting room. Most of the patrons held silent vigil around the bar, but some sat apart in groups of two or three, segregated by language, and nervously conversed in hushed tones.

The Spanish speakers crossed themselves and dutifully recited the rosary, for this president was one of their own. Some among the Anglos present weren't exactly Kennedy supporters. They knew for a fact that he was a Yankee and a Catholic, and they reckoned that he was probably a Communist to boot, but he *was* the president of the United States and this was happening in Texas, damn it, in Dallas, fewer than three hundred miles up the interstate. Only the day before they had all proudly watched the evening news as he addressed the nation from their fair city. That made this national crisis personal somehow. Late arrivals didn't have to be told that something was terribly wrong; they could feel it as soon as they walked through the door. One after another, they wordlessly found themselves places to sit where they could see or at least hear the television coverage. The static CBS logo had been replaced by a stark, monochromatic image of an unusually harried Cronkite holding his earphone in place with one hand and receiving Teletype printouts from someone offscreen with the other. Everyone in the beer joint and the entire nation watched and waited and held its collective breath as one terrible rumor after another turned out to be true.

"... *witnesses at the scene report that multiple shots rang out as the presidential motorcade approached Dealey Plaza* ..."

"... *the president and Texas governor John Connally, who was also wounded, have been rushed to Parkland Memorial Hospital, where at this hour both are undergoing emergency surgery* ..."

"... *the First Lady, who was not, I repeat, not injured, is at her husband's side* ..."

When the bad news finally came, it was delivered in halting phrases by an obviously stunned Walter Cronkite, who removed his reading glasses to note the time on the studio clock.

"*It's official, then. John Fitzgerald Kennedy, the thirty-fifth president of the United States, is dead, at just after one o'clock East Coast time . . ."*

There were only a handful of women in the room, but each and every one spontaneously burst into tears. Some cried out loud, even sobbed, hysterically. Others only managed whimpers. Teresa covered her mouth with both of her hands in an attempt to stem the flood, but it was no use. Her grief spilled out in a sustained, piteous wail, interspersed with barely intelligible curses and prayers. Some of the men cried too. Manny certainly did. Great big tears rolled down his great big cheeks; his lower lip trembled like a frightened child's. But most only stared silently at the television screen and shook their heads in disbelief.

"Damn shame," said Doc, sinking back into his chair. The half a bag of dope wasn't holding up like it had been a few minutes ago. He was a hairsbreadth from buttonholing Manny when he suddenly remembered that there was no television in his room at the boarding house.

"Graciela!"

Doc jumped up, nearly upending the table and sending dominoes clattering to the floor as he headed for the door at a dead run. Then he stopped suddenly and turned on his heel, sending Manny, who'd followed a little too closely behind, tumbling ass over teakettle and sprawling.

"Sorry about that, amigo," Doc apologized, "but it just occurred to me that, well, no offense intended, that you might not be the ideal interpreter in a delicate situation such as this."

Manny's eyes widened. "No offense taken, Doc. Let's get Teresa."

But Teresa continued to wail inconsolably behind the bar, slapping away the well-intentioned touches and embraces of her regular clientele and stamping her feet like a spoiled toddler in the throes of a tantrum.

"Well, first things first." Doc sighed.

He strode across the room and dashed around behind the bar, sidestepping a wild uppercut as he wrapped the surprisingly strong little woman in a powerful bear hug, burying her face in his chest and muffling her screams. He held her there until she stopped struggling and then freed one arm to smooth her hair and wipe her face with his handkerchief.

"There, there, now. I know, I know. The world is an awful place sometimes. But you've got to pull yourself together, girl. I need your help down at the boarding house."

When Teresa stifled a sob, snatched the handkerchief, and wiped away the last traces of mascara herself, Doc knew that she understood.

"Graciela?" she inquired.

"She doesn't know," Doc confirmed.

Teresa opened the cash register, scooped up the big bills, and tucked them deep into her brassiere. *"¡Vamos!"* she hollered in her best last-call-for-alcohol contralto. "Go on! You don't have to go home but you can't stay here! This shit hole is closed in memory of the president and in honor of Yah-kee!"

They found Graciela in the hallway, a basket of wet laundry balanced on her shoulder as she pushed the back door open with her free hand, her right. Doc immediately focused on the bandage on her wrist and reached for the basket.

"Here, child, let me give you a hand with that."

Graciela resisted playfully for an instant before suddenly releasing the basket, catching Doc off-guard and sending him stumbling backward beneath the burden she had borne so effortlessly. She laughed out loud, a child's laugh, spontaneous and musical with no guile in it, but no one else was laughing and the final notes rang sour and died. She looked from one somber face to another and found foreboding but no answers. Manny couldn't even look her in the eye. So Graciela turned to Teresa.

"¿Qué pasa?"

Teresa took Graciela's hands in hers, kissed the bandaged wrist, crossed herself, and began speaking to her in low, reassuring Spanish the way her mother always had when the news wasn't good. Placing one arm around her waist from behind and pulling her close to her, like a bird taking a fledgling under its wing, she gently but firmly guided Graciela down the hallway and up the stairs. Manny grabbed the laundry basket, and he and Doc followed behind. They couldn't hear what was being said but when Graciela's knees buckled slightly about halfway up they knew that the message had been delivered, and they were both thankful that Teresa had drawn the short straw. Teresa only wrapped her other arm around Graciela and locked her wrists together for support and continued to shepherd her to the top of the stairs and into Doc's room.

Marge and Dallas had been watching the coverage on the TV in the parlor. "Oh, you've heard," Marge surmised, and Dallas hurried up the stairs behind Manny and Doc.

Graciela sat on the edge of Doc's bed with her head on Teresa's shoulder and cried hard for an hour and a half. There was nothing that anyone could do or say to console her, so they simply waited until she was spent and then Teresa helped her to lay her head down on the pillow and covered her with a corner of the quilt and soon she was asleep.

．　．　．

There was nothing more Teresa could do, so Doc sent her home.

"You better go on too, Manny," he said. "Better go get your re-up before those dope fiends burn this whole goddamn place down. We'll be all right."

Marge kept a pot of coffee going, and now and then Doc popped down for a fresh cup and the latest news.

"They got him," Marge reported some time in the late afternoon. "Some ugly little motherfucker name of Oswald they found hidin' in the picture show. Said he killed a cop too."

"Did he confess?" Doc wondered.

"No, but they say he's a Communist and he used to live in Russia. Even got him a Russian wife."

"Russian, huh? How's that son of a bitch Connally?"

"They say he's restin' comfortably."

Doc shook his head. "That figures. And now Lyndon Johnson's the president of the United States."

When he returned Graciela was awake.

"Well, hello there!"

Graciela didn't respond, so he tried Spanish.

"¡Hola! ¿Qué tal?"

She just lay there on her side, her black eyes staring at nothing. Doc reached for his bag and went through the motions of a cursory physical examination. He checked her pulse, listened to her heart and lungs through his stethoscope, made sure that her pupils were responding to light the way that they should. All that looked fine and Doc wasn't surprised. He reckoned they'd just have to wait this one out, so he pulled his chair up alongside the bed, just like he had when she had first come to him. How long ago now? He remembered that it had been hotter than hell, so it must have been September. It couldn't have been August, could it? *Well, I'll be damned,* he thought. Over three months. A season, they call it. Long enough to bring about a change. He shook his head.

He'd always helped people who had nowhere else to turn, but he did it for money and dope and to secure himself a place in the scheme of things. Practicing medicine in the straight world was no different. That sheepskin not only assured him of a handsome income but also got him into the country club, where he could rub elbows with lawyers, judges, oilmen, and real estate tycoons, the kind of friends that are handy to have on your way up. On the way down there had been the Bossier crew, the bartenders and the working girls, and the *Hayride* yahoos like Hank. Truth was, Doc didn't make a habit of doing anything for anybody who couldn't do something for him.

It was hard to see Graciela like this.

She lay there motionless and silent for another four hours, and then just after midnight she closed her eyes and drifted off to sleep. Doc wasn't far behind. He put up a halfhearted fight, shaking his head and shifting his weight around in the chair, but finally his chin dropped down on his chest.

VIII

Doc's around somewhere, but Hank can't tune him in like he usually can. It's heartbreak that Hank homes in on, the singular frequency of hopelessness emitted by denizens of the half-light like Doc. But tonight there's some kind of static in the air, millions of voices out there, and they're all hopeless, all hurting, and Hank can't tell one from the other. They've found one another somehow, and now they cry out together, tortured souls in concert, united in their fear and their anguish.

And Doc's nothing but another needle in the heartbroken haystack.

IX

✳

Graciela finally opened her eyes and spoke just as a sunbeam knifed through the grime on the boarding-house windows.

"Quisiera ir a la iglesia a rezar," she said.

She would like to go to church to pray.

The little church had been a Spanish mission once, a place where the local Indians could barter their souls to the Franciscan friars for enough corn to feed their families and a modicum of protection from their more aggressive and still unconquered neighbors. Doc dutifully followed Graciela down the aisle. His footsteps fell like thunderclaps, ricocheting from floor to vault, and in the hushed intervals he could swear that he heard the whisper of moccasins and sandals.

He was surrounded by objects of devotion, the Stations of the Cross, the shrines, the ancient oak crucifix that had no doubt been lovingly carved by a newly baptized Indian artisan. Row after row of tiny candles struggled for oxygen in blackened glass votives casting Halloween-colored shadows that danced on the edge of the darkness. Each was a personal beacon kindled by the hand of an individual believer in hopes of opening a private channel for communication with his or her God. They came and lit their candles and then they sank to their knees and silently waited. Not for a sign or a miracle, for these were not Sunday Christians offering up foxhole prayers. Most had prayed every day of their lives, and they knew no such vulgar display was forthcoming. They expected no remedy. No answers. They prayed only for affirmation, the peace that comes from unconditional and unwavering faith. It was enough to believe that God indeed heard them cry out in their hour of darkness.

Graciela took her place at the kneeler. Doc stood awkwardly for a moment and then followed suit. Not sure what to do with his hands, he glanced sideways at Graciela.

It was as if he were seeing her for the very first time. A white mantilla covered her head and cascaded over her shoulders and arms, leaving only her folded hands exposed; a simple wooden rosary was woven in and out of her fingers. When she prayed, her hands covered her nose and mouth so that only her upturned eyes were visible. He recalled a picture he'd seen somewhere of some saint or another, or maybe it was the Lady of Guadalupe that he was reminded of, the vision of the Blessed Virgin who had appeared to an Indian in central Mexico four hundred years before and who was now the patron of all Mexican Catholics. Graciela said her Our Fathers and Hail Marys in Spanish, and Doc tried to follow along, translating in his head, but at some point he lost the thread and then drifted for a while, his mind wandering aimlessly the way it used to in church or school when he was a kid. He'd just check out. As he got older and learned what the world was really like, it got harder and harder to find that place.

Whiskey helped. It gave him the courage to talk to girls, even the really pretty ones, though he never cared for the taste of it. As he got older, friends and family alike chided him for adulterating good sour mash with Coca-Cola.

Then in the first year of his residency he befriended a crazy old pathologist who worked the midnight shift in the county morgue, and it was he who introduced Doc to the miracle of morphine. From that very first shot it was as if he'd discovered the one vital ingredient that God had left out when He'd sent Doc kicking and screaming into the cold, cruel world.

So here he was in church, and damn near sober. How long had it been?

A lifetime, and a long, hard one at that. He was suddenly certain that on this day he was the only agnostic in the house, God's house. Wait a minute. Did he believe in God or not?

Sure, why not?

He believed in ghosts. And he damn sure believed in the devil. He had seen sufficient evidence that something evil was, indeed, abroad in the world, men murdering one another over money or dope or simply because they felt like killing. But he had never encountered anything that felt remotely like God in any of the churches he'd ever attended.

Back in Louisiana, he'd been to Catholic weddings and funerals held in big, fancy cathedrals, and as far as he could tell those affairs were no more spiritual than their Protestant counterparts. They were pageants. Fashion shows held in sanctified country clubs. Just another place to see and be seen by all the right people; they said the words and sang the songs, but they were too busy trying to cultivate the appearance of piety to actually pray.

But everybody in this little church was praying. It was eight o'clock on a Saturday morning and there'd been no call to worship and no priest was presiding, but they came of their own free will and they got down on their knees and they prayed. They closed their eyes and they opened their hearts and they praised their God unconditionally, asking only for His will for them. Simple people though they were, they knew that attempting to make sense of the events of the previous twenty-four hours was futile.

For over an hour, Graciela prayed, and Doc watched in awe of her faith and in envy of her tenacity.

But whom was she praying to? This Catholic God, Whose functionaries on earth would excommunicate her and see her cast into hellfire if they knew what she had done?

And whom was she praying for? Jackie? Caroline? John-John? That would be just like Graciela. The Kennedys had one another and the sympathy of an entire nation, and Graciela had nothing. No family, no friends except for a raggedy band of half-assed outlaws with no hope and no future.

Doc wanted to pray too, but he didn't know how. The only prayer that he knew was the Child's Prayer that his mother made him say before he went to bed every night.

> *Now I lay me down to sleep*
> *I pray to God my soul to keep*
> *If I should die before I wake . . .*

What the fuck was that all about, anyway. He clearly remembered lying awake for hours terrified that if he closed his eyes, even for an instant, he might never open them again.

And what should Doc pray for?

That God might forgive Graciela? Wash away even her great sin and restore her to the fold? Then she could go home to her mother . . . or maybe one of the good people of this congregation would take her in and rescue her from the guilt and the shame and carry her far away from the South Presa Strip.

Doc could never pray for that. He was nowhere near that self-less.

Well, he was here, so he might as well give it a shot, he reckoned. He closed his eyes and he bowed his head . . . and at first he just listened.

The air was filled with prayer, soft sibilant whisperings and low murmuring echoes all around him. He could make out a word of Spanish here and there and he tried to divine their secret meaning but he found, to his frustration, that he was ultimately fixated on the steady thud of his own heartbeat. Maybe he should just start out by introducing himself.

"Lord, You don't know me —" The deep voice rumbled in the limestone chamber, and the entire congregation turned and stared as if some fugitive beast of the field had suddenly desecrated the sanctuary, bellowing at the top of its lungs. Every one of those black eyes, reflecting the light of a thousand candles, was brought to bear, rousing Doc from his fitful meditation, and it was only then that he realized that the offending voice was his own. Graciela stared like everyone else, but there was no judgment in her eyes, and, Doc thought, the faintest hint of a smile at the corners of her mouth, even the telltale twitch of suppressed laughter. She reached across to offer a reassuring pat on the back of Doc's hand and then she and the rest of the faithful returned to their prayers as if nothing had happened.

Doc sheepishly bowed his head and tried again, taking care to keep his feeble efforts to himself.

Like I was saying, Lord, You don't know me . . .

A quick look around to ascertain that he was indeed praying silently this time.

. . . I mean, I don't get to church much and, well, I'm . . . well, I don't have to tell You that I'm a sinner. I'm certain that You can see that for Yourself. I've probably committed every sin that there is at one time or another, and if there's a hell then there's no doubt in my mind that I am going there, and when my time comes I'll go quietly. I think. It's just that, I'm only here today because of this little girl, see, and she could use a little help right now. She's taking this whole thing pretty hard and she's had a pretty rough go of it here lately, I mean, she was in trouble, Lord, and she didn't know who to turn to and, well, look at her! She's not much more than a child herself. Now, Lord, I know You don't approve of me and what I do to get by in this world and I can't say that I blame You because I struggle with the moral ramifications myself from time to time, but please, please, don't punish the girl, Lord. She hasn't got a mean bone in her body and her only sin as far as I know is being young and foolish and scared and putting her trust in an old quack like me. So if there is to be a reckoning, Lord, here I am. Take me, for it was my hands that offended You, Lord, not hers . . . but of course You already know that because You know everything, I reckon, but I'm just saying. Well, uh, I didn't mean to go on so, Lord, I guess I'm starting to sound like some kinda preacher or something; well, You know, not a preacher but . . . well, hell . . . thanks for listening . . . Amen.

There was no light. No angels singing from on high. Neither was there a bolt of retributive lightning. Doc was not at all surprised and only mildly disappointed. Years of lowered expectations had inoculated him against any hope of divine intervention. He expected little of himself and therefore nothing at all from God.

Graciela crossed herself and rose, placing her hand on Doc's shoulder for support. Doc instinctively gripped her wrist, gently, he thought, but she flinched in obvious discomfort.

"Let me see that, child."

The bandage, which Doc had changed just before they left the boarding house that morning, was soaked through with fresh red blood. Graciela shrugged it off.

"Let's go home," she said.

The yellow-white morning sun is blinding as they step out of the church, and in the instant just before his eyes adjust, Doc can make out the figure of an ambulatory skeleton leaning against a cottonwood tree in the shadow of the mission wall. He shades his eyes with his hand and squints against the glare but Hank is gone.

Back at the boarding house Doc carefully removed Graciela's dressing and was surprised to find that there was no new injury, no puncture or laceration to account for the bloody bandage. There was only the original abrasion, a scrape really, like children get on their knees and elbows every day. The area was clean and there was no sign of infection. There was also no indication that the wound was healing the way that it should. The abrasions appeared fresh, the flesh still raw and pink. Graciela had nearly bled to death during her termination procedure, but Doc knew that true hemophilia was a condition that only men suffered from. Stranger still, the new bleeding had inexplicably stopped on its own; no clotting, no scabbing, none of the usual signs that Doc usually depended on to formulate any kind of a prognosis. Doc was completely baffled but he cleaned and rebandaged the wrist, doing his best to conceal his concern.

Marge and Dallas were still glued to the TV. Dallas glanced up long enough to look over Graciela for a moment.

"You feelin' any better, honey?"

Graciela only dragged up a metal chair and joined them. Doc stood in the doorway and watched for a minute or two, then slipped out the back and down the street to Manny's spot.

Manny wasn't there. Doc beelined for the beer joint, fighting off a mild panic that began to subside only when he got close enough to recognize Manny's Ford parked out front.

Manny never varied his routine. Seven days a week, three hundred and sixty-five days a year, including holidays. Roll in at nine, open the shop, flip the pack, and then stop by the beer joint for a beer and a game of bones around lunchtime. Here it was not even eleven, and the big man was sitting at the bar jawing with Teresa, already on his second beer.

"Goddamn, Manny! You scared the bejesus out of me. I thought the vice squad had rolled up on you when you weren't looking, or worse. You on vacation or what?" Doc offered Manny his hand, a neatly folded five-dollar bill tucked discreetly between his thumb and palm. Manny glanced over his shoulder for an instant, but his hand never left the longneck beer bottle resting on the bar before him. "Sorry, Doc. I sold out about an hour ago."

"Sold out?" Doc bellowed. "What the fuck is that? First come, first served? Is that how it is? Sold out! What the fuck's the matter with you, Manny? I reckon I deserve some kind of fucking consideration around here. Turn around and face me when I'm talking to you, goddamn it!"

Every eye in the bar was on Doc. Though most folks considered the old sawbones to be more than a little prickly, no one in the beer joint had ever seen him lose his cool before. If anything, he was known as the lone voice of reason on many a South Presa

Saturday night. Now he was scaring the hell out of everybody in the joint. Manny shook his head, pivoted on his stool, and stood up.

"Hold your horses, Doc," he said calmly. "I was just getting ready to go re-up. You can ride with me if you want."

Doc rocked back and forth on his heels in the shadow of the much larger man once or twice and then, pulling his hat down low over his eyes, mumbled, "Well, all right, then. Let's get moving."

The oppressive combination of Manny's shock and Doc's embarrassment made for a virtually silent ride across town. Doc didn't know what to say, and besides, he was still more than a little preoccupied with Graciela's persistently bleeding wrist.

Fifteen excruciating minutes later they parked across from a nondescript frame house on the deep west side. Doc waited in the car while Manny went inside and took care of his business, returning in a little under half an hour with a small grocery bag that he unceremoniously tossed onto the seat between himself and Doc. They were halfway back to the beer joint when Doc broke the ice.

"Manny, I don't know what to tell you. You weren't at your spot and . . . I mean, you never sold out at a quarter to eleven before . . ."

"I know! It's crazy. I can't bag the shit up fast enough. Bad news, I guess. Makes people want to get high. That and good news. I would have saved you one, Doc, if I had known. But, hell, I ain't seen you fix in the middle of the day in a couple of months."

All that was true enough. A bag a day. Half in the morning, half around suppertime. Hell, Doc used to do twice that much before breakfast. But this morning's fix wasn't hanging in there like it had been. Maybe Manny was stepping on it a little too hard, or maybe all the goings-on of the last couple of days were just a little more than Doc's nerves and a half a bag of dope could handle.

They rolled.

"Manny, you believe in God?"

"Sure." The big man shrugged.

"You ever go to church?"

"Not since I was a kid. If I was to go after all this time, the confession would take half a day all by itself. I'd feel bad for the priest. Besides, somebody's got to go to hell, I guess."

"Yeah, I guess so," Doc agreed. "Well, tell me this, then. You believe in miracles? Maybe not like the burning-bush kind of deal but, you know, signs?"

"Oh, I don't know, Doc. My aunt and uncle drove all the way down to the valley when I was a kid to see a tortilla with Jesus's face on it. They brought back pictures. Looked like a burnt tortilla to me. I guess when it's all said and done, I reckon God's God and He don't need to prove nothin' to nobody. Least of all me."

Manny reached into the paper sack and handed Doc a bag of dope.

"If you want me to I can pull into this Texaco station up here so you can get yourself straight, Doc. This neighborhood's pretty cool."

"Naw, I reckon I can hang on to this one until suppertime."

The next morning Marge, Dallas, Graciela, and Doc all watched Jack Ruby shoot Lee Harvey Oswald dead on the same black-and-white TV, and not one of them saw the same thing.

"Didn't they see the goddamn gun?" Doc wondered. "I saw it! Stuck out there in front of him like that, just as plain as day!"

Marge didn't care. She believed that what they had all witnessed was not only justice but a particular brand of retribution that she approved of wholeheartedly. "Serves the Commie son of a bitch right!" she said with a snort as she poured herself a second cup of coffee.

Dallas wasn't so sure.

Her real name was Dorothy. She was called Dallas because that was, indeed, where she came from, and when Jack Ruby's name and likeness flashed across the screen she shook her head and wrung her hands and wondered out loud what the world was coming to. "Did you see that? The way the bastard just walked right in there! Into the police station and shot that poor man on TV and all! In front of God and everybody! At the very least he had the right to expect a fair trial. Ain't that how it's supposed to be?"

"No," Doc said matter-of-factly. "He saw it coming. You could tell. You could see it in his eyes." Before anybody had a chance to ask what the hell he meant by that, he retired to the bathroom in the hall for a little lick of dope. He caught his own eye in the corner of the mirror and he shivered when he saw the same resignation there that he had seen on Oswald's face just before the bullets bent him double.

Graciela only wept silently and bled through the second bandage that Doc had applied that morning. She bled intermittently all that day and into the next, whenever, it seemed to Doc, another heartbreaking monochromatic image flickered across Marge's TV: the president's daughter kneeling beside her mother to kiss the flag that draped her father's coffin; his three-year-old son standing soldier straight and saluting as the funeral cortege rolled through Washington, DC. Doc changed her bandages each time, carefully avoiding conversation with Graciela or anyone else who might acknowledge that something extraordinary was taking place.

· · ·

Thanksgiving that year, coming as it did on the heels of a national tragedy, went almost unobserved in much of the country, not that any holiday constituted much more than a slow business day on South Presa. If it weren't for the Macy's parade and the football games preempting Teresa's soaps on the beer-joint TV, it could have been any Thursday.

Sometime Friday afternoon Marge and Dallas abandoned their vigil in front of the TV and drifted back into the daily logistics of running a combination hotel, brothel, and emergency room. By nine o'clock that night, Teresa was busily slinging handfuls of pitchers of draft beer, and Doc had extracted a .22-caliber slug from the hand of a small-time thief who had evidently not heard that it was customary in the barrio to ask the husband for permission to dance with his wife. Then, just before midnight, he scrubbed for the first of three terminations that he would perform before Sunday.

The girl was young and frightened and she sobbed softly through the entire procedure. When it was all over she broke down and bawled, and there was nothing that Doc could do to console her. At his wits' end he hollered for Dallas, but it was Graciela who burst through the door and intervened. Doc's first impulse was to shoo her out of the room, to shelter her from the bloodstained sheets, not to mention complicity in the procedure. But before he could object she climbed up into the big iron bed, cradled the young girl's head in her lap, and began softly singing in Spanish and rocking her like a baby. The girl stopped crying within seconds and the sudden silence rang in Doc's ears as he gazed in wonder at the tableau before him, a living breathing Pietà. Somehow he managed to scribble instructions on a scrap of notebook paper, fold it into a makeshift envelope, and enclose a dozen penicillin capsules while Graciela tenderly helped the girl dress.

That night, without a word exchanged between them, Graciela became the extra pair of hands that boiled the water, rolled the bandages, and changed the sheets, as well as the better half of Doc's bedside manner. Doc was careful to limit her involvement in termination procedures to holding the girls' hands, but she was quickly up to her elbows in all other surgeries, no matter how gruesome. Her English improved daily, but by and large she and Doc spoke very little when they were working, each instinctively augmenting the actions of the other as the situation required. Doc's livelihood had always depended on the consequences of his fellow humans' transgressions, and being no angel himself, he was slow to judge his patients on anything like a moral basis. He did, however, suffer from a low tolerance for stupidity and a temper, which had been exacerbated of late by an inadequate level of opiates in his bloodstream. Graciela compensated for these occasional lapses with a gentler hand and a kind word, and to Doc's amazement she seemed to be able to locate the source of any complaint instinctively, though her methodology left him more than a little uncomfortable.

She simply closed her eyes and laid her right hand over the patient's forehead as if she were checking for a fever, except that her skin never actually came in contact with the patient's. That is, until she opened her eyes and moved her hand so it came to rest directly on the affected area. Sometimes Doc could swear that a wave of relief washed over the face of the afflicted. All of the patients they treated together recovered quickly, too quickly perhaps, most up and able to leave under their own power within hours if not minutes. Once the patient had been tended to and sent on his or her way, Doc knew even before he examined Graciela that he would find her bandage once again soaked through with fresh red blood.

There was a fair amount of talk out on the strip about miracles.

But that, Doc would tell the curious, was ridiculous. He was just a defrocked country doctor of some minor gifts, and Graciela was just a child. A child who, for some perfectly sound medical reason beyond his diagnostic skill, didn't heal very well.

"She's some kind of sorceress, that's what!" Hank hisses, hovering *maliciously above Graciela's cot as she sleeps on her side, her face turned toward the wall. "A she-devil! It ain't natural, the things she can do."*

"Natural!" Doc barks, raking his paraphernalia back into the bag. Hank's spoiling his wake-up shot. "Now if that ain't the pot callin' the kettle black!"

Hank self-consciously descends to floor level, smoothes the front of his jacket, and straightens his tie. "It ain't right, that's all. There'll be a reckonin' for all this somewhere down the road. You mark my words!"

"Yeah, well, that's true enough," Doc concedes. "The reckoning part, I mean, but that little girl there will be way behind you and me in that line." Doc looks at his hands, turning the palms down and back up again. "I used to believe that that's why you were here, Hank. To punish me for all the harm I've done in this world."

"What makes you think I ain't?" Hank rasps, trying to sound as threatening as possible.

"Come off it, Hank. I told you. You don't scare me and you never did. As a matter of fact, I've grown rather fond of you over the years, although you could call in the ghosts of George Armstrong Custer and the entire Seventh Calvary and never get me to admit it to a living human being. At any rate, I've gotten kind of used to

*you being underfoot, or overhead . . . well, you know what I mean.
I even miss you some when you're not around. Come to think of
it, where do you go, Hank? When you're not making a nuisance of
yourself around here, I mean."*

*"Oh, I'm always around. You just don't always pay attention,
that's all. Especially since that little witchy girl turned up and
glamoured you."*

*Doc cocks his head and closes one eye, as if bringing the ap-
parition into sharper focus will make his ramblings any easier
to understand. "Is that what you think? That she's got me under
some kind of spell?"*

*"Go ahead, Doc. Make fun. But you'll live to cuss the day that
little Jezebel from hell walked through your door. You mark my
words!"*

"Shh! You'll wake her up."

"Oh, don't you dare, Doc. You know she can't —"

Graciela yawned and stretched, extended her arm as far up as she
could reach, then let it fall to the edge of her covers. Then, suddenly, she rolled over and sat up, peeling back the bedspread in
one motion.

"There, there. It's okay, child. You had a bad dream is all."

Graciela said nothing, but she knew better. She sensed something between a mood and a smell hanging in the atmosphere
that the ghost had only just vacated.

Christmas was a multicultural affair. There was no discussion, no
consensus. Nobody invited anybody anywhere. But on Christmas
Eve, Marge assembled the ingredients for eggnog according to
her daddy's special recipe, which called for copious quantities of
sour mash whiskey rather than rum, and poured them into a small

washtub. Dallas had spent the day baking sugar cookies shaped like Christmas trees and stars, transforming the boarding-house kitchen into a confectionery wonderland; every surface was covered in a dusting of powdered sugar and glittering red and green sprinkles. Graciela and Teresa made several varieties of tamales, some savory and some sweet, under the watchful eye of the more experienced but arthritic Maria. A pot of frijoles simmered on the stove, filling the air with the aroma of cumin and red chili.

Doc and Manny went out and bought a tree, one of the last half dozen on the lot, a little flat on one side but priced to move as the sun set on the last shopping day before Christmas.

The delegation assembled at the beer joint just after dark and decorated the tree with strings of popcorn and pull-tabs and multicolored lights appropriated from their year-round position behind the bar. The joint was open but there was nobody around. Doc, Manny, and Santo broke out the dominoes and started up a game at the table in the back. Teresa loaded the jukebox with quarters and punched in both sides of every Christmas record on offer. Unable to interest any of the men in joining her in a two-step to "Rockin' Around the Christmas Tree," she grabbed Graciela and walked her through the steps.

Graciela was a natural. Within minutes she glided effortlessly from corner to corner of the tiny dance floor, creating delicate floral tracings in the fresh sawdust beneath her feet. Teresa had only to imply a turn or a spin and Graciela was there, pirouetting beneath her up-stretched arm like an exquisitely animated marionette, stopping and changing direction without missing a beat, until she suddenly became self-conscious. She was being watched.

It was Doc. She wondered how long he'd been staring at her like that and why it didn't make her more uncomfortable than it did. She shifted her left hand from Teresa's shoulder to her waist, and the older woman surrendered and allowed her to lead. Marge and Dallas were the next to hit the floor and it was immediately obvious to everyone present that the pair had danced together before. Maria collected old Santo from the domino table and dragged him into the fray, and as they danced, one anticipating the other's every nuanced maneuver, the question of why they had stayed together for all those years, cuttings and beatings notwithstanding, was answered in two turns around the floor. Doc was still transfixed, unable to take his eyes off Graciela, so Manny finally gave up and shoved his hand to the middle of the table.

"Well, fuck it, Doc. If nobody wants to play, then I'm gonna dance!"

The big man lumbered across the floor, catching Teresa in mid-spin and excusing himself to Graciela, who smiled and acquiesced, giving her partner a barely perceptible push into Manny's arms. Their first few steps were tentative until Teresa overcame an understandable fear of being crushed and her genuine surprise at how smoothly Manny moved once they got going. Graciela watched them for a moment before retreating in a series of fluid, sliding motions, still in time with the music, and pivoting on her toe like a music-box ballerina to face Doc and then curtsying expectantly. When Doc remained in his chair, suddenly unable to look her in the eye, she hid her disappointment behind an understanding smile and sat down at the table.

"Merry Christmas, Doc," Graciela intoned perfectly.

"And merry Christmas to you, child."

That's right, Doc reminded himself. She was only a child.

Doc and Graciela watched the others dance until all of Teresa's quarters were spent. After the presents were opened — dime-store purchases mostly: chocolate-covered cherries, cheap cologne, and the like – there was more dancing and drinking and grazing on tamales and beans.

The party broke up about eleven. Dallas and Marge finished off the eggnog and steadied each other for the short stumble home. The Mexican women freshened up in the ladies' room, covered their heads with lace mantillas, and then, accompanied by Santo, headed downtown in Teresa's car to midnight Mass at San Fernando Cathedral. Doc, who had seen enough of church recently to last him awhile, politely declined and offered to lock up the beer joint on his way out. Manny stayed behind to keep Doc company.

Once the women were gone, the spirit of the occasion evaporated instantly. The joint was suddenly dark and dirty and quiet. Too quiet.

"Game of bones?" Doc offered, mainly to hear the reassuring sound of his own voice.

Manny grunted agreement and shoved the tiles around in circles, drowning the oppressive silence in the satisfying scrape of Bakelite across the metal tabletop.

It was amazing, Doc mused to himself, how addictive fellowship was. Most of his life he had functioned as a standalone entity, interacting with others only out of need and self-interest. Now he had to admit, at least to himself, that he was becoming accustomed to company and that Graciela's absence in particular was excruciating. How long had it been since she had been out of his sight for more than a few minutes? Weeks? No. Months! But this was ridiculous. She'd only just left, and she'd be back directly.

Manny won the first game and then, snorting, shoved back from the table.

"I got to take a piss but you need to get your head in the game, Doc, or I'm goin' home."

As soon as the men's room door closed behind Manny, Doc, no stranger to the joint, was aware of a cacophony of rattling and humming that he had never noticed before. The worn-out compressor in the beer box. The neon buzzing in the window. A barely perceptible whisper, dry and brittle like a last breath.

"You got to help me, Doc! I'm tellin' you, I'm in a bad way!"

Doc ignored the voice. He never answered Hank when he was reasonably sober and anybody else could hear. Instead, he noisily shuffled and reshuffled the dominoes until Manny returned to the table.

The two played for the better part of an hour, speaking only when they added up their scores. Doc was less distracted and played marginally better than before, going domino a time or two, but Manny knew something was wrong.

"You okay, Doc? If you need a little somethin', I got a bag or two left."

It was only then that Doc realized that he hadn't had a shot since his wake-up, and that had been over twelve hours ago. Doc took a quick inventory. Head hurt. Legs ached. Nose was running. Yep, he was sick.

"Well, now that you bring it up, I don't feel all that great, but I reckon I've almost made it through the day already. Maybe it can wait until morning."

Manny whistled. "You're really pulling up, ain't you, Doc?"

Doc ignored the observation. "Hey, Manny, tell me something. The other day, when we were riding back from the west side? You mean what you said? You really believe you're going to hell when you die?"

The big Mexican shrugged.

"You reckon it's going to be like Dante?"

"Like who?"

Doc shook off the familiar sting of guilt he felt whenever he caught himself talking over Manny's head. Truth be told, Manny, despite his lack of education, was one of the smartest people Doc had ever met.

"Dante Alighieri," Doc explained, "an Italian poet. Hell, *the* Italian poet when all's said and done. He was the first to describe heaven and hell in a language other than Latin. Everything that ordinary folks know about eternal damnation comes from him. You know. Lakes of fire. Lost souls tortured by demons and writhing in eternal agony."

"I dunno, Doc. Maybe it's different for everybody. Like . . . maybe I'll have to stand behind the liquor store forever while every junkie that ever dropped dead from a shot of dope I sold 'im passes by like a parade and I'll have to look 'em all right in the eye and no matter how hard I try I won't be able to look away. But when I look in there I won't see nothin', just empty and black and cold."

Doc's jaw dropped. "Holy shit, Manny!"

Manny kept going, rescuing the abortionist from a procession of shattered fetuses that danced in his head.

"But that can't be right, Doc, can it? I mean, them bein' there with me? It wouldn't be fair."

Doc shook his head.

"I don't get it."

"Well, no offense, Doc, but junkies are already in hell. I see 'em go through it every day. It's hard work bein' a dope fiend. Hustle all day and all night . . . Robbin'. Stealin'. Sellin' themselves. You're lucky, Doc. You got a gift so you get by all right. But all them other poor hopheads out there on the street? There ain't no way God'd make 'em pay any more than they already paid when they die." Manny drew a long breath. "Me? I done all right sellin' *chiva*. Nice house. Good car. Never served more than ninety days in jail in my whole life. I take care of my mama all right, but that ain't gonna get me into heaven. No, Doc. I reckon I'm probably fucked."

He clapped a handful of black-and-white tiles down on the table.

The loud metallic *clack!* was answered with a hollow click from behind them.

"What the . . ."

Both men turned around at once. The sound came from the jukebox, which had awakened seemingly of its own accord and begun rifling through its repertoire.

"Did you?"

"Wasn't me, Doc. Maybe one of them quarters Teresa dropped in there got stuck."

Another click and they watched the sickle-shaped selector pick up a disc and place it on the turntable, and the needle dropped with a crackle and a hiss like the final warning of a poisonous snake.

If you lu-u-u-ved me half as much as I love you

Doc told himself that it would be all right.

You wouldn't w-u-ury me half as much as you do.

But it wasn't.

Doc was on the other side of the room in flash, sliding across the sawdust-covered floor. His hand shook as he reached behind the jukebox and groped blindly for the Reject button on the back. Where was it? Down low on the right somewhere. He had seen Teresa perform the operation a thousand times, but now he couldn't seem to lay his hand on the damn thing. He finally resorted to pulling the plug.

"Sorry, Hank," Doc muttered as the record growled to a halt in the middle of the fiddle break. "I guess I'm not that well yet."

He fumbled in his pocket for Teresa's keys and held them out for Manny.

"Manny, I think I'll take you up on that bag after all. You wouldn't mind locking up for me, would you?"

Manny swallowed a question and shook his head, taking the keys and trading him a balloon from the top of his sock.

Back at the boarding house, Doc fished the balloon from the sweatband of his hat on his way up the stairs. What was he thinking about? Sure, he'd cut back. Way back, but Christmas Eve or not, he still needed what he needed. Pulling up was one thing. It felt good not to walk around in a fog all the time, not to mention having the extra cash in his pocket.

Sometimes he even felt like he was getting his touch back, like he was really helping people instead of merely going through the motions to feed the monkey on his back. And there was Graciela. There was something that was at once humbling and empowering about her very presence in his life. The way she watched intently as he worked to piece together torn flesh or stanch the flow of blood from a lacerated artery, and just last night when he had his hands full treating both combatants of a barroom cutting contest and was rapidly losing one of them, Graciela had stepped in and applied what she had learned from watching Doc *with those hands* of hers, especially that right hand, and the result was, well, miraculous.

Miraculous: having the power to perform miracles.

Now he really needed a fix.

Then, when he reached under his mattress to retrieve his outfit, he discovered that Santa Claus had left him a little something extra for Christmas.

It was a bag of dope, one of Manny's trademark red balloons, that Doc had somehow managed to hide from himself, not an easy thing for a junkie to do. There was no telling how long the thing had been there, and Doc couldn't imagine how he had missed it. Maybe it had slipped out of his hat when he was flush and too high to accurately inventory his supply. Or maybe somebody else left it there before he had moved down the hall from his old room last spring.

The previous occupant was an old hophead named Amos whom Marge found dead one morning in that very bed. Doc hadn't been able to rule out an overdose, as Amos's outfit was still out on the table beside the bed, but if he'd had to bet, Doc's money was on a heart attack. Marge had cussed Amos for a son of a bitch because he had departed this world owing her two weeks' rent. Doc hadn't even packed his stethoscope away before he asked Marge if it was all right if he moved into the bigger, better-lit room.

Anyway, hermetically sealed in plastic, heroin had a hell of a shelf life. Now Doc had two bags of dope. His habit was covered for the next seventy-two hours.

Or maybe not. After all, it was Christmas. He'd been good. In fact, he'd been very good by his own standards, and a little extra Christmas cheer in his spoon couldn't hurt anything, now could it?

Two bags. He used to do three in one shot when he could afford it. Now it looked like a mountain of brown powder in the spoon. It cooked up dark and thick and sickeningly sweet, and

108

Doc was immediately sucked in by the big lie that all junkies want to believe in spite of daily evidence to the contrary, that this shot was going to be like that first shot all those years ago. He tied off, found the money vein in the back of his arm, well rested now because he had always reserved that one for the big shots, the teeth rattlers, and it stood at attention like a soldier on payday. He pierced the flesh, backed off the plunger, and let it go.

Doc knew he'd fucked up before he had the needle out of his arm. Sweat instantly erupted in tiny drops across his forehead, and the floor seemed to open beneath his feet like a gaping trapdoor. He stood up and lurched for his bag on the dresser, though he wasn't sure why because he knew that there was no remedy there that could bring him back. Not from this place. He didn't make it anyway. His legs buckled beneath him and he crashed to the floor, conscious only for the instant it took him to roll over on his back. The last thing that he saw was the bare 40-watt bulb suspended from the ceiling, flickering and failing as it spiraled away into a vortex of collapsing black . . . and then there was cold night air slapping him in the face and the voice of doom.

"You don't look too good, Doc."

Hank hovers over Doc, his spectral visage only inches away. Near enough to make Doc acutely aware of the absence of any breath emanating from behind a picket of ragged yellow teeth. From Doc's vantage point, Hank appears even more skeletal than usual, squatting on his haunches, his arms akimbo on his knees, his elbows jutting out at unnatural angles. Almost comical, though Doc isn't laughing. But Hank is. Right in Doc's face.

"What's the matter? Feelin' poorly? Maybe that shot had a little too much kick to it. But I've seen you take a lot more dope than that before. I guess all that playin' house with that hot little enchi-

lada of yours is makin' you soft. Can't hold your dope no more. What was it you used to say? 'As high as I can get is flat on my back'? Well, you're sure 'nough flat on your back now."

The ghost glances over his shoulder to some point in space behind him.

"Tell me, Doc. You see a light? I mean, when you crossed over. I always heard that there's this beautiful light and when you walk into it the Lord Jesus is there waitin' for you with open arms. You see anything like that, Doc?"

Hank doesn't wait for an answer. Shakes his head.

"Me neither. Didn't see a damn thing, Well, heh, heh, I did see a pair of taillights . . . but I don't think that's what the preacher was talkin' about. Do you, Doc?"

Doc tries in vain to sit up but every muscle in his body burns and quivers like the third day of a cold-turkey kick. He collapses in a heap on the asphalt, his elbows scraped raw and stinging. Asphalt? He looks around and finds that he's lying in the middle of a blacktop road that stretches out for an indeterminate distance in both directions before disappearing into darkling hills.

"Where the fuck am I?" Doc gasps, immediately regretting that he's acknowledged the apparition for the first time in months and praying that no answer is forthcoming. No such luck.

"Hell if I know, Doc. You tell me. Could be Eleven West or Highway Nineteen, maybe. Somewhere in West Virginia, I reckon. Or maybe not. Maybe this ain't nowhere. Kind of lonesome, ain't it? Out here in the middle of nothin'. Makes a body feel lost and forsaken. Like there ain't nothin' . . ."

Doc knows the words to this one so he joins right in.

"Ain't nothin' gonna be all right no how."

Hank snaps to his feet as if he's been shot from a tautly stretched rubber band and spits out his words in angry, sibilant bursts, like a demon christened with holy water.

"Mock me? Sass me? Where the hell you think you are? I'm the head honcho around here, Doc. This here's my highway and from now on you go where I go. I'm sick and tired of followin' you around."

With a supreme effort Doc stands up.

"Then don't. Go on, Hank. Go on back wherever it is that you came from and leave me alone."

"Heh! Go back?" Hank cackles. "You still don't get it, do you? There ain't no back! This is it! What do you think I've been waitin' on? Misery loves company. Ain't that what they say, Doc? Well, I'm one miserable son of a bitch and from here on out you're keeping me company whether you like it or not."

"Why?" Doc pants.

"So I don't have to be alone. So I don't have to wander up and down this road all by my lonesome until Gabriel blows his goddamn horn."

"What I meant was, why me, Hank?"

Hank looks at Doc like he's just asked the stupidest question in the world.

"Why not you, Doc?"

It's beginning to sink in. Hank's got him now. The tables are turned, and nobody, not Graciela, not even God, can help him. The first pangs of despair reach up from within and Doc wants to scream but before he has a chance he's blinded by a light, and it's not beautiful but it's certainly brilliant and awesome and it's coming right at them, rolling down the highway, or is it streaming down from the sky? Hard to tell, but it's getting closer, bearing down at a tremendous rate of speed. Gargantuan shadows

111

of naked tree trunks line the highway, shattering the onrushing luminosity into stroboscopic shards. Hank is visible now only intermittently as a vaguely human-shaped hole, blacker than black against flashing luminous white. Doc tries to turn and flee but in spite of his terror finds that neither his feet nor his spirit are willing and he falls back to his knees.

"Goddamn it, Hank! There's something coming! We've got to get out of this road!"

But the shadow that was Hank isn't listening, and the light overwhelms them both.

A scream was still ringing in Doc's ears as he gasped for the first breath of a new life.

Graciela was beside him, her right hand on his chest and tears of joy and relief in her eyes. Manny and Teresa helped him into the bed, and Dallas and Marge hovered around for a while, chattering like grackles, desperate to convince the others that they'd been sound asleep and had heard nothing when Doc fell out. Graciela shooed everyone from the room, closing and bolting the door against any further intrusions. She helped Doc undress and then literally tucked him into bed, pulling the quilt up under his chin. When Doc tried to apologize, Graciela stopped him before he could get out a single word.

"It is okay," she enunciated carefully and then smiled, pleased with herself for answering in English. "Don't talk now."

Graciela had amassed a collection of candles in brightly painted jars emblazoned with the images of various saints and inscribed with assorted blessings in Spanish. She kindled them all and distributed them in strategic positions around the room, chanting softly under her breath, now in Spanish, now in Latin, now in a language that Doc didn't recognize. She crossed to the bus tray on the dresser where Doc kept his supplies and produced a half a quart of clear liquid and a cigarette lighter, and before he could object she had upended the bottle and atomized a mouthful of pure grain alcohol over the open flame, projecting a plume of blue fire to each of the four corners of the room. Then she sprinkled a little of the remaining liquor over Doc and herself and in a semicircle around Doc's bed, using her fingers as her aspergillum. She then knelt beside Doc's bed and whispered every prayer to every saint and spirit that she knew.

Doc drifted in and out of wakefulness until morning. In one instant of clarity, deep in the night, he recognized the part of Graciela's story where he had come in, except now the principal roles were reversed.

X

✳

Doc slept through the daylight hours of Christmas Day 1963. When he finally came around it was a little after eight in the evening and Graciela was there, kneeling on the floor beside him, her head bowed low and resting on the bed. At first Doc assumed, somewhat self-consciously, that she must be deep in contemplation or prayer. Then in one luxurious catlike motion she yawned and stretched and rubbed the sleep from her eyes.

"*¿Cómo están?*" she half whispered and then: "No, no, I must English! I mean — I must say in English!" She muttered to herself as she applied a cool, damp washrag to Doc's forehead and settled beside him on the edge of the bed. She knitted her brow in concentration, silently mouthing the words one more time before committing to another attempt.

"How do you f-fee-ul?" she finally offered, wide-eyed, searching Doc's features for any sign that she had managed to make herself understood.

"I feel fine, child," Doc lied. "Very well, thank you very much."

In point of fact, it was now nearly twenty hours since the shot of dope that had nearly killed him, and he was beginning to get the chills. Still, he was more tired than he was sick, so at Graciela's urging he rolled up in his covers and turned his face toward the wall and was soon asleep again.

When he awoke the following morning he was in the very teeth of withdrawal. He hurt nearly everywhere: his head, his back; his skin felt like an acid-lined exoskeleton, unshed and at least two sizes too small. He sneezed and he coughed, his stomach roiled, and his bowels rumbled. Experience told him that as miserable as he was, it was nothing compared to what was in store.

So what was he waiting for? There was no urgency, no relentless beat of the drum he had marched to for most of his life. He knew good and well that if he didn't haul his ass out of bed that instant and hustle up a bag of dope it would only get worse, but he was still lying there. All of the usual symptoms that served as constant reminders that his life was not his own were present and accounted for, with one notable exception.

There was no funk. No blues. No blackness on the horizon that he couldn't see past or dread rising up with the bile in the back of his throat. No terror to motivate trembling arms and leaden legs and set the tedious routine in motion. Doc grimaced as he was caught off-guard by a strong cramp, and Graciela understood at once. "I go for Manny," she assured him, but when she removed her hand from his forehead it was as if all of the color had suddenly drained out of the world. Graciela winced as Doc desperately grasped her injured wrist and replaced it by force.

"No, child. Just don't go anywhere right now."

Manny showed up anyway, a little after ten o'clock, and stood at the foot of Doc's bed with his hat in his hand, looking sheepish.

"You okay, Doc?"

"Well, *okay* would be an overstatement, but I reckon I'll live."

The big man glanced over his shoulder, moved around to the side of the bed, and bent over Doc, lowering his voice as if he were about to impart some sensitive piece of information.

"I asked around, Doc," he began, a puzzled expression on his face. "All my regular customers. Nobody else fell out. I cut that stuff myself. It was just my usual — "

"I know that, Manny," Doc interrupted, struggling to sit up. Graciela hurried to his assistance, propping him up with a couple of extra pillows. "Are you cold?" she asked, noticing that Doc groped for the covers as they slipped down. He nodded and she tucked the thin blanket up under his chin. "I'll get another blanket." On her way out the door she collected a couple of washcloths in the basin. "I'll be right back," she assured Doc.

Alone with Manny, Doc did his best to assuage the big man's guilt.

"It's not your fault. I had an extra bag lying around and I . . . well, I was just stupid. I mean, it's Pharmacology 101. Increasingly higher doses of morphine, or anything else for that matter, result in an exponential increase in tolerance over time. That same theory applies to decreasing doses, though I must admit that I have no practical experience in that area. But, hell, Manny, I knew better. It's not your fault. Just put that out of your mind." A peculiar look spread over Doc's face; he stumbled over the words as if they were being issued from someone else's mouth: "Anyway, the thing is, I don't know but I . . . well, I think I might be done."

Manny nodded. "You thinkin' about kickin'?"

Doc blanched and threw back the covers. "Well, technically, I think I already am."

Supported by Manny, Doc only just made it down the hall before the next spasm racked him like a toothpaste tube squeezed in the middle, the contents issuing simultaneously from both ends.

He rocked back and forth on the toilet vomiting violently in a galvanized mop bucket that Marge kept under the chronically leaking sink. Christmas dinner had long since been purged but that didn't stop the relentless rhythmic contractions and Doc half expected to look down in the bucket and identify fragments of various vital organs. In fact, nothing was coming up anymore and wave after wave of dry heaves shook him to his marrow. At some point in the ordeal Doc looked up through watering eyes and he could just make out Graciela standing in the doorway. He was mortified.

"For chrissake, Manny, I'm fucking indisposed here!"

Manny, who was fully occupied keeping Doc on the toilet and the bucket in position, managed to swat at the door with one giant pawlike hand, and it slammed shut with a loud bang in Graciela's face.

The room darkened, not a complete blackout that could be explained away by the flip of a switch or a blown fuse, but a subtle graying, a pall descending over everything. Doc didn't even have to open his eyes to name the beast.

"Feelin' poorly, are you, Doc?"

"Ah, there you are, Hank, you lousy cocksucker. Stands to reason you'd come around to kick me when I'm down."

Manny thought Doc was talking to him. "You don't have to talk ugly like that, Doc. I'm just tryin' to help, that's all."

Doc can't make out what Manny's saying but there's a voice inside his head, maybe it's Hank's or maybe it's his own, hissing, "Just roll up your sleeve, Doc! That's all you got to do!"

"Yeah, and then what?" Doc answers. "Then I have to start all over again."

"Start what? Who you tryin' to kid, Doc?"

Definitely Hank. And he's right. The puking and shitting is the easy part.

Doc grabbed Manny by his lapels and pulled himself up off the toilet; the big man stumbled backward but Doc held on tight, like a desperate animal.

"You've got to help me, Manny!" He gasped.

Hank's still there, just above and behind the big Mexican, and he's egging Doc on.

"Yeah, that's the way, buddy! You know what to do! Ain't but one thing gonna cure what ails you."

Doc finally threw in the towel but not because of any ghost. It was the darkness that lurked inside him that brought Doc to his knees as soon as Graciela was out of the room. "Come on, Manny, I know you've got something on you! Just a taste. That's all I need. Just a taste, to get straight!"

Manny was repulsed and perhaps a little disappointed although not surprised by Doc's sudden about-face, but he never had a chance to reply.

Doc's first instinct was that it might be a raid and the police were breaking down the bathroom door. Then the hook-and-eye latch tore out of the doorjamb and whistled past his ear like a ricocheting bullet. The door swung wide open and a fiercely determined Graciela stood in the breach.

· · ·

Both Hank and the darkness give ground.

Stunned and embarrassed, Doc released Manny from the death grip, and the big man stepped aside.

Hank spits like a terrified cat and evaporates as the room begins to spin and Doc falls face-down on the cold tile floor.

Later Doc would only vaguely remember Manny's picking him up and carrying him to bed and then retreating before Graciela, backing out of the room like a captivity-addled circus elephant.

Graciela wedged a chair against the door and lit more candles and fetched the basin from the table, and now there was the aroma of steeping herbs that Doc had come to identify with healing rising up from the warm water. All of Doc's senses seemed to be intensified and he could smell fresh blood on her bandage as she placed the washrag on his forehead, and at that exact moment the horror that had gripped him so suddenly miraculously vanished into thin air.

Miraculously. Miraculous. Miracle.

But it was a miracle. There was no other word for it.

That night, he ran the gauntlet — pain, nausea, diarrhea, and respiratory distress — fully cognizant that these were passing physical symptoms that he would certainly survive if he could only overcome his own fear. As a physician, he was well aware that no one ever died of withdrawal from morphine. Alcohol? Sometimes. Barbiturates? Often. But never from morphine in any of its forms, including heroin. It was truly only fear itself that stood between him and freedom.

And when Graciela touched Doc, he was never afraid.

The next day passed in vignettes, ragged shards of consciousness that segued suddenly from nightmare to fitful wakefulness and back again. When Doc occasionally opened his eyes, he was never certain into which realm he had drifted, but Graciela was always there and she smiled and whispered reassuringly and he'd take a deep breath and re-immerse himself in the stream.

Then, sometime deep in the third night, Doc sat bolt upright and wild-eyed to find that he had outrun some unnamed denizen of his dreams only to awaken in palpable agony in the world of light. Pain the likes of which he had imagined in only the most twisted of his medical-school horror fantasies assailed him, as if his spinal cord had been neatly but not necessarily painlessly removed, leaving him raw and empty for an instant before the hollow was filled with alternating layers of fire and ice that froze him and burned him, and he writhed and thrashed until the sheets hung damp and twisted from the bedposts. But in an incongruous moment of clarity, Doc perceived that this was indeed the penultimate penance and that he need only buck up and stay the course and it would all soon be over. The pain fell on him in waves now, one after another, and there was no time to recover before the next one came crashing down. Another epiphany: Graciela indeed possessed the power to spare him all this, but she only watched and waited, crouching sphinxlike on her knees and elbows at the foot of the bed. The physical agony was somehow amplified by Doc's complete lack of fear. There was no shivering or shaking anymore, no mercifully mind-numbing shock. Then, just when Doc was certain that he could bear no more but before he could open his mouth to scream, Graciela uncoiled herself and slowly crawled toward him on all fours. She was naked, and her hair was ringed in light, a halo one instant, a circle of fire the next, and in the constantly moving candlelight, her skin ranged in hue from something between honey and caramel on her shoulders to deep sienna along the shadows on her inner thighs where they lay alongside Doc's hips. He was, at once, intensely aroused and deeply ashamed, his erection hard and painful, and when Graciela grasped his wrists to guide his hands to their perfect places on either side of her tiny waist and lowered herself down on him he gasped out loud. She arched her back and then fell on him again, her mouth closing on his, breathing in precisely as he breathed out. *Succubus!* Doc had heard the word back home. It referred to a she-demon who came to men in their sleep and sucked their spirits from their bodies. *Spirits. Demons. Saints.* In New Orleans, as in Dolores Hidalgo, these words were synonyms, and the very concept of good and evil was far more ambiguous than in the civilized places of the world. Perhaps it *was* Doc's immortal soul that Graciela was devouring, but the physician knew disease when he tasted it and he couldn't help but believe that he was better shed of it. He climaxed almost immediately and the pain was unmitigated, but there was release and he screamed, and when he stopped the silence was profound.

Doc slept the rest of that night and half of the next day, his head resting in Graciela's lap as she kept watch over him in both wakefulness and dreams.

XI

Hank's standing in the middle of South Presa Street and it's dark and dirty and deserted.

Not like the highway. The highway's lonesome too, but at least it's clean, and once a body gets going he can keep right on going even if it doesn't really take him anywhere.

What the hell happened, anyway? Hank had finally had Doc right where he wanted him, out in the open with no skirt to hide behind, and then something went terribly wrong. Doc was there one second and then, just like that, he was gone, and to add insult to injury, he had somehow managed to drag Hank back to this godforsaken place with him. Makes a body wonder who's haunting who around here.

Hank scans the boarding-house windows up above and finds a rumor of light behind one; faint, flickering amber casting shapes that dance like fairies, or at least butterflies, fluttering behind the colorless curtains. He takes a step closer, hoping for a better look, but the shadows converge and form a single shape, human and feminine, darkening and growing until it fills the entire window.

When the curtains open, the girl stands there, framed in the glow of a hundred unseen candles. Hank recoils but he can't look away because she is achingly beautiful and wearing nothing except a bloodstained bandage around one wrist; she folds her hands as if in prayer and looks out through black eyes that cut through the night like beacons and find Hank and she sees him. She sees him, and in that instant he realizes that she has always seen him, and there is no fear or awe in those eyes to give him any power over her whatsoever, and when she draws the curtains Hank is left alone in the dark.

XII

The voice was female, neither young nor old, appropriately anonymous.

"Bless me, Father, for I have sinned. It's been fourteen years since my last confession."

The priest would have been shocked or at the very least surprised if he weren't hearing the third confession of a long-term apostate in as many days.

"Go on then, child," he encouraged her. The priest's accent had moderated little in the ten years since he'd arrived in America fresh from an Irish seminary, and the woman continued, encouraged as much by the music in the disembodied voice as the kindly words.

"Well, I don't know exactly where to start, Father. The beginnin', I guess. When I was eleven — "

"Perhaps," the priest interrupted, "we need only concern ourselves with the sins that you have committed *since* your last confession."

"Oh, okay. Let's see then . . . Well, to begin with, I've taken the

Lord's name in vain about a million times; well, maybe not a million, Father, but you know what I mean. I guess you hear that all the time, don't you, but it is a sin, ain't it?"

"Yes, child," the priest agreed. "It is indeed a sin and as good a place to start as any."

"Well then, I've taken the Lord's name in vain *many* times, Father," the woman reiterated, and as she continued, the overtone of anxiety in her voice gradually gave way to relief, and the priest settled back in the narrow wooden seat for what the experience of the past few weeks had taught him would be the better part of an hour.

"Well, I've lied a lot, that's for sure, sometimes when there wasn't even nothin' to be lyin' about. Just to stay in practice, I reckon . . ."

He had known that something was afoot as early as February; unfamiliar voices on the other side of the screen, new faces in the nave at Mass. He had originally dismissed it as an anomaly, an unusually enthusiastic observance of Lent by well-meaning chronic backsliders, perhaps. But now it was the Saturday before Holy Week and they were still coming.

" . . . and I guess I don't have to tell you, Padre, that I stole my share of anything that wasn't tied down, I mean, well, I do have to tell you, so I'm tellin' you: I used to steal. From perfect strangers on the street. From so-called friends of mine. It didn't matter. As soon as their backs were turned I stole 'em all blind. I even stole from my own mama and now she won't even allow me in her house no more . . ."

They were easy to spot, these newcomers. At first, they sat in the back of the little church in little knots of two or three. By mid-March they occupied the last four rows and it was hard to ignore the gulf of empty pews that separated them from the regular congregation. After Mass one day, the priest asked an elderly parishioner why this was, and he was taken by surprise when she spat on the ground and hissed, *"¡Putas!"* — whores — indicating a small group of the strangers who were making their way across the little plaza before the church. "They do not belong here."

" . . . of course I drank a little, well, more than a little, I guess, but that was before I got on that dope, and then, well, I just couldn't get enough of that shit — oh! Pardon me, Father! — but, well, anyway I was only seventeen and I didn't have no job or nothin' and there's only so much a girl can steal and it was just a matter of time before I figured out that there's only one way that a poor girl like me can make that kind of money if you know what I mean . . ."

The priest knew of course that a semi-notorious red-light district thrived a little over a mile away from his church, but until recently he had never given it much, if any, thought. He had been elevated to pastor only a year earlier, at the rather precocious age of thirty-six, upon the sudden death of his predecessor, Father Cantu. Since then he'd had his hands full winning the hearts and minds of the mission's all-Hispanic, mostly female, middle-aged-to-elderly congregation. Some, he sensed, still saw him as the fresh-faced curate who had served at their longtime padre's side for nearly a decade. In truth, he had been loath to squander the hard-earned goodwill of the faithful on a handful of heathen hoping to mitigate a lifetime of sin by putting in an appearance on alternate Christmases and Easters, but in the end his calling won out over parish politics. He had vowed to minister to all comers. Young and old, rich and poor. The wretched as well as the righteous. Of course he would hear the confession of this sinner, just as he heard all the other newcomers'. That was his job.

As usual, he made no attempt to keep a tally of the transgressions as they flew by, offering only the occasional semiverbal encouragement or comment, an "I see" or an "um-hum" here and there. Indeed, the stories of these strangers were much the same, including this poor girl's, and he was ashamed to realize that he had been only half listening until she suddenly burst into tears.

"Oh, Father! Please tell me that it's not too late! I swear that I can change, really, truly change! And I promise that I'll try to do good from here on out. Maybe not like *she* does. I mean, something like that must be a gift from God, don't you reckon, Father? A great gift that not everyone — ?"

The priest was caught completely off-guard. The litany had droned on for long enough that he found it necessary to clear his throat before he interrupted.

"Um-humm! I-I beg your pardon, child! Just so that I'm sure that I understand . . . who is *she?*"

"Oh, I'm sorry, Father! I guess I thought — well, you know. The girl, Father. Everybody's talkin' about her, from one end of the strip to the other!"

"One of the other, uh, working girls, then?"

"Oh no, Father. Not Graciela! I don't reckon she's ever turned a trick in her life and one thing's for sure, Father, she ain't from around here! What I heard was that she comes from way down deep in Mexico somewheres and that she has powers, Father — "

"Now, now, child!" the priest interjected. "One can't be too careful about the stories that one hears, especially the ones that come up from, well, dark places."

"But that's just it, Father," the voice insisted, whispering for the first time, forcing the priest to lean in close, his ear only inches from the screen. "This ain't no story. I seen it with my own two eyes! It's in her hands. She just lays her little hand on 'em, wherever they hurt. All she had to do was touch me and, well . . ."

"A trick. A sideshow act."

"But it wasn't like that! Take it from me, Father. I traveled with a carnival for a while. There weren't no smoke nor flash nor none of that! She just touched me was all, and she smiled at me, and I went away from there knowing, Father! Knowing that I could kick. I mean, I was still sick as a dog for three solid days but I toughed it out this time and whenever I felt like I couldn't take any more I only had to close my eyes and I could see her face and I just knew that everything was going to be all right! It was a miracle, Father!"

"Now, see here, child — "

"I know, Father, I know it sounds crazy, but how else do you explain a thing like that? I tried everything to kick dope. Had myself locked up in hospitals. Loony bins. Hell, I even handcuffed myself to a Murphy bed once. Damn near pulled my arm out of the socket tryin' to get loose. Probably would have gnawed it off if the cops hadn't showed up with a key. Oh, I got all the way through the sick part a couple of times but it was never more than a week before I was right back on the street again. But this time, it's been over a month and I don't even think about dope anymore, not even when I see the other girls line up at the spot to get their wake-up. I give it up, Father. I give it up once and for all. And now that I give up the dope there ain't no need for me to be, well, you know, hustlin' no more. Truth is, Father, I haven't turned a trick since that night. It's like everything changed the minute she touched me, and the funny thing is, Father, I didn't even go down there for myself. I just carried my girlfriend Esther there so Doc could look after her . . ."

"To the hospital?"

"No, Father, to the boarding house, the Yellow Rose, down at the end of the strip."

"But you said that your friend was ill."

"Beggin' your pardon, Father, and the Lord's forgiveness, but I never said nobody was sick. She was . . . well, it's just that Doc ain't that kind of a doctor and if you don't mind I'd rather not say anything else bein' that this is my confession and not Esther's!"

She was right. He had forgotten himself entirely and it had been necessary for a member of his own flock to remind him that his curiosity was threatening the sanctity of the confessional.

"Uh, well, then, is there anything else that you'd like to unburden yourself of, child?"

"No, I guess that's all I got, Father. I mean, right off the top of my head."

"Tell me, then, are you sorry for the sins that you have committed?"

"Yes, Padre, with all my heart."

"Then make an act of contrition. Do you remember how it goes? Come on now, I'll help you. O my God, I am heartily sorry for having offended Thee and I detest all my sins because I dread the loss of heaven and the pains of hell," he began, and on the other side of the screen the voice joined in. ". . . But most of all because they offend Thee, my God, Who are all good and deserving of all my love. I firmly resolve, with the help of Thy grace, to confess my sins, to do penance, and to amend my life. Amen."

"Good," the priest affirmed. "Now I want you to go say a decade of the rosary every day for a week, and not just an Our Father, ten Hail Marys, and a Glory Be to the Father and then about your business, but a proper decade, meditating on all five of the appropriate Mysteries for the day. Do you remember your Mysteries, child? Beginning with Monday, they go Joyful, Sorrowful, Glorious, Joyful, Sorrowful, Glorious, Glorious. It'll come back to you. Now go in peace."

Though he knew it was a sin that he would have to deal with in his own confession, he was unable to keep himself from peeping through the curtain to watch the woman cross the nave, earnestly repeating the order of the Mysteries to herself.

Joyful, Sorrowful, Glorious, Joyful, Sorrowful, Glorious, Glorious.

XIII

Doc couldn't see, but the smell of blood filled the air, warm and salty as it settled on his tongue, and he nearly gagged.

"Graciela!" Doc shouted, loud enough, he could only hope, that the girl could hear him over his patient's screams. In any case she responded again and again, wiping his glasses with a length of gauze wrapped around her hand like a bright red mitten.

Somebody had really done a job on the kid. The bullet had evidently entered at the point of the back of his hip, just missing his kidney, and exited from his groin. Doc reckoned that it had nicked one of the branches of the femoral artery, too high and too deep for a tourniquet to do any good, so the only hope was to locate the lacerated vessel and close it with a stitch or two. Unfortunately there was so much blood that locating the bleeder was proving to be difficult. He probed the wound with his fingers, not really knowing what he was searching for. He wasn't a surgeon, after all, and he'd seen just enough emergency room action during his residency to know that he wasn't cut out for it. He was in way over his head and he knew it, but he had to do something or this kid was going to bleed to death. Right here. Right now. He closed his eyes, took a deep breath, and, ignoring the loudening screams, forced his way past torn flesh until . . . there it was! He could feel it, a faint quiver of a pulse.

"Hemostat, goddamn it!" he barked.

Graciela had stood beside Doc through enough procedures to know which instrument was needed and not to take offense at his tone. He was cussing the blood, not her. She slapped the long-handled stainless steel clamp into the palm of Doc's hand the way she had been taught, waiting for him to close his fingers securely around it before she released it. Among her many gifts was an unfailing calmness under pressure, but it wasn't the cool detachment of a good scrub nurse so highly prized in a modern operating room; it was more like the warm, loving patience of the caregivers of another culture, if not another time. She performed each and every task that was asked of her flawlessly and gracefully; no matter how chaotic her surroundings became, she never stopped praying.

"*Santa María de Guadalupe, Mistica Rosa, intercede por la Iglesia, protege al Soberano Pontifice . . .*"

Doc knew this one. It was a prayer to the Virgin of Guadalupe. Graciela always began with it, her voice rising and falling in accordance with the urgency of the situation at hand. Scattered among the Hail Marys and the Our Fathers were less familiar passages, some in Spanish, some in that other language that she sometimes recited. He had asked her, once, what the words meant and she had answered that she didn't know. She had learned them by rote from Grandfather. Still, he found the very sound of Graciela's voice reassuring and was grateful that she never stopped praying until the procedure was completed.

"Got ya, you slippery little motherfucker!"

The clamp snapped into place.

"*. . . Danos un amor ardiente y la gracia de la perseverancia final. Amén!*"

That was how they worked together: Doc cussed and Graciela prayed. There were nights when they were literally awash in blood and the screams continued to ring in their ears long after the procedure was completed, but Doc kept cussing and Graciela kept praying and not a single life had slipped through their fingers so far.

Six months ago Doc would have told the kid that there was nothing he could do and retired to the boarding house to shoot a lick of dope big enough to assuage his Hippocratic guilt, and the ghost would have hovered above the scene and agreed.

"There ain't nothin' you can do, Doc. Hell, you can't save yourself, let alone nobody else!"

Oh, Hank was around, all right. Doc would catch a glimpse of him once in a while, lurking in some shadow, but he didn't hear him anymore or, more accurately, he didn't listen.

Doc was pretty sure that Graciela saw him too, but they never spoke of it so he didn't know that she did not perceive the shade of a great hillbilly singer or even the shape of a man.

She had always seen the ghost, and those like him, had seen them since she was a little girl, and her grandfather had recognized her gift. The first day that she'd laid eyes on Doc, back at the beer joint, she had glimpsed something hovering above him. Like a shadow on the ceiling but at least a shade too dark, and whatever it was, it occasionally failed to accurately mimic the shape actions of its host. Sometimes it fleetingly took on the vague form of an animal cowering on the edges of consciousness, a coyote or a feral dog.

Perhaps it was the *onza*, the wolf-cat her grandfather had told her about. The ancient Mexicans called it *cuitlamiztli* and it was only one of many animal spirits in the world, and though they were worthy of respect, the presence of any of them was natural and rarely cause for trepidation. All the same, she instinctively imposed herself between Doc and any encroaching shadow. Whatever was out there, if it was coming for Doc and intended him harm, it was going to have to get through Graciela first.

Hank is seething, helplessly pacing from corner to corner. Just who the hell does she think she is, anyway? Doesn't she know? Doesn't she see?

But there's the fly in the buttermilk. She does see. Nobody else but Doc has ever seen Hank.

But the girl sees and she tracks every move Hank makes and watches over Doc every waking moment.

Well, Hank reckons there's more than one way to skin a cat.

Manny was waiting in the parlor and he hauled himself up to his considerable height and followed Doc out onto the porch. He knew better than to ask about the kid's condition, reckoning that a report would be forthcoming just as soon Doc was good and ready. He scrambled to light a crooked Camel that dangled from Doc's lower lip.

"Well, he's lost a hell of a lot of blood, Manny," Doc lectured. "And he needs to be in a fucking hospital!" He took a deep drag on the cigarette, held it, and then let it go, long and slow, the thick white smoke issuing from his nose as well as his mouth along with the words. "But the bleeding has stopped, for now, and he's resting, so we'll just have to wait and see." He offered one of his cigarettes and Manny accepted it gratefully.

"Thanks, Doc! I owe you! And my sister — "

"You don't owe *me* shit. But Marge is another story. And Graciela, her being illegal and all. Hell, nobody in this place needs the police to come snoopin' around. What happened, anyway?"

The kid was Manny's nineteen-year-old nephew David, his sister's oldest boy. He and a carload of his friends had double-dog-dared one another to rob a liquor store that night, and for a minute there it had looked like they would get away with it. The owner had politely handed over $256 and a case of beer and then waited until the fleeing desperados were piling into their car before opening up with a .357 magnum and hitting only young David, who, as shitty luck would have it, was bringing up the rear. His partners in crime had intended to dump him in the emergency room driveway but he was on probation for a previous charge and he had begged them to drive him to South Presa instead. His uncle Manny, he said, was a big man down there. He would know what to do.

"I didn't know where else to go, Doc."

"Yeah, well, I'll tell you where you're fixin' to go now. Out there in the street and put your ear to the ground and make damn sure that nobody's going to show up here looking for this boy. No bondsmen, no *migra*, no local John Law! I swear to God, Manny, I'll haul him downtown myself if I have so much as an inkling that something's getting ready to come down, you hear me?"

"I hear you, Doc, I hear you, but don't you worry about nothin'. He had a stockin' over his face and I know that old *boleo* that owns that liquor store. He's like all the rest, can't tell one Mexican from another. No offense, Doc. Anyways, I'll talk to my man downtown, just to be on the safe side." He dropped the butt of his smoke on the porch and stepped on it. "So . . . you reckon he's gonna be all right then, Doc?"

"I've done everything I know to do, Manny. It's out of my hands now." He cocked his head in the direction of the bedroom upstairs where Graciela continued to pray at the kid's bedside. "But she hasn't lost one yet."

The big man grinned but Doc wagged a blood-and-nicotine-stained finger in his face.

"Just as soon as he's well enough to be moved he's out of here, Manny, you hear what I'm sayin'? Now, come on, it sounds like Marge is up. You can settle with her for the room."

Marge was back in the kitchen presiding over a skillet full of sausage while the oven heated up to receive a cookie sheet full of drop biscuits. The coffeepot had just stopped percolating. Doc poured Manny a cup and one for himself and then sat down hard, leaning so far back in the chair that the front legs hovered a foot off the floor.

"Don't do my chair like that, Doc! You'll break it down."

Doc straightened up, spilling a little hot coffee in his lap. "Sorry, Marge." Doc winced and he and Manny exchanged shrugs. Marge had never turned around.

"I heard it creak. It's bad for 'em to lean 'em back like that. Not to mention dangerous. Long night?"

Doc shook his head. "Trust me. You don't want to know. I am going to need room five for a week or so, though. Manny'll be pickin' up that tab. He'll pay you up front."

Marge never looked up from the stove. She did trust Doc and she had learned years ago that it didn't pay to know about everything that transpired under her own roof. Simply looking the other way had always been a way of life at the Yellow Rose. In her father's day it was simply a courtesy extended to the establishment's regular clientele. As the South Presa Strip continued to decline, plausible deniability became, more and more, a matter of legal expediency. And since Graciela had arrived, events had transpired in the old firetrap that Marge intuitively felt she was more comfortable knowing little or nothing about.

"That'll be twenty-five bucks through Saturday, another five if you need linens."

"That's another thing." Doc motioned to Manny, rubbing his thumb and forefinger together, and the big man hauled out a roll of bills and began peeling them off. "Those old sheets are about ruined, I reckon. The pillowcases too, along with every last towel that was in that room and a couple that we had to borrow from seven."

"I see — well, new linens is ten. The extra towels two and a half, plus the two from next door, that comes to — "

"Forty-five dollars. Manny, pay the woman."

And Manny laid the money on the table without complaint and then, turning up the collar of his sport coat against the pre-dawn chill, left to tell his sister the good news.

Marge finally turned around long enough to give Doc a quick look up and down.

"You hungry, Doc? I could fry you a couple of eggs to go with some of this sausage."

"No, thank you, Marge. I'm about whipped. I think I'll lie down for a while."

Doc left a half a cup of coffee sitting on the table and climbed back up the stairs. He looked in on his patient and went through the motions but he knew what he'd find. Stable pulse, steady and strong, respirations normal, no fever, no nothing. And Graciela down on her knees by his side, her hands folded, her rosary beads entwined between her fingers, and fresh blood spotting her bandage. Six months had passed and Graciela's wound still hadn't healed.

But the kid's would. It would heal quickly and cleanly without any trace of a scar.

The kid was going to make it. There wasn't the slightest doubt in Doc's mind. It didn't make any sense. By all rights the kid should be dead, or at least in a coma. An irreversible coma. Hell, he wasn't even in shock.

In fact, Doc reckoned that David would not only live but probably thrive, maybe even turn over a new leaf that very day and never steal or cheat or lie ever again. He would, against all odds, in spite of where he came from and one hell of a bad start, amount to something someday and make his mother very proud. He might not become rich or famous but he would certainly keep safe for the rest of his days and get married and have children, and when his time came he would go peacefully and face his Maker with his eyes wide open.

Doc couldn't credit any science or craft, certainly no skill of his own, for young David's inevitable recovery. It wasn't a matter of faith because Doc reckoned faith was the act of believing in something without any physical proof, the proverbial leap beyond ration and reason. Doc still didn't believe in much of anything, unless it was Graciela herself. But he had personally witnessed her perform one miracle after another, so no suspension of disbelief was necessary. He knew from experience that the kid would pull through, just like that redheaded girl last week.

Her old man had cracked her head like an egg without leaving a mark on her face. A smart pimp never hit a girl anyplace that might show because it damaged the merchandise. The girl couldn't see her way clear to calling the law dogs down on the son of a bitch so she refused to go to the hospital and she damn near died before somehow she wound up on Marge's front porch and Marge and Dallas had helped her up the stairs and banged on Doc and Graciela's door. Graciela had taken the girl's hand and begun to pray and Doc had shined his little light into one of her eyes and then the other, and though it defied what sixteen years of formal education and a lifetime of misery had taught him, he knew that she'd make it. He knew because they all made it. All they had to do was get through that door. Sometimes he would perform the procedures that he'd been taught, but he was never sure if he was really contributing anything. The first few times cold chills ran down his spine but eventually he became accustomed to knowing. Now he just knew and that was all and that was that. The girl made it. And when she was up and around she left her pimp and left town and began a new life somewhere else.

And David would make it too.

"I'll be down the hall if you need me," Doc whispered, and Graciela nodded affirmatively, but he knew Graciela wouldn't be coming to bed and he was too tired to undress so he lay diagonally across the four-poster and fell asleep.

Doc's back in his old office above the liquor store in Bossier and he's drawing down a shot of straw-colored liquid from a bottle marked with crossed bones and a grinning skull into his big glass syringe. He thumps the syringe just below the needle with the back of his index finger and squeezes out the last tiny bubbles of air. Clenching the loaded syringe between his teeth like a pirate's dirk, he's just about to wrap the rubber tube around his arm and summon up a suitable vein to receive the dose when someone clears his throat. He knows the voice before a word is uttered.

"What the hell are you waitin' on, Doc? Christmas?"

Hank's leaning against the examining table, his pants down to his knees, his shorts pulled down just far enough to expose a patch of translucent flesh the size of a half-dollar. He looks like hell, eat up with the gaunt-ass, Doc used to call it, his skin the color of spoiled milk, but he does appear to be solid enough to stick a needle in and when Hank turns and glares back over his shoulder, Doc can only stare slack-jawed in return.

"I swear to God Almighty, Doc. You gonna stand there and stare at my ass all night or are you gonna give me a shot?"

Doc looks down at the loaded syringe, then over at Hank, sighs, and crosses the room.

"Sure thing, Hank. Take a deep breath." He deftly stabs the needle into the spare flesh, pressing the plunger with his thumb and watching the liquid disappear into Hank's hip. What a waste. It won't even help the pain. Nothing helps Hank's pain.

Hank's tucking in his shirt and eyeing Doc suspiciously. "You ain't turnin' queer on me, are you, Doc?"

Doc's still disoriented but he has managed to regain the power of speech. "I wouldn't worry too much if I were you, Hank. Even if I were a little light in my loafers you wouldn't be my type. I've always been partial to an ass with some meat on it."

Hank looks Doc up and down. "You all right, Doc? You ain't actin' like yourself."

"Yeah, I'm okay. It's just that, well, I'm a little bit . . ."

Fuck it, Doc decides. Just ask him.

"Is this a dream?"

Hank manages half a smile and shrugs. "For you, maybe. For me it's just a place that I can follow you and she can't get in the way."

"But you're alive. I mean, you look as alive as you ever did."

"I'm only alive because it's your dream and you're dreamin' that you're back in Louisiana, and in Louisiana I was alive. That is" — Hank surveys the office with distaste — "if you call this livin'."

"So — when I wake up, you'll be dead again, and we'll be back in Texas?"

Hank's up and moving now. Restless, pacing the worn linoleum floor.

"I reckon. It don't make no never mind to me, Doc, but for the life of me I can't figure out what would ever make you want to go back to a place like that. All that bleedin' and screamin', one hard-luck case after another. And what do you got to show for it? Nothin'. Bean money, at best, and nothin' to knock the edge off at the end of a long, hard night." Hank stops, freezing for an instant before turning and closing in on Doc in one long, sliding step, leaning in close, grinning from jug-handle ear to jug-handle ear.

"Big ol' shot of dope'd be good right now, wouldn't it, Doc? Just what the doctor ordered? Well, you're the doctor!"

Hank steps aside and with a flourish reveals the medication cabinet, its doors open wide to showcase an army of glistening amber soldiers dressed in shining glass armor. Doc crosses the room in a step or two and reaches for a bottle, half expecting, even hoping, that it will melt in his hand, but it doesn't. It's hard and cold to the touch, every bit as solid as Hank is in this topsy-turvy dream of Doc's. Without bothering to sterilize his syringe he turns the bottle upside down and pushes the needle through the rubber cap.

"There you go, Doc! Live a little. I don't understand the attraction myself. That stuff's just medicine to me. It does wonders for the pain in my back but then it puts me right to sleep. Give me a drink of whiskey any ol' day of the week."

Doc's got the tourniquet wrapped around his arm again and he's found a vein but Hank's rattling is getting on his nerves . . .

"What the hell are you waitin' on, Doc? Christmas?"

Hank's leaning against the examining table again, *his pants down to his knees, his shorts pulled down just far enough to expose a patch of translucent flesh the size of a half-dollar . . .*

"Goddamn it, Hank! That's not funny!"

"Heh, heh, heh! I'm sorry, Doc. If you could've seen the look on your face just now. Go on. Do yourself up a good one . . ."

"Yeah, right! And then there I'll be, starin' at your narrow hairy ass again. And again, over and over until hell freezes over, I guess, and you'll still be laughin' and I won't be any higher than I am right now! No, thanks, amigo!"

Hank pulls up his pants, buckles his belt, and takes a purposeful step toward Doc.

"Miss it, don't you, Doc."

"Sometimes." *He shrugs.* "But I don't miss waking up sick, or getting rousted by the cops, or hustling all day and all night."

"You're still hustlin', Doc. Harder than you ever have. Harder, now that you've decided to take the weight of the whole goddamn world on your shoulders. Tell me, what did any of them lowlifes ever do for you?"

"It's not about them, Hank. It's about her."

"Well, that's about the first true thing to come out of your mouth in a coon's age, Doc. It's all about her. She's got you, all right. You and everybody else she casts that evil eye of hers on. You don't, none of you, take a piss without she gives you leave first."

"That's a lie!"

"Oh yeah? Then prove it. Take a shot of dope, Doc. You know you want to."

"I don't! I don't want to live like that anymore!"

"Sure you do, Doc. Otherwise, how come you're here?"

"Even if I did . . . I can't. She touched me and now I can't. Even if I w-wanted to!"

"Well, she ain't here, Doc. You can have one here! This is your dream."

"No, I can't! I tried!"

"That wasn't her, Doc. That was my handiwork. Try again, Doc. I promise, I won't mess with you this time. I just wanted you to know what it felt like. To not be able to get what you need."

"And you won't stop me."

"I can't stop you forever. Like I said, I was just messin' with you. It's your dream, Doc."

Doc looked around. It was still his office and the syringe was still full.

"Well, all right, then. And you go on and have yourself a drink, Hank, by all means."

"Huh! Well, if that ain't the meanest thing anybody ever said to me. Don't you know that I would if I could, but I can't."

"Why the hell not?"

"Because there ain't no whiskey in this goddamn hophead dream of yours. I've looked all over this place and there ain't nothin' around here but dope."

Hank's right. There's nothing in the medication cabinet but morphine. Not even an aspirin.

"Well, if it's my dream then it's my dream, Hank, and I never thought I'd ever be the one to say this, but if you'll just shut the fuck up and let me shoot this one good lick of dope in peace you can have all the whiskey you want."

Hank reaches inside his coat and his face lights up. "Well, what have we got here?" He produces a pint of Four Roses and twists off the cap.

"Well, thank you, Doc! I don't mind if I do."

Doc only nods and focuses on the business at hand, his first shot of dope in nearly four months. It always annoys him when other

junkies equate injecting narcotics with the sexual act. He reckons
a good shot of dope is a far superior sensation. But then the needle
slips into the vein on the first try and Doc realizes that his dick is
as hard as a rock. He lets the load of dope go and then . . .

. . . Doc woke up to find that he had, indeed, come in his sleep, the first wet dream of his life at age fifty-six. To his surprise, he was deeply ashamed. He changed his shorts, depositing the soiled ones in the garbage. He wasn't sure exactly why. After all, it was Graciela who sat by Doc's side for seventy-two solid hours when he was kicking, emptying buckets of puke and cleaning up when he soiled himself and the bed, but he kept the dream to himself, a trail of bread crumbs back to his old life. Just in case.

XIV

The corner of South Presa Street and Chicago Boulevard was the bargain basement of prostitution in San Antonio, Texas, and the girls that worked it were reminded of their lowly status every time they looked in a mirror. The corner girls didn't keep well, exposed to the elements as they were, summer sun blazing down on asphalt until pools of oil simmered in the potholes, bone-chilling wind and needle-like rain in the winter taking their toll. The wear and tear was visible even to the drivers of the vehicles that slowed down for a better look as they approached and then sped away, showering the girls with gravel as they accelerated, adding injury to insult. When a car did stop, the girls pounced on it, knowing that whoever got her hand on the door handle first would turn the trick.

Collecting their money was another matter. They were freelancers for the most part, no pimps to enforce a pay-up-front policy and protect them from johns who got a little too rough. The right to retain 100 percent of their earnings was small consolation because the pickings were slim and most of the customers were first-timers who would never come back once they discovered that the girls who worked out of the boarding house and the motels were younger, prettier, and only marginally more expensive. The only repeat business on the corner came from the deadbeats and nut jobs who'd already been eighty-sixed from every respectable den of iniquity on the strip.

Some of the girls on the corner weren't girls at all, and it was a tall, angular black transvestite sporting a tight-fitting gold lamé dress and a five o'clock shadow who muscled his way up to the late-model Ford station wagon first, but for once, it wasn't the customer who was in for a surprise.

"Oh my Lord!" the creature gasped, straightening up to his full six feet and backpedaling when the priest's collar flashed, white against black, as he reached across to roll the window down. "One of y'all gonna have to get this one, ladies. Miss Tiffany's goin' to hell but not today, honey, uh-uh!" He smoothed his skirt as he teetered away, traveling quickly if not quietly on heels that would have crippled half the real girls on the strip. The others filled the void, jostling and elbowing for position.

After all, Tiff figured, a hustler's got to have a code. Even the lowest of the low have a line they won't cross. What would his grandmama say if she looked down from heaven and saw her baby boy rolling around in the back of a station wagon with a man of the cloth!

The priest proffered a bill grasped tightly in his fist; he thrust it out the window and waved it as if it emitted an alluring aroma and then snatched it back again, and the sharks moved in. "Twenty dollars just to take a ride and talk. It's only information I'm after. I'm trying to find someone."

"Hold up!" the he-she bellowed like a bull, breaking character to make sure that he was heard and clattering back to the car.

Only a tough bleached-orange-headed Mexican girl that every-body called Sweaty Betty took exception.

"That ain't right, Tiff! You know it ain't! You walked away!"

Truer words were rarely spoken on South Presa, but twenty dollars was equivalent to four blowjobs, the better part of an hour's work, so the lanky hustler stepped up on the curb, tower-ing over the competition, and made a show of reaching into his beaded purse.

"Yeah, well, who died and left you Jiminy fuckin' Cricket? Move on, y'all, before you make me get this razor out an' cut one of you silly bitches a new pussy! You know that I will!" There was some grumbling but everyone stepped aside as he slid into the passenger seat next to the priest, slammed the door, and rolled the window up. "If I were you, I'd drive, Padre, before these hos tear up your nice car."

Everybody on South Presa knew that Tiffany wasn't really a girl. Some knew that he had once been Daryl Dennis, a big foot-ball star back at Eastside High in Longview, Texas, heavily re-cruited throughout the Southwest Conference. Some cracked jokes about his having played tailback but never to his face. Most called him Big Tiff in order to distinguish him from another Tif-fany for the purpose of conversation, not that anyone who actu-ally knew the two was ever confused.

Little Tiff was white and actually female, a lipstick lesbian who literally held her nose as she swallowed one cock after another in order to support a fifty-dollar-a-day heroin habit. Big Tiff, on the other hand, never touched dope but constantly nursed a half-pint of gin in a brown paper bag and enjoyed his work immensely.

Nevertheless, the two Tiffanys were in pretty much the same boat on South Presa Street.

Big Tiffany was a little too muscular to ever really pass for female. Most of his customers were latent-homosexual specialty tricks who still required at least the pretext of femininity before they fucked a man in the ass. Little Tiff hated men, but as far as she knew, women didn't pay other women for sex. Her constitutional inability to hide her contempt for her clients consigned her to a place alongside the other oddities at the dark end of the street. In a more open-minded city, New Orleans or New York City, perhaps, the pair might have been exotic selections in the stable of an upscale establishment. But not in the home of the Alamo and legendary lines drawn in the sand. Texans liked to keep their freaks in the freak show.

Whatever his intentions, the priest was no different than any other rookie on South Presa. Not knowing the lay of the land, he gravitated toward the obvious, the activity that was visible to the untrained eye. The plan was to find a girl that he could pay to tell him what he wanted to know, so he'd driven up and down the strip several times a day for weeks. Now that he had finally worked up the nerve to stop, the result was wholly unexpected.

"You . . . you aren't really a woman, are you?"

Tiffany reached over and nudged the steering wheel back to the center as the wagon veered uncomfortably close to a parked car.

"No, I ain't, but I'm really a ho, so come on with that twenty, honey! And keep your eyes on the road before you hurt somebody out here."

The priest realized that his hands were trembling and the steering wheel was slick with sweat. He was beginning to decide that his little fishing expedition wasn't such a good idea after all and maybe he'd seen enough of the seamier side of his parish for one day. He laid the twenty on the seat between them. "Well, here then, just take this and I'll drop you off right — "

Tiff reached over and snatched the twenty and added it to the padding in his bra. "Oh, hell no, you won't! The least you can do is turn this thing around and carry me to the spot where you picked me up! I ain't walking all the way back up this raggedy-ass street in these heels, honey."

The priest turned into the beer joint and circled the parking lot, eager to release this monster he had mistakenly netted. His leg cramped and twitched as he strained to hold down the clutch, and his heart pounded in his ears so loud that he couldn't concentrate enough to even pray. Finally, there was a break in the traffic and he pulled out and headed back up the strip toward the corner.

"Slow down, honey!" Tiff admonished. "You're gonna mess around and get us pulled over and then how you going to explain that to your congregation."

The priest backed off the accelerator. He said one Our Father and two Hail Marys to himself to calm his nerves, and it helped him some. It wasn't primarily fear that caused his ears to ring and his heart to pound but carefully suppressed anger. Anger at himself for being so inept, and anger at Tiff for being what he was and treating the priest like a taxi driver. The nerve of this abomination! He followed the prayers with a series of long, slow deep breaths, in through his nose and out through his mouth, the way his boxing coach back at seminary had taught him. He began to feel better immediately and somehow, somewhere halfway between the beer joint and the corner, he recovered his resolve and he remembered that it was his calling that had brought him to this terrible place. That this was his parish and these people were his flock and the children of God, no matter what the old women in the congregation believed. Even this aberration that now rode by his side was worth saving . . . and maybe she, or he, could at least tell him what he wanted to know. He had to find this girl everyone was talking about and see for himself if the stories were true. He said another Hail Mary, out loud this time, and suddenly gunned the station wagon, accelerating into a hard left turn into a side street followed by a right into an unpaved alley.

"*Uh-uh,* honey!" Tiffany warned, one hand reaching for the door and the other into his purse to produce an ivory-handled straight razor. "You better stop this thing right now!"

The priest complied, bracing himself against the steering wheel, slamming on the brakes, and tossing Tiff into the dashboard like a rag doll. The razor clattered down into the tight space between the seat and the door. Then, before his passenger had a chance to recover his equilibrium, the priest mashed on the gas and drove down the alley until he spotted an abandoned garage. He wheeled the station wagon around back and parked parallel to a blank cinder-block wall, so close that Tiff couldn't open his door more than a couple of inches. Realizing he had nowhere to go, Big Tiff fished desperately for the razor, and . . . found it! He brandished the six-inch blade, obviously determined to exit through the priest if necessary.

"I will fuck you up, you freak, if you don't get out of my way!"

The priest held up both hands, palms out, so that Tiff could see that they were empty, and he struggled to catch his breath.

"I assure you I *am* a priest and I mean you no harm! I only want to talk!"

"Yeah, right!" Tiff snarled, lashing out with the razor but coming up short as the priest recoiled, narrowly avoiding the blade. Tiff couldn't help being impressed that the priest, unarmed, continued to stand his ground.

"If you're a for-real priest, then show me some kind of ID."

For an instant the priest was insulted, but then he realized where he was and whom he was talking to. "Well, I don't, I mean, I never . . ."

"Aw, come on! You got to have something on you that proves that you're what you say you are. A bingo card, somethin'?"

The priest laughed a little at that, but Tiff wasn't even smiling and he still had the razor. The priest waved the fingers of his left hand.

"I'm going to get out my wallet."

Tiff nodded but extended the razor to arm's length.

The priest pulled out a plain black wallet, rifled through it, and in a moment produced a dog-eared pale green document stamped with the seal of the U.S. Immigration and Naturalization Service and bearing the name of one Father Padraig Killen, born in Letterfrack, County Galway, Ireland, on the third of March in 1927, and he handed it over to Tiffany.

"You see right there, under 'occupation,' it clearly says 'clergy.'"

Tiff scanned the document, comparing the vital statistics listed — brown hair, brown eyes, five foot eight, a hundred and sixty pounds — with the man who was still blocking his escape.

"Ireland, huh? I knew you wasn't from around here." He tossed it back. "Okay, so maybe you're a priest." Tiffany folded the razor. "But that don't mean you ain't a freak, so keep your ass over there. You say you're lookin' for somebody? Well, honey, I know everybody down here and everybody know me. You won't get nothin' out of them bitches back there, no way. Most of 'em illegal and and half of 'em can't even speak American! Whoever it is you're lookin' for, if they down here I can find 'em. Tell you what. For another twenty . . . Now, don't you look at me like that! Just a little somethin' extra for scarin' a girl half to death!"

The priest replaced the card in his wallet, opened it wide, and found one more bill.

"Well, my resources are somewhat limited just now. Would you settle for a tenner?"

Tiff eyed the bill for about a beat and then shrugged and extended his hand, now empty of the razor, palm up.

"Who you tryin' to find, honey?"

The priest smiled faintly, released the bill, and rolled down his window to let in some fresh air.

"I'm looking for a girl. A Mexican girl."

"Well, there's plenty of girls down here and most of 'em's Meskin."

"This one would be young. About eighteen or nineteen. Her name is Graciela."

Big Tiff stiffened, and the priest felt it all the way across the car.

"Humph! So that's what you like, huh? Young, narrow-ass thing. Hell, if that's what you want, I know a girl that does the whole thing, honey, plaid skirt, pigtails, and all —"

"No!" the priest interrupted, loudly enough that a faint ringing reverberated from the cocoon of glass and steel that surrounded them. "I told you, I just want to talk. To this one particular girl. I need to speak with her about a matter of some importance."

"Well, I ain't no snitch, and if you —"

"No, it's nothing like that! She's not in any kind of trouble. I only want to meet her because, well, I understand that she's a Catholic and I want to offer her my assistance in any, uh, spiritual matter that she might —"

"Yeah, well, I don't know nothin' about that, bein' raised up in the AME myself, and you know what else? I might have heard something somewhere about a girl like that, but for thirty dollars, that's all I can remember right now."

The priest struggled to control his temper. He'd always had to, ever his since his seminary days. He repeated the breathing exercise he'd been taught — *in through your nose, out through your mouth* — until he was at least outwardly calm. "That's all the money I have with me."

Tiff was certain that Father Killen was telling the truth but Tiff's survival instincts had kicked into overdrive and he was acutely aware that continuing to converse with a customer who was willing to pay him to talk was tantamount to giving away a piece of ass and against his deepest principles. "Then that will conclude show-and-tell for today, honey. Feel free to come back on payday and aks me again, and in the meantime I'd appreciate it if you'd carry me back up to my spot now."

The priest felt like he was entitled to an answer to at least one more question for his money, but he took in the determined look in Tiff's eye and remembered the razor and thought better of saying so. He grudgingly ground the car into gear and rolled down the alley to the street. They pulled up opposite the corner where he had picked Tiff up, and the hustler reached for the door handle but then stopped, turned, and leaned back, lounging with his head lolling against the passenger-side window. His eyes narrowed to near slits, as if he were sizing the priest up. "You sure there ain't nothin' else I can do for you, Padre? I can suck the chrome off a trailer hitch."

"Get out," ordered the priest.

"Suit yourself!" Tiff snorted through elevated nostrils and then he glanced across the street to make sure that the girls were all watching before he got out of the car. Before the priest could drive away, Tiff leaned back in through the window, winked, and said loudly enough for the whole neighborhood to hear, "Thank you, honey, come on back an' see me now, you hear?"

Tiff barely managed to avoid decapitation as the wagon peeled away.

The priest was back on the strip the next day, and the day after, and the day after that. He came at odd times, whenever his schedule allowed, and he witnessed much activity that intrigued him but almost none that he understood. In the name of discretion he parked in a different place every day, alternating between one side of the street and the other, but within a week everybody on South Presa had noticed the rather conspicuous vehicle.

For his part, Big Tiff was telling anybody who would listen that the stranger in the white Ford wagon was just a rich freak who liked to play dress-up and was queer as a three-dollar bill. Even looking at him, Tiff assured them all, would be a waste of their time, not to mention an invitation to serious bodily harm.

But truth be told, nobody on the strip was worried about the priest. Deeper mysteries were unfolding.

People were disappearing. Not that anyone on the strip suspected foul play. That had happened before, monsters that preyed on those whom no one would bother to avenge, but this wasn't like that. Some did indeed simply vanish without a word or a trace, but most said goodbye to somebody, and that somebody told somebody else, and, hope being contagious, word got around.

Folks were getting out. Simply walking away. Everybody you asked had his or her own theory as to where everybody was going and why, but they all added up to something to do with the Mexican girl who stayed down the street at the Yellow Rose.

Tiff didn't get it. What was all the fuss about? A skinny little gal from some rat hole in Mexico with no hustle. She didn't fuck, she didn't suck, and she didn't have to, because everybody on the strip was lined up to kiss her Meskin ass! Fuck that bitch! She was nothing!

But who knew what went on behind closed doors up there in that big old ugly-ass house.

Not Tiff, that was for sure, and he reckoned he never would because that bull dyke Marge didn't allow niggers past the porch.

Father Killen had heard the same stories as Tiff had and received them every bit as skeptically. It was 1964, after all, and a modern seminary education had taught the priest that the days when God had any need of proving His existence by supernatural demonstration were long gone. His own faith was based on an unquestioning acceptance of a vocation that ran in his family, his older brother having been ordained a decade before him. The fact was that, where he came from, jobs were scarce. His calling was practical as well as spiritual.

When the South Presa girls began to turn up in his church, he was intrigued but he didn't dwell on it. He never saw some of them ever again; he'd hear their confessions and then they'd waft out the door as if the weight of their sins were the only things keeping them in Texas. He often wondered about them, even included some in his prayers. He feared that most slipped and went back to their old lives on the South Presa Strip, but he liked to believe that some returned to their families or moved far away and started all over again.

But a few stayed around, took Communion, and joined the newcomers at the back of the nave. They came to Mass every Sunday, and with each passing week the priest watched in wonder as they were transformed. They greeted everyone that they met with kind words and smiling faces, and even the older parishioners were won over in time. They volunteered for any good works that presented themselves, and they did them with prayer and praise for God on their lips.

It was from them that the priest first heard of the blood on the bandage and the name Graciela, the miracle worker of South Presa Street. Finally, he had determined to find her and see for himself.

Father Killen grew more desperate with every passing day. The strip was less than a mile and a half long from one end to the other, and, toxic environment that it was, its roots in the surrounding neighborhood weren't deep. One had to travel only a block east or west before malignant blight gave way to honest working-class squalor. It was ridiculous, thought the priest, that after driving from one end of the narrow corridor to the other, day after day and night after night, he had yet to lay eyes on the girl. Maybe he was wasting his time after all. Maybe she didn't exist.

Occasionally he'd work up the nerve to make another pass at Chicago Boulevard. If Big Tiff was out, the priest wouldn't even slow down. Even when he wasn't, none of the girls would get anywhere near the priest's car, no matter how much money he waved out the window, for fear of tangling with the intimidating transvestite. It was inevitable that a morning would come when Father Killen gave up, crossed himself, invoked the Holy Mother, and pulled the wagon over at the corner. All the girls stood aside, and Big Tiff climbed into the shotgun seat, unchallenged, the market successfully cornered.

Tiff's triumph soon gave way to disgust. Father Killen was just like everybody else. All he wanted to talk about was the Mexican girl.

Tiff didn't understand. If souls were precious and the priest's stock-in-trade, then it stood to reason that there was more than one sinner on the south side worth saving. South Presa Street had a thousand tales to tell, ruminations on ruined lives that, like all refuse, were worth something to somebody, and Tiff knew them all. There were at least a hundred girls on the strip in no less mortal peril. After all, neither Big Tiff nor anyone on South Presa had any firsthand (or even secondhand) knowledge of Doc's girl accepting so much as a peso in return for sex. Nothing to tell, nothing to sell, Tiff figured, but the priest would have none of it. He would pay to hear only what Tiff could tell him about the Mexican girl.

Tiff heaved a sigh. "I know the bitch. So what?"

"So, do you know where I might find her?"

"She at the Yellow Rose."

The priest held out a twenty "The Yellow . . ."

"Rose, honey." Tiff banked it beneath his blouse. "Boardin' house at the bottom of the strip. She shacked up down there with a junkie name of Doc."

For some reason, that information struck Father Killen physically, a pang down low in his gut. What was he thinking? That she'd be a virgin?

"Doc, you say?" As much to cover his discomfort as anything else, he reached into the glove compartment and pulled out a small notebook, the kind reporters used, and a pencil. "Do you mind?"

"You sure you ain't a cop?"

"If I were, don't you suppose you'd already be locked up? Doc who?"

Tiff shrugged and lit a cigarette. "Doc's the onlyest name I know. Used to be a MD, they say, before the dope took him down. Now he patches up folks that can't go to no hospital and he takes care of the girls when they . . ." Tiff realized he had nearly misspoken. That information was worth a twenty by itself. He backpedaled a little. "Uh, well, you know, when they come down with the clap or the general cunt infection. He a bad dope fiend. Shoot a half a yard a day, or at least he did before she come along."

"She?"

"The Meskin girl! The one you're lookin' for! That Gracy Ella or whatever her name is. She give me the creeps. I don't go nowhere near the Yellow Rose. If you're lookin' for that hoodoo bitch, that's where you'll find her. But if I was you I'd swing back by the church first and pick up about a gallon and a half of holy water and some silver bullets and shit and you can drop me off right here, honey."

He slammed the door and was gone before Father Killen could ask what *hoodoo* meant.

The priest found himself a parking spot on School Street where he had a clear view of both the front and back doors of the Yellow Rose. He'd learned quickly that arriving before noon was a waste of time. If he was in his spot by one or two in the afternoon he could witness the stirrings of the boarding house's early risers, usually the elusive Graciela herself.

He saw her first in the dusty backyard hanging laundry out to dry. She wore a yellow floral cotton shift and nothing on her feet; her arms were stretched up to hold the corner of a sheet in place, and a pair of wooden clothespins were clenched in the corner of her mouth. There was nothing vaguely threatening about the girl as far as the priest could tell. On the contrary, Graciela was ethereally beautiful, even from a distance, the image of innocence, barefoot in the dirt and broken glass like a blossom in the waste-land. She seemed unaffected by her decrepit surroundings, even gay. Her very name sounded beautiful and fresh and clean, and the priest caught himself repeating it over and over to himself.

Graciela left the house infrequently, two or three times weekly at best, but when she did the priest followed on foot, and he found that her itinerary rarely varied.

First stop: the pawnshop up the street on the right. She'd stay for as much as an hour, sometimes more, but her business there was obviously of a personal nature, as she always arrived and de-parted empty-handed. After that she visited the beer joint. Some-times she was in and out. Sometimes she stayed awhile, but she always at least dropped by on her way to her final destination, the grocery store. Some days she'd stop back by the bar or the pawnshop on her way home and leave some part of what she'd purchased behind. Acts of charity, the priest hypothesized. Inter-esting.

The other human traffic that Father Killen continued to wit-ness on his daily stakeouts presented more questions for subse-quent sessions with Big Tiff, at twenty dollars a pop, than it did clear answers.

"Who's the old man, then?" the priest asked as he and his infor-mant sat parked in the same blind alley where they had become acquainted. "The fat one with the scar on his face, always about a half step behind a rather bent-over old woman. I've never seen him before, but the woman's a parishioner of mine."

"You mean Santo. He run the pawnshop, him and that mean-ass wife of his."

"Mean, you say? Surely we're not talking about the same per-son! I see her at Mass every Sunday and she seems like as sweet an old lady as you would ever hope to meet."

Tiff's mouth opened with a pronounced clucking sound whenever he delivered a piece of what he considered to be particularly juicy information. "Yeah, well, where the hell you think ol' Santo got that scar from?"

Father Killen whistled, genuinely impressed. "Well, what about the big Mexican fellow then, in the black four-door Ford?"

The priest had known before he asked the question that no answer would be forthcoming. Not today in any case. Tiff did his best to ration his answers, always careful to hold something back for the next visit. He knew that the time was rapidly approaching when his rather shallow pool of marketable information would run dry. "I don't know nobody like that," he lied. "I be glad to ask around, though. Stop by tomorrow evenin' and we'll see."

Father Killen's patience was dissipating rapidly as well, but he knew it wouldn't do to push. There was still much to learn, but sometimes it was all the priest could manage not to strangle the transvestite with his bare hands. He continued to rely on the breathing technique and prayer to control his revulsion and calm him whenever it became obvious that Tiff was holding out on him. Sometimes he found it necessary to dig even deeper into his boxing coach's toolbox.

Before coming to Maynooth Seminary to teach theology and coach the boxing team, Father Stephen Walsh had traveled extensively in Asia as a missionary. He had recognized in the young seminarian Padraig Killen a genuine athletic talent, as well as a dark and dangerous streak of anger that unchecked, he feared, might result in an unfortunate incident if not a tragedy in the ring. He taught the young man techniques that he had learned from a yogi in an ashram in Ceylon, touting them as a means to improve his pugilistic performance. "If you lose your temper like that out there, you're at the mercy of your opponent, son. You've got to focus! Find your center and wait for the other man's weaknesses to reveal themselves. Then you pick them apart, one by one."

"Well, all right," the priest told Tiff now. "Tomorrow, then? A little earlier, say, three? I've catechism at six."

At the next meeting they picked up right where they'd left off, over a thermos of coffee that the priest had brought along with the customary twenty-dollar bill.

"Big man's name is Manny. Short for *Man-u-el*. Manuel Castro, like the Cuban. Peddles dope, they say, but I don't fuck with that."

"And what's his business at the boarding house? Who's he see there?"

Tiff shook his head. "Used to be Doc, for sure, but the street say Doc ain't gettin' high no more. But shee-it, I don't believe that for a minute. He still on South Presa and folks still go to see him down to the Rose. Him and that hoodoo girl."

This time the priest asked. "Hoodoo?"

"Hoodoo! Voodoo! Mumbo jumbo! Whatever you want to call it." Tiff motioned for the priest to come closer and clucked. "Some say that girl got powers. Healin' powers, you know, layin' on hands and shit. Humph! She ain't touchin' me!"

The priest's pulse quickened again. This was it! This was what he'd been waiting for! This deviate stank of gin and worse and made his skin crawl, but he was so close now.

In through your nose! Out through your mouth!

"She'll see!" Tiff rattled on. "Somethin' bad'll come of all of that carryin' on! And Marge and Dallas — "

"Marge and . . . ?"

"Dallas. They run the joint. But I reckon that Meskin girl's got 'em all hoodooed, and it's her that calls the shots down to the Yellow Rose nowadays."

"And these healings that you speak of, you've witnessed them firsthand, then? Seen them with your own eyes?"

"Witnessed?" Tiff weighed the word, framed as it was in a direct question. "I ain't 'witnessed' shit. Like I told you, I don't go near that joint."

"You've never been inside? Not once?"

"Hell, no!"

"Well, what have you heard, then? Surely you know someone –"

"I know a lot of people that's *white* that been down to the Yellow Rose for one reason or another . . ."

Of course. It was a boarding house: no coloreds allowed.

". . . and they got all kinds of stories they tell about healin's and haints and who knows what else and I don't believe none of that but that don't mean there ain't nothin' goin' on down there!" Out of breath or bile or both, Tiff took a break long enough to fish a pack of Marlboros out of his bag and offer one to the priest, who shook his head but pushed in the cigarette lighter on the dashboard. "I ain't *seen* nothin', but I'll tell you what I *know*," Tiff went on. "Folks go in there all tore up and then walk out again and heal up too soon to be natural! Nothin' like that happened down here before that Meskin girl come along" – he took a quick look over each shoulder – "and I'll tell you what else. Ever since she come, some girls go in that place and nobody ever hears from 'em ever again!"

The priest rolled his eyes and shifted impatiently in his seat. He'd heard that kind of wild innuendo from Big Tiffany before and he wasn't interested. "Ah, Tiff. I told you, I've been watching the place for weeks now."

Tiff reared up and howled, "Just aks around! Aks if anybody seen Marylou lately! Or Fat Alice. And where the hell Lupe at, 'cause that bitch owe me twenty dollars!" The lighter popped out with a muted *ping* and the priest handed it to Tiff with a shaking hand. Tiff captured the priest's wrist, steadied it, and lit his smoke. He took a long deep drag, and his head disappeared momentarily in a cloud of thick gray smoke. When he reappeared, there were precisely two tears rolling down Tiff's cheek and for a moment Father Killen thought the creature would break down and bawl. But he only sniffed, and the priest reached out and offered his handkerchief.

"Here."

Tiff looked up and accepted it, wiped his makeup-smeared face, and then covered his nose with the freshly laundered cotton square and blew loudly.

"Thank you," Tiff fairly purred, offering to return the handkerchief to the priest. Father Killen shook his head and Tiff kept going. "You know how fucked up that is, Padre, pardon my Cherokee. Suckin' girls in there like she do? Usin' Doc as bait, that's what she's doin' 'cause he's the onlyest place these girls got to go when they in trouble!"

Father Killen choked on a mouthful of cold coffee. As he usually did when Tiff began to expound on his own theories about the Yellow Rose, the priest had tuned him out . . . but what exactly had the abomination meant by *trouble*?

"Surely you don't . . . ?" Then the priest put it all together, and he named the beast. "Doc!"

Tiff did a double take.

"What? Naw! Don't tell me you didn't . . . Damn, Padre! I reckoned you'd figured that out by now, skulkin' around the Rose the way you do!"

The priest's mind reeled. He had sat outside the boarding house, day after day, night after night, and watched the comings and goings of the damned. He'd known that Graciela was surrounded by serpents; by harlots, thieves, and deviants. But . . . an abortionist.

Big Tiff watched as realization spread across the priest's face. "Damn!" He complained, "See, now I feel stupid, Padre, 'cause if you'da aksed me that question outright, that information woulda cost you at least another twenty-dollar bill!"

Father Killen wasn't listening anymore. He was preoccupied with chastising himself. How could he have been so stupid! He had sat there in his car night after night doing nothing while the greatest of all sins, atrocity of atrocities, unforgivable in the eyes of God, was committed over and over again beneath the very same roof that sheltered a living miracle. His miracle . . .

"Hell, Padre! What did you think all those girls were doin', in and out Doc's place like that?"

And this monster knew! He'd known all along! *In through your nose! Out through your . . . Forgive me, Lord.*

A storm of fists and elbows fell on Tiff, the blows raining down in staccato flurries of four, one-two-three, hook-hook-hook, followed by a vicious uppercut. Just like Father Walsh had taught him. As big and strong as Tiff was, he had no chance whatsoever of defending himself. The terrified hustler's head snapped backward and forward like a rag doll's, rebounding off of the window again and again until the safety glass cracked, crystallizing into a spider-web-shaped halo. But the beast that had slept inside the priest for a couple of decades was not yet sated. Father Killen ratcheted the driver-side door open with a bleeding left hand and rounded the front of the car in a couple of steps. Tiff tumbled out backward as the passenger door was yanked open but the priest caught him before he hit the ground and dragged him around the corner of the cinder-block garage and stood him up against the wall. One-two-three-*four*, the onslaught continued for a quarter of an hour more and it was only the frequency of the blows that kept Tiff on his feet. Blood flooded both of his eyes and his nose, and he gulped air mixed with blood in through his mouth and expelled in a piteous wail, *"Ma-a-a-m-m-a-a!"* but another merciless blow shut him up and he realized that the priest intended to kill him, right there, right then.

But he didn't.

The punishment suddenly stopped and there was the slightest delay before Tiff slid down the wall and folded into a heap at Father Killen's feet. The priest stood there panting and sucking on his bleeding right hand for a moment, trying to reconcile the scene before him, but it was no use. He wished that he could tell himself that he had blacked out, but it simply wasn't so. He had, in fact, been hyperconscious of his actions the entire time, relishing every blow that he had meted out to the deviate he despised, and luxuriating in the release of the pent-up rage of a lifetime. He scanned his prostrate victim for signs of life but made no move to offer any aid. When Big Tiff softly groaned and tried in vain to lift his head, Father Killen crossed himself and turned and ran to his car.

XV

✳

Hank's surprised. "So you're talkin' to me again?"

Doc shrugs. "Well, technically, I'm not talking to anybody. If you'll notice, my lips aren't moving."

"Oh! So this is just another one of your crazy dreams."

"Maybe, but I don't think so. It just occurred to me that, being as nobody but me can hear you when you talk, maybe not everybody needs to hear me when I'm talkin' to you . . . or something like that. Anyway, as far as I know, Hank, I'm wide awake and sitting on Marge's front porch rockin' up a storm, and you're perched up there on the rail like a crow, just like always."

"Course I am, Doc. That's what I do. I just follow you around like a goddamn dog. And now I'm a crow to boot!"

"Or a cat."

Hank hops down off of the rail, both feet landing simultaneously on the porch without a sound. "A what?"

"A cat. Graciela says you're some kind of a cat. She sees you, you know."

Hank paces to the end of the porch, one, two, three, four long paces, turns on his heel, and instantly snaps back into his starting position. "She stares at me," he whines. "Long and hard. I can feel it." The ghost reaches out and buries a long thin finger deep in the solid oak door. "Almost." He yanks his hand back, and, cradling it as if it's newly injured, he's pacing again, one, two, three, four, snap! "Well, if she can see me then how come she don't talk? I've tried talkin' to her but she don't never say nothin'!"

The physician taps a Camel out of the pack, lights it, and drags deep. "Maybe she can't hear you, Hank. You know, she told me once that you're only here for me."

"Huh! That so? How come she can see me then?"

"I don't know, Hank. Because she sees things . . . folks . . . entities like you . . ."

"I ain't no en-ti-whatchamacallit, and I ain't no cat and I ain't no crow! I'm Hank goddamn Williams, goddamn it! A great singer and songwriter and entertainer!" Pacing again, one, two, three, four, snap! One, two, three, four, snap!

Doc nods in agreement. "Yeah, I know. Doesn't make sense, does it? But then, neither does me sitting on the porch talking to you. She sees you all right and you can take my word for that. She sees everything."

Hank settles dejectedly back onto his perch on the rail. "Well, at least you're talkin' to me again."

Doc stands up and stretches, arms out, twisting at the waist, to the left and then the right. "Yeah, well, you've got Graciela to thank for that. She says you're here for me and I'm here for you. Reckons we're supposed to learn something from one another, something like that. What you say we take us a little walk and 'learn' what's going on up at the beer joint?"

Doc hollered, "Marge!" and the answer came from way back in the kitchen but loud and clear.

"Yeah, Doc?"

"Tell Graciela I'm up to the beer joint for a spell! Be back directly!"

The game was draw dominoes, childlike in its simplicity: match the spots, or pips, on your tiles, or bones, to those of your opponent until one of you has no tiles left or until there's no place left to play. But in the beer joint, it was played and watched by grown men in deadly earnest.

Doc shook his head as he totaled up the score and then pushed his remaining bones back into the middle of the table.

"Manny, my friend, another draw like that last one and I'm going to make you turn out your pockets!"

Manny only grinned and grunted and offered two ham-size closed fists. Doc chose the right, and Manny opened his hand to reveal a white ivory tile divided in half by a line with three black spots on one end and four on the other. "Seven," the big man acknowledged before clapping the remaining hand down hard on the table and then rolling it to one side to reveal a double-six. "Twelve, Doc. I guess it just ain't your day." Having earned the right to draw first, Manny shoved the tiles back to the center. Doc then shuffled them in a couple of halfhearted circular motions, and Manny drew his seven bones and stood them on their edges, his forehead pinched into several rows of deep furrows as he contemplated his hand.

Doc was rapidly losing interest in the contest. He had seen Manny on a roll like this too many times to believe that anything, including cheating, could spare him the beating that he was taking at the hands of his bearlike opponent. Perhaps Doc would have stood a chance at one of the more sophisticated forms of dominoes, the bidding games like moon or forty-two. But Manny only played draw, and he played draw only for money.

"You forgettin' somethin', Doc?"

Doc winced as he drew his bones one by one, lifting each one up in the vain search for the high double necessary to begin the game.

"I didn't forget a goddamn thing, Manny. I guess I just reckoned that my credit was good around here and that we could settle up all at once, but now that I see how it is . . ." He leaned back, groaning and muttering under his breath to exaggerate the effort, and finally produced a wrinkled dollar bill, wadded it up in a ball, and rolled it across the table. "There you go, Amarillo Slim! Don't spend it all in one place."

"Thank you, Doc." Manny chuckled, smoothing the bill out on the table's edge. "You know, as bad as you play dominoes, it still don't even come close to makin' up for the dope you used to buy. But every little bit helps." And then he led with a double-six.

"How is business, Manny?"

The big man's smile faded. "Steady Eddie, Doc. Nine to five. Same poor fuckers come by every day until one day they don't. If you ask around somebody'll tell you why but I don't 'cause I don't want to know. If they got busted they'll do their stretch and they'll line up the day they get out. If they . . . well, if somethin' else happened then somebody else will take their place in the line." The big man brightened a little. "Some of 'em pull up. Get clean. You did, Doc. Some funny things goin' on around here, Doc, that's for sure." Manny sighed. "But people still get high, Doc. Every day. All day long."

169

Doc squinted at the Pearl Beer clock behind the bar. "Now that you mention it, Manny, it is a little early for you to be sitting on your ass down here playin' dominoes. Who's watching the spot?"

"Ramón."

Doc's cigarette dangled from his lower lip as his jaw dropped. "Ramón? Junkie Ramón? Run-off-with-the-pack-and-bring-it-back-light your nephew Ramón?"

"Yeah," Manny admitted. "He's been fuckin' up. But he don't take much. Not so far, anyway. And he's family. To tell you the truth, Doc, I'm sick of sittin' down there all day. Thinkin' about givin' it up."

Doc leaned back as if to get a better look at the big Mexican and came to the realization that he was indeed serious.

"But what'll you do, Manny? How'll you live?"

Manny shrugged. "I got a little money put by. Enough to keep Mama in beans and bingo cards for the rest of her life, and the house is paid for. Maybe I'll get a job."

Doc, as well as several bystanders, convulsed in belly laughs, long and loud and uncontrollable.

"What's so funny about that?" Manny fumed. "I got skills! Hey, I can drive. I could drive a eighteen-wheeler. Truck drivers make good money; I can get a commercial license, no problem. I ain't got no felony record or nothin'."

As if on cue, the front door burst open and Teresa whistled, loud and piercing, two fingers of her right hand in her mouth, and hollered, "Hugo!" A handful of patrons bolted for the back door, a couple for the bathroom. Detective Hugo Ackerman ignored them all and headed straight for the table where Doc and Manny sat with their hands already raised.

"Relax, relax. Put your hands down. I ain't here on business, Doc." He did a double take back to Manny. "Well, not my busi-

170

ness, anyway. Manny, shouldn't you be up the street peddlin' that poison of yours? Why don't you take a hike and let me have a word with Doc here."

Manny waited for Doc's okay, a barely perceptible tilt of the head, before shoving back from the table and lumbering toward the door. The remaining bystanders cleared the area.

Detective Ackerman dragged Manny's chair around the table and planted it perpendicular to Doc's. He pivoted it around backward, and the wooden chair groaned as he straddled the seat and rested his arms on the back. After checking to make sure that no one remained within eavesdropping range, he leaned forward until he was only inches from Doc's ear and nearly whispered, "I need your help, Doc."

Doc squirmed in his chair and fiddled with the dominoes. "Well, I don't know exactly how to say this, Detective, and I'm sure you won't believe me, but I don't shoot dope anymore, and I doubt very seriously if there's anything I can tell you — "

Hugo interrupted. "I heard that. I didn't believe it, but now that I hear it from you . . . look at me, Doc." Doc pivoted in his chair and the cop squinted, looking into Doc's eyes, first one and then the other. "But that's not what I meant, Doc. I don't need you to tell me nothin'. What I need is . . . is your services."

A quick hustler's read of Hugo's face detected no obvious tell unless it was the openness Doc had never seen there before. "Well, all right then . . ." Doc glanced over each shoulder. "So, you've got someone in trouble." That was interesting, mused Doc. The cop actually blushed!

"Well, uh, someone's in trouble, that's true enough, but you can help me, can't you, Doc? Folks around here say you're really good at . . . what it is you do. I've asked around and everybody reckons that somebody, a girl, I mean, that was in trouble would be in good hands if she come to you for help, I mean, if that's what she needed." Now Hugo was searching Doc's face for answers.

"I may be able to help you," said Doc, "and your friend. I'd obviously have to examine her. Would you happen to know how far along . . . ?"

"Six weeks. Exactly."

Doc thought that there was something disconcerting about the cop's certainty. "Six? Well, that's good, then, the earlier, the better. Of course, there's the matter of my fee."

"Yeah." Hugo nodded. "I understand that the going rate is a yard. Your arrangement with me has always been fifty a week but I'm willing to suspend your payments until – "

Doc was already shaking his head. "No."

Hugo raised both hands, palms up, in genuine surprise. "I-I don't understand!"

"That'll be cash. Fifty now. Fifty on completion of the procedure. Same as anybody else."

"But – "

"But nothin'. Like I said, I quit shootin' dope so I don't need any more, uh, protection from your intrusions into my personal life. Yeah, you could plant something in my room but you won't because if I'm locked up I can't help you with your little problem, can I? As far as my professional activities are concerned I reckon that you're no longer in a position to be pointing any fingers. Let's face it, Hugo, your options are somewhat limited. If you were one of those Alamo Heights swells, then things might be different, but the truth is that when a regular everyday hard-working guy like yourself knocks up his little girlfriend, I'm the only game in town. After me, all you'll find out there is some butcher with a wire coat hanger or an enema bag full of lye. That being said, I'll be glad to help you and your lady friend out, but I'll sleep better sleep if we keep this transaction on a cash basis, from my hand to yours. That way nobody gets confused."

Hugo hung his head for an instant, then reached in his pocket, pulled out a small stack of bills, and counted out two twenties and a ten.

Doc raked them up and tucked them into his hatband. "Seven o'clock at the Yellow Rose. Bring the rest of the money."

Detective Ackerman stood up and walked out of the bar without a word. Manny and the other domino players migrated back to the table. Doc checked the bar clock and determined that there was enough time for at least a couple of hands before he had to punch in, but Graciela, he knew, liked a little warning before patients arrived. He surveyed the room for a likely courier. Not sticking every extra dime one made in one's arm afforded one luxuries.

"Precious!"

The skinny working girl spun on her barstool to face the domino table. "Yeah, Doc?"

"You reckon you could stick your head in the door up at the boarding house and let Marge and Graciela know that we got company coming at about seven?" He held up a neatly folded ten-dollar bill.

"I'd be glad to, Doc, and you just hang on to your money, hon. I pass right by there on my way home anyway."

"I'll be damned!" Doc muttered, shaking his head and pocketing the ten. Manny grunted. "Told you, Doc! Somethin' funny's goin' on around here."

Graciela ran through the list in her head, checking off some items in Spanish and some in English, as she knew no words in her native tongue for *hemostat* or even . . .

"Stethoscope, stethoscope, stethoscope," she repeated under

173

her breath in an attempt to maintain her concentration as Marge bellowed at her from below.

"Graciela! Where you at, girl!"

It was Marge's nature to act put out. She usually did whatever she was asked to do, within reason, but she reserved the right to bitch, at least to herself.

The stairs above rumbled softly and then bare feet slapped on the linoleum floor as a smiling Graciela stood catching her breath in the kitchen door. "Yes?"

Marge clucked and harrumphed and glanced over her shoulder. She still wasn't sure what to make of the Mexican girl and the strange goings-on that seemed to follow her around. "You're gonna mess around and break your fool neck, you keep flyin' down them stairs like that!" She pulled her apron off over her head and hung it on the nail in the wall by the stove. "I'm off to meet Dallas and I reckon we'll stop for a Mexican meal at Mi Tierra while we're downtown."

"Okay, Marge."

Normally Marge would have helped prepare for the arrival of a client, but tonight Doc and Graciela were on their own. Marge's gal, Dallas, was getting out of jail later that evening. She'd been picked up in a vice sweep on her way home from the store one night a month earlier, just swinging innocently down Presa Street with a bag of groceries on her hip. She couldn't help but attract attention, Marge reckoned. She just walked like that. As it turned out, Dallas had an outstanding warrant from a year and a half back. Given the choice between a fine plus six months' probation or thirty days in the Bexar County jail, Dallas had cheerfully opted to serve the time and walk away with a clean slate. Marge had shaken her head and spat on the ground and proclaimed, "Everybody's goin' crazy 'round here, I swear to God!"

But now that Dallas was getting out, Marge had scrubbed the floors and washed the windows and was fixing to catch the South Presa bus downtown and be waiting for her sweetie when she walked out the jailhouse door.

Graciela spoke English now with almost no accent, unless it was a hint of Doc's antebellum drawl.

"Kiss Dallas for me, Marge!"

The remark drew a sideways glance from Marge that Graciela never saw. The screen door slammed, and Graciela was alone.

Graciela relished the rare moments of solitude afforded by her life at the Yellow Rose. Doc, Marge, Dallas, and even Helen-Anne hovered over Graciela constantly, like hawks defending a fledgling. Manny was every bit as overprotective when he was around. But today she was alone. No boarders. No patients.

No pilgrims.

The word was out, and they had been coming for weeks, not in droves but alone for the most part and in twos or threes at most. They were mostly working girls with heroin habits. They came asking after a Mexican girl and then, later, asking for Graciela by name. They had heard that they might find hope for a new life if they really wanted it and none was turned away and no one left disappointed.

But on this day everything was quiet and Graciela reckoned that she had a couple of hours before Doc arrived to scrub for the procedure. She closed her eyes and breathed the silence in. When she breathed out again, the dust that she disturbed danced in a column of sunlight and she was reminded of lying on a blanket watching falling stars with her grandfather back home in Dolores. Long ago and far away. She sighed. Further still since her grandfather had died.

She had received no word from her family since she'd come to

South Presa, nearly a year ago. She wasn't even certain that her mother was alive. But there was no doubt in her mind that her grandfather had passed away in April.

She had awakened in the middle of the night calling for him. When Doc woke up and asked, she told him that she was certain that her grandfather was dead. What she didn't say was that he had come to her, or at least his words had, in the mouth of a jaguar spirit. She didn't ask, but she knew that she would never again see him in his human form, in this world or any other. Now for all intents and purposes, Doc was all the family she had, and the Yellow Rose was home.

And for the moment she had her home to herself and there was no time to waste.

It was like a dance without rhythm, deliberate and slow. She moved from room to room tracing faint figure eights on the dusty floor. She scanned the shadows, sniffed the air, and listened without and within, searching for any weakness in her own handiwork, the defenses that she maintained around the house and all who entered there. She burned sage against malice and secreted cedar cuttings beneath beds to protect against nightmares. She lit candles in honor of saints and animal spirits alike. Her grandfather had said, "There are no evil spirits in this world, child, only people who aren't listening to what God is trying to tell them." Graciela prayed for people like that. She invoked spirits to protect them from themselves. Not just for Doc and Dallas and Manny. She certainly mentioned them still, but they needed her prayers less and less every day. She concentrated her intercessions on Marge and Helen-Anne and that boyfriend/pimp of hers, Wayman. She even said prayers for the souls of Jack Ruby and Lee Harvey Oswald, and when she did the blood flowed freely from the wound on her wrist and the bandage soaked through.

Bang! Rattle! Bang! Rattle! Bang! Rattle!

It never failed. Somebody was knocking on the screen door downstairs. She sighed but she knew that she was alone in the place and that if she didn't answer it, no one would.

She padded down the stairs but before she reached the landing where she'd have a clear view of the front door, something nameless whispered in her ear. The voice was softer but more credible than Marge admonishing her not to run down the stairs, and she stopped and leaned around the corner and peeked under the banister. The silhouette of a man in a dark suit stood on the other side of the screen. When he leaned forward to knock once again, his features came into focus and Graciela stifled a gasp when she recognized the pastor from the mission church. In nearly a year that Graciela had lived in the Yellow Rose, no member of the clergy had ever come calling.

The young priest shaded his eyes and peered into the half-light where the small noise had come from.

"Is there anyone at home?"

Graciela took a couple of steps downstairs into the light.

"Well, hello there!" he began, and then, "Uh, *buenos días*, señorita."

She responded mostly out of pride in her English and regretted it immediately.

"May I help you, Padre? I was working. Cleaning. Upstairs, and I didn't hear you knock, Padre . . ."

It was several seconds before the priest realized that Graciela was speaking rather than singing.

"Killen. Yes! So! You speak, uh, well, yes, I'm Father Killen. From the mission church." He pointed vaguely behind him and then self-consciously covered his bandaged right hand. His instinct was correct but it came too late. Graciela had noticed it immediately. "I was just in the neighborhood and I, well . . ." He leaned closer to the screen and then retreated. Graciela had yet to blink. "I wonder, would it be all right if I came in? It's a little awkward standing out here like I'm selling something, if you follow me. And I'm not . . ."

The voice in Graciela's ear hadn't given her permission to allow the priest past the threshold. "I can come out," she offered, and when she pushed the screen open the priest noticed her own bandage, bright red with fresh blood.

"Well, uh, okay then. Please, I would appreciate that . . . Are you all right?"

"It's nothing. I bleed too much," she explained. "It doesn't hurt."

Father Killen stepped back a full two paces, twice the distance necessary to allow the door to open. He stumbled a step farther back when the screen door swept aside like a galvanized veil to reveal that Graciela had the face of an angel, both innocence and experience peering back at him through unblinking black eyes that seemed to assay his intentions. Still he lied without hesitation when she inquired after his own injury.

"An accident," he said. "Gardening. I—well, I just wasn't very careful. It's a nuisance but it isn't painful." As if to corroborate his story, he offered Graciela the injured hand in greeting. "Well, it's very nice to meet you," he said. Graciela held his hand for only an instant before she let it go as if it were hot, but the priest was so mesmerized that he took no notice and prattled nervously on. Up close she was even more beautiful than he could possibly have imagined. He found that he was able to maintain eye contact for just a few seconds at a time. He would glance away at intervals to avoid drowning in infatuation, only to look back and ecstatically submerge again. Words came to him, but very nearly randomly, and he found himself nervously anticipating the endings of his own sentences. "Like I said, I was in the neighborhood and I've always wondered about this big old house. I drive by it nearly every day and I, well, is it yours?"

Graciela smiled at the absurd suggestion, and Father Killen's heart nearly stopped. "No, Padre. It's a boarding house. I rent a room here."

"Well, of course it is! The sign in the yard. How silly of me. Oh, I'm sorry, did I introduce myself? Before Graciela could remind him that he had, he went on. "Let's just start over, then, shall we? I'm Father Padraig Killen from the mission church, and you are . . . ?" He extended the bandaged hand again but Graciela ignored it this time.

"Graciela."

"Graciela!" He pronounced it correctly. "That's a beautiful name. Are you called Grace sometimes?"

"No."

"Well, fair play to you. It's a beautiful name. Your Christian name, I take it? You were christened in the Catholic Church?"

"Yes, Padre."

"And confirmed?"

"Yes, Padre. When I was seven."

"And how long have you lived here? In the parish, I mean."

Graciela said nothing to that, and the priest silently panicked. He had searched for this girl for weeks and he knew too well how easy it would be for her to simply vanish into the streets if he allowed her to slip away. If he couldn't keep her talking, it was only a matter of time before she closed the door in his face.

"And why, then, have you never come to Mass?"

Graciela smiled again, even though she had already made up her mind that there was something about this priest that she didn't like.

"Forgive me, Padre, but I have."

It was true that Graciela attended Mass at the mission church from time to time, but it didn't surprise her that the priest had never seen her there. Coming and going without being noticed was part and parcel of her gift.

Naturally it was her grandfather who had first recognized that spirits of all kinds were drawn to Graciela like moths to a flame and that she possessed the rare ability to see and hear them all. That same internal beacon attracted human attention as well, and her grandfather had told her that if she was to have any peace in this world, she had to learn how not to be noticed when she didn't wish to be. It was simply a matter, he said, of damping down that inner light.

Graciela took a step forward and the priest retreated again, blithely unaware that only inches separated him from a nasty tumble backward down the steps.

"I am sorry, Padre," the girl began, wringing her hands nervously, her eyes downcast as she shifted her weight from one foot to the other. "I know I should come to Mass more than I do but I work on some Sundays and most Saturdays, which is why I haven't been to confession in such a long time."

The priest looked down on the small figure standing before him, her hair hanging limply, her dress wrinkled and soiled, and her bare feet caked with yellowish dirt. The face that he had thought so fair only a moment before seemed rather plain now, and when the girl made excuses for her lack of devotion there was no longer any music in her voice. Even the bandage around her wrist had faded, going from a flaming red to a muted brown and dirty white in the light of the dying day, as had his conviction that he was in the presence of anything remotely miraculous. The girl droned on for some indeterminate period, responding to his questions without really answering, until, no longer able to recall what had been so urgent about his errand that day, the priest produced his card and offered it to Graciela. "Well then, we'll have to try to do better about getting ourselves to Mass, won't we?" The girl made no reply except to shuffle her feet some more. "Right. I'll keep an eye out for you, and, of course, you don't have to wait for Saturday or Sunday. You know where I am, so feel free to come call whenever you like. My door is always open."

Graciela didn't even look at the card. She backed inside and the screen rattled as the heavy oak door closed in Father Killen's face.

Somehow the priest managed to make his way down the steps and back to his car, though later he would remember only finding himself behind the wheel and navigating the moral wreckage that was the strip through the gauzy haze that had suddenly descended on South Presa Street. He rolled past the beer joint and the pawnshop, paying no attention to the whores on the corner and the dope fiends lined up behind the liquor store. Some of the girls recognized the station wagon; the word was out that nobody had seen Big Tiff for a while, so maybe her special trick was fair game now. But the priest never even slowed down. Once he crossed Roosevelt Avenue he could easily have pretended that he'd never heard of anyone called Graciela, and he was beginning to wish that he never had. He was ashamed. He had spent weeks chasing after smoke from one end of hell on earth to the other on the words of a handful of degenerate strangers, and for what? She was only a girl. An ordinary Mexican girl. How could he have been so stupid? He pounded the dashboard with his bandaged fist as hard as he could.

And it didn't hurt. Not even a little. He yanked the wheel to the right and slammed on the brakes, grunting out loud as the Ford lurched to a stop. He held his hand up so that the grimy bandage caught the light and he noticed a bright red smear and he knew instantly that the blood wasn't his own, and his heart began to pound. He frantically unwound the bandage and turned his hand front to back and then back to front again. He shouldered the door open, activating the dome light, and repeated the inspection of the hand that Graciela had touched, but there was nothing to see. Not a scab. Not a scar. Not a trace.

Graciela hurried up the stairs. She knew that the camouflage she had conjured was temporary and permeable, and it was only a matter of time before the priest returned.

In a basket beneath her bed she found a Mason jar half filled with *milagros,* tiny, shining lead charms. She shook them out across her bed and selected four.

The Eyes of Santa Lucia. The saint sentenced to be defiled in a brothel, then blinded and martyred when her persecutors found they could not move her there.

The Praying Man. For her grandfather, that the old *curandero*'s wisdom and knowledge might flow through her.

The Sacred Heart of the Blessed Virgin. For her devoted mother, who said the rosary every day of her life, expecting nothing in return.

The House. For the protection of the Yellow Rose and all who dwelt within its walls.

She fastened them with straight pins to a thick white candle, kindled it, tilted it at odd angles to nurture the flame until it was tall and bright, and then anchored it in a puddle of molten wax on a saucer that she stationed on the windowsill, where it would be visible from the street.

She selected the herbs required to help repel the onslaught

that was coming: manzanilla, verbena, and more sage. While the water boiled on the hot plate, she bruised them between her fingers, occasionally glancing out the window to scan the street below.

The priest was nowhere to be seen. But he would be back, if not today, then tomorrow, or the day after that. But he would come. Graciela was certain of that. She had known a priest who felt like this.

Back home in Dolores, Father Gutiérrez, the old parish priest who had christened her and all of her brothers and sisters, had died suddenly, without ever having had a day of illness though he was well into his eighties. He had simply gone to sleep at the end of a typically long day of service to his flock and failed to awaken in this world. Even Graciela's grandfather attended the old priest's funeral Mass, and afterward Graciela realized that in all of her life she had never seen the old man inside a church before, and she asked him why.

"There are those among these" — he took a breath as he chose an appropriate word — "women . . . who are uncomfortable sharing their God with an old *curandero* like me. At least, until they have a boil on their backside or an unfaithful husband. Then they come and see me after dark when they think no one is watching." He had winked and nudged Graciela playfully and rolled his eyes up to heaven. "But I think He knows!" The old man crooked his finger, drawing Graciela into whispering range. "Even Father Gutiérrez visited me from time to time, when his back was acting up."

The old priest's replacement, Father Contreras, although he was fifty years younger and ostensibly more progressive, was nowhere near as open-minded when it came to spiritual matters. Her grandfather had dismissed him as a *sacerdote mundano*, a "worldly priest" more concerned with canon than creed but harmless. For his part, the new pastor, after canvassing the local gossips, had wasted no time in focusing his attention on the old man's occupation. He preached sermon after sermon on the evils of superstition and the practice of all manner of unholy rite and ritual, no matter how mundane. "Satan," the new priest exhorted, "is subtle and cunning and comes to us cloaked in familiarity."

Of course, the new priest found no duplicity in the long-established practice of co-opting indigenous tradition and mythology whenever there were souls at stake. He even told his own version the tale of La Llorona, clearly targeting the young women in his congregation, and Graciela's older sisters stared at the floor and fingered their rosaries whenever the priest preached on chastity or the sanctity of life.

But Graciela, even at her tender age, knew hypocrisy when she encountered it, and she avoided Father Contreras whenever possible. Still, he cornered her at every opportunity and submitted her to barrages of questions about her grandfather and the comings and goings at the family's house — especially those that transpired after dark. Why was her grandfather never at Mass? Graciela answered the questions vaguely or not at all. One day the priest, in his frustration, lost his temper. Graciela would follow her grandfather into hell if she wasn't careful, the zealot warned her, and his long fingernails had left a mark on her arm when she wrenched it from his grasp and ran away. From that occasion forward she had never set foot in the little church again. She traveled by bus to San Miguel Allende to take Communion and give her confessions.

Bang! Rattle! Bang! Rattle! Bang! Rattle!

"Marge! Open the goddamn door!"

It was Doc. Graciela dropped the herbs in the water and inhaled the cloud of vapor that arose in one long deep breath before racing down the stairs.

Bang! Rattle! Bang! Rattle! Bang! Rattle!

"Goddamn it, Marge! We got a client comin'!"

He was just about to rip through the screen when Graciela opened the door.

"Marge ain't here!" She panted. "She went to meet Dallas at the jell. But Doc—"

"Marge *isn't* here," Doc corrected. "And it's *jail*. Long *a*, child, not *eh*." That was how Graciela had learned to speak English: Doc patiently pointed out her mistakes, and Graciela didn't take his corrections personally. But this was no time for an English lesson.

"Doc, there was a priest here!"

"A priest?"

"A bad priest!"

"What the Sam Hill are you talkin' about?"

"He was asking a lot of questions!"

"Here? This evening?"

"Just now!" The girl nodded, following him to the kitchen and back, wringing her hands and biting her lip.

Doc stepped out on the porch and squinted into the failing light. "Well, he's gone now. Sheets and towels, hon, and boil some water, could you? We got a girl in trouble on her way down here."

Graciela gave up. She knew that there was no time to make Doc understand, especially when she wasn't sure exactly what it was about the priest that she found so unsettling. She bobbed her head in acknowledgment and resignation and disappeared in a whirl. She rematerialized an instant later with an armload of linens and took the staircase in a few nearly silent bounds. She dumped the spent herbs in the wastebasket and refilled the pot with water before she replaced it on the hot plate. In a box atop a homemade bookshelf, she found a Zippo lighter and an unused taper candle, long and red. She kindled it and completed her rounds of the altars in the four corners of the room. Then she replaced the bloody bandage around her wrist with a double thickness of fresh, clean gauze and white medical tape before gliding down the stairs and, for the second time that day, being stopped in her tracks by the figure of a man darkening the screen door.

"Doc!" she yelped. "It's the cops!"

Doc was behind her now. "It's all right, honey," he assured her. "Detective Ackerman is accompanying our patient. Come on in, Hugo. It's open."

The cop was so massive that he had to lead with one shoulder in order to fit through the door. He took a step inside and then stopped, eclipsing the porch light. Doc had never seen the cop act like this before, fidgeting uncomfortably in the parlor, his hat literally in his hand until Doc reached the bottom of the stairs and offered his own.

"You alone? Where's your girlfriend, Hugo?"

At first, Doc thought the detective was blushing. His ears and his cheeks were edged in brilliant red, and drops of sweat popped out of every pore on his face. He wore an anguished expression, as if he were desperately trying to put exactly the right sentence together and failing miserably. Doc took a moment to assess the situation. On second glance, Hugo may well have been embarrassed, but he was angry too; he took a stiff step to one side and somebody in back of him moved with him, maintaining the cover that the massive man afforded. Hugo reached behind and tugged gently on a skinny arm, and a young girl, a very young girl, with tears overflowing both eyes, peeked around at Doc and Graciela.

"Come on out, honey. This man's a doctor. He's going to help you." He tugged again and the girl stood out in the open, twisting in his gentle but unyielding grip and covering her face as best she could with one hand.

Graciela glided past Doc and was on her knees with her arms wrapped around the tiny figure before Doc could open his mouth.

"My God, Hugo! How old is this child?"

There was a sharp, deliberate, threatening intake of breath, followed by a long, slow release as the big cop replied in carefully measured words.

"It ain't my baby, if that's what you're thinking."

The girl wrestled free of Graciela, a look of horror on her face as she realized what was being suggested, and she retreated to her haven behind Hugo. The cop's cheeks and ears were blazing now.

"I don't know who the daddy is and she won't tell me." He dropped to one knee and guided the girl around in front of him once more, and after hugging her and whispering in her ear he slowly turned her around.

"But the answer to your first question is she's fourteen. This is Elaine. She's my daughter."

Hank watches from his perch on the rail around the boarding-house porch as Doc lowers himself wearily into the rocking chair and lights up a smoke. A ribbon of opaque white seeps from the physician's nostrils to the corners of his mouth, and in and out again, wasting nearly nothing as he holds the rapidly disappearing cigarette in place between bloody fingers.

"You ought to wash that off," Hank observes.

Doc drops the hand long enough to glance at it, front and back. "You're kidding, right?"

"Hell no, I'm serious as a heart attack!" The ghost checks over

one shoulder and then the other before alighting on the porch.
"Somebody might be watchin'!"

"Oh yeah!" Doc chuckles. "Somebody's always watching, all
right."

"I meant somebody like the Law!"

Doc takes another, deeper drag and lets it go.

"The Law just left here, Hank, after aiding and abetting a crime
against the people of Texas and God Almighty. I don't reckon we
need to worry about the cops tonight." Doc cocks his head as he
considers the ghost's motives. "What's it to you, anyway?"

The screen door swings open and it appears that Graciela and
the ghost are of the same mind. She carries a basin of warm soapy
water. She nods in acknowledgment of the onza *cat spirit. "Tell*
him!" It hisses, every hair on its back standing on end. Doc doesn't
hear the spirit's cat form, and Graciela ignores it and kneels be-
fore Doc and waits expectantly. Neither she nor the ghost flinches
when the physician flicks his cigarette over both their heads and
surrenders a bloody hand.

Graciela wrung out the washcloth and gently probed every fold
and crevice between Doc's oaken-colored fingers, tracking down
all hidden traces of blame by feel and excising them by means of
gentle steady pressure and whispered incantations in Nahuatl.
She believed it to be her vocation, the purging of the residue
of death from Doc's skin, though she held no illusions that she
could offer him anything like absolution. There would be a price
to pay for all of this, she reckoned. Maybe Doc had been paying
all along and she herself had only just begun. A part of her, perhaps her most worldly part, the part that aspired to her grandfather's constancy, believed that by keeping Doc's hands clean she
was helping to forestall any retributive atrophy that the powers

might visit upon him. One thing was for certain: Graciela shared whatever debt was owed for the death of her own unborn child equally with Doc, and she and the physician would carry that common stain for the rest of their days and nothing would ever wash it away.

She struggled within herself to reconcile feelings in Spanish with an inadequate arsenal of English words. It had become her and Doc's custom not to speak at such times, but she could still taste the tang of malevolence that the afternoon's encounter with the priest had left hanging in the air.

The onza/*Hank insists, "Tell him, goddamn it! Tell him about the priest!"*

"Doc, we need to talk . . ." she began.

Tires grinding gravel. V-8 rumbling and rattling to a stop. Headlights on high beam cut the Hank/cat in half and blind Doc while encircling Graciela's head with light.

The old house shivered as Manny bounded up the steps and planted a shiny size-15 tangerine-colored shoe on the porch. The big Mexican headed for the front door until he spotted Doc and Graciela and lurched to a halt. In a glance he took in the rusty-colored water in the basin Graciela cradled in her lap.

"All done here, then?" he asked.

Doc stood up. "Let's go for a ride, Manny. I need some air."

Graciela sighs and rises and retreats indoors, leaving the cat to take the next watch alone.

• • •

189

Manny drove and Doc rode shotgun in silence for a half an hour; downtown to Commerce Street, west to Zarzamora, then north and west again out Culebra Road. They rolled over the very underpaved streets where Manny had learned to drive, a cloud of bone-colored limestone dust following behind them. Kids recognized the car, stopped playing, and waved from nearly grassless yards in front of neat, flat-roofed frame houses painted bright shades of blue, yellow, and purple. This was the west side, Manny's San Antonio. He felt safe here, and the big Ford practically steered itself. The big man broke the silence first.

"You see that house, Doc? The yellow one with the blue mailbox?"

Doc squinted and shrugged. "Yeah."

"That's where I grew up. My sister and her husband live there now. My daddy died when I was fourteen, and my mama finished raisin' eight kids in that house all by herself. Everybody finished high school except for me. Even the girls. I'm the only one that ever been in any kind of trouble with the law, not that I'm complainin', as lucky as I been."

Manny knocked on his head with his great knuckles, and Doc had to smile.

"Anyway, when you raise eight kids around here on nothin' and only one goes bad you got to be doin' somethin' right. Look, I know that shit I peddle hurts a lot of folks. Good folks, a lot of 'em, who'd never hurt a fly if it wasn't for a hundred-dollar habit. Most people that sell this shit as long I have eventually get locked up or shot dead. Even if nothin' bad happens to 'em right off, it's just a matter of time before they end up gettin' high on their own supply and then they get what's comin' to 'em on the installment plan." Manny saw Doc's eyes widen in the rearview mirror. "What? You think I ain't never been tempted by a taste now and then, as much of that shit passes through my hands every day? Shit! I ain't no saint, Doc. Anyway . . ."

They were stopped at a four-way at the corner of Twenty-sixth and Delgado streets when the big man finally began to home in on his point. He looked back to the mirror and met Doc's eyes again.

"Doc, how long you been clean now?"

Doc shifted in his seat, trying to escape the big man's reflected gaze, but couldn't. "I don't know. Six, maybe seven months?" He was lying. He knew damn well it was precisely eight months and seventeen days.

"Without a slip?" Manny persisted. "Not even a sniff?"

"Manny, you know me better than that. I wouldn't bother — "

"You ever think you'd be able to do that? Pull up and not shoot dope for seven months?"

Doc shrugged again, then cracked a smile that matured into a nervous laugh. "Well, no, to tell the truth."

Manny trumped him with a grin. "Me neither. No offense!"

"None taken."

"It's just that . . . I'm kind of the same way. Ever since Graciela came, or maybe it was when we all rode out to the airport — hell, Doc, I can't tell you exactly. I just know my heart ain't in the hustle no more. Truth is, here lately I can't bring myself to sell a single solitary dime bag of dope, and it just don't feel right lettin' other people do my dirty work for me! I mean, that boy Ramón is a retard, Doc, but he's my sister's kid. Hard as I tried to school him, he's already strung out, and you know as well as I do that it's just a matter of time before he gets pinched and gives me up. That's the main reason why I've always done it all myself. No loose ends, see? I always figured as long as I kept my eyes open and my mouth shut and greased Hugo whenever he came around I was all right.

But hell, I know my luck can't hold out forever. The thing is, after everything my mama went through raising eight kids, it sure would be a shame if she had to watch my dumb ass, the only bad apple in the bunch, go away to the penitentiary just because I lost my hustle. And that's exactly where I'm headed, Doc, if I keep this shit up."

Doc didn't answer right away. He looked down at his hands and followed the scars along the veins in the backs of his hands around his wrists as he rotated them, palms up. He reached across and shoved his sleeve up above his elbow, exposing the inside of his left arm. More scars. If he lived forever, they would never go away. But there were no new marks. No swellings. No flecks of fresh blood on his sleeves. "You really believe Graciela's got something to do with all this?"

Manny snorted. "You don't?"

"That's not what I asked you. You don't even want to know what I believe. I'm not even sure I know what that is anymore. The question was, what do you believe?"

Manny paused, as if taking an internal inventory of some sort.

"I believe that Graciela touched me somewhere deep inside and now I can't stand to sell poison just to make a buck no more. I believe she touched you too, Doc, and now you can't poison yourself."

"Yeah, all that may be true, but then how do you explain that I'm still getting paid for killing babies?"

Manny sighed, relieved that Doc had come out and said it first.

"I used to worry about that, Doc. Worry for you, for the girls. I mean, just because I don't never go to Mass don't mean I ain't a Catholic! But, you know, Doc, every girl you've laid hands on since Graciela came has changed, really changed. I believe that, Doc, with all my heart! So maybe some good comes from what you do. Maybe as long as Graciela's standin' next to you it's all right, Doc, I don't know. But me? As far as I know there ain't no good that's ever come from any piece of dope I ever sold." He ended the sentence with an emphatic sigh, obviously intended to be a period. Then a smile spread across his wide, brown face from ear to ear. "Unless it was them two bags that killed that asshole Jaime. You remember that *pendejo,* Doc? Used to beat the girls up and rob 'em all the time?"

"Yeah." Doc chuckled. "He was a monumental prick."

When they pulled up to the curb outside the boarding house Manny and Doc turned to face each other without the mirror between them.

"You really going to give it up, Manny?"

"I'm done, Doc. I can't sell dope no more."

"Well, that's that, then. But that brings us to the sixty-four-dollar question. What *will* you do? You say you've got your mama taken care of, but what about you? You're a young man, Manny. You can't just do nothing for the rest of your life."

"Oh, I don't know, Doc. I think you'd be surprised. But I've been thinkin' about that too. Maybe I'll just . . . drive."

"Oh, your big-rig scheme. I don't know, Manny. You don't see that many Mexicans — "

"Naw, Doc! I ain't talkin' about no job . . . I mean, maybe later. There's plenty of time for all that, but for right now, I got a little extra change and this old Ford runs like a top. So what's wrong with the idea of just hittin' the road for a while? Do a little travelin'."

"Well, nothing, I guess," Doc scoffed. "But where would you go?"

"Nowhere. Everywhere. Just go. See the country before I settle down. Hell, Doc, I ain't never been nowhere. I hear California's nice and there's plenty to see between here and there. Carlsbad Caverns! I ain't so sure I really wanna go *down* in no cave. Get the creepers when things get close like that, but they say that if you get there right at sunset you can watch a million bats fill up the whole sky! And the Grand Canyon, Doc. That's on the way to California, ain't it? Hey, you know what? What if you and Graciela was to go with me?"

Doc's reaction was startlingly visceral. "Me? Aw, hell, no, Manny! I never was much of a traveler."

"Aw, come on, Doc. Don't you ever wanna just roll down that highway to wherever it goes?"

"Not really. In my experience, wanderlust is vastly overrated. Every time I've ever taken to the road it's carried me to someplace worse than where I was before. When I finally wound up on South Presa I decided that I better quit while I'm ahead . . . more or less."

"You don't ever think you might be pushin' your luck, Doc? Doin' business, illegal business, in the same spot, day after day, year after year? I know I do. I'm hotter than a two-dollar pistol; I can feel it, Doc. And you got an awful lot of traffic runnin' in and out of that boarding house every day. Somebody's bound to notice. And it ain't just you. Graciela's illegal, and what about Marge and Dallas?"

"What about 'em?"

"I mean, what's gonna happen to them if the police shut the Rose down?"

"For chrissake, Manny! Nobody is shutting anything or anybody down. Hugo's got our backs — "

"Hugo ain't nothin' but a broke-down ol' vice cop, Doc. He can't help you once the big dogs downtown get on your trail."

"Big dogs? Aw, Manny, no big dog, downtown or up, is even remotely concerned with anything that's happening here at the ass end of South Presa Street. Besides, like you said yourself, maybe, just maybe, I'm beginning to do some good in this fucked-up world. Maybe some of these girls will go on to make something of themselves or do some small kindness for somebody else, and, who knows, maybe all this will add up to something someday. Hell, I don't know. All I'm saying is that something—I don't know what you call it, Manny; instinct, maybe—all I know is it's telling me to stay right where I am and keep on doing exactly what I'm doing until the day that I die. And even though I've never had a single solitary notion of my own steer me anywhere but dead-center wrong in my entire life, that's exactly what I intend to do."

"What about Graciela?" Manny sighed in a last halfhearted effort.

"Graciela's grown. She can stay or go, as she pleases."

"She won't go without you."

"Look, Manny, Graciela's going to do what Graciela's going to do and you're going to do what you're going to do no matter how many times I tell you that there's nothing out there on that highway except for maybe ghosts."

"Ghosts?" Manny scoffed.

"Yeah, well, never mind, Manny. You go! See the bats and the Grand Canyon. Roll down the highway until your wheels come off, if that's what you've got in your mind to do. But first drop me off at the Yellow Rose."

Doc stepped out of his shoes and carried them as he tiptoed up the stairs. He even undressed in the hallway and gingerly backed onto the edge of the bed in hopes of not disturbing Graciela, but it was no use. She was awake.

"Can we talk now?" she began before his head even hit the pillow.

"I'm listening." Doc sighed and turned to find Graciela lying on her back, the sheet pulled up nearly to her chin, her eyes wide open as if she were contemplating the ceiling fan above. Her tone was quiet, matter-of-fact, but deadly serious.

"We need to go, Doc. We need to leave this place."

"Oh, hell, Graciela. Not you too!"

"Please, Doc!" Graciela implored him. "You said that you would listen."

Doc growled softly, took a deep breath, and then literally held his tongue between his teeth. Graciela went on.

"Do you remember when I came here? How frightened I was? I had no money, no English. I didn't even understand what this place was at first, this South Presa Street. There is no street like this back home in Dolores. Maybe in Guanajuato or Querétaro, I don't know. So much pain. So much shame. And I brought my own shame with me and then I made it worse by taking the life of an innocent – "

"No!" Doc interrupted. "That's not fair! It was me who – "

"It was my decision, Doc, and we both will pay a price, not only for my child but for every other life that we have taken together!"

Doc turned his back to Graciela and faced the empty darkness. "You only assisted. You never touched an instrument during a termination procedure."

"Do you really think that matters, Doc? I've been watching you. I'm a fast learner. I could do it myself! I know I could. There's no need for all the blood to be on your hands."

"Absolutely fucking not!"

"Why, Doc? We share this. It is what brought us together and we will both pay for it for the rest of our lives. It is a great sin,

196

this thing we do in this house, maybe the greatest of all sins, but my child, for one, was spared a life of paying for the mistakes of his mother, and what if I hadn't found you? What if Armando had taken me to someone else or simply abandoned me on the strip? Someone would have found me. Someone like Wayman, some animal, and my story would be like Helen-Anne's or worse. It was my choice, Doc, and I made it before you ever laid eyes on me. My mother hated Armando. She tried to warn me about him but I wouldn't listen. When the worst she could imagine came to pass, I only knew that I couldn't bear to bring up Armando's child in my mother's house where he would be unwanted and unloved through no fault of his own. And you saved my child from that. And you've saved at least a hundred others from worse. There was a reason, I believe, that you came to this place dragging your little black bag and your cat-man ghost and a reason that I found you here and we came together to help all of these people who somehow find their way to us here in this place at this time. But now, I fear, that time is past and it is time for us to go."

"That can't be right," Doc said, ruminating. "All these years stumbling and falling farther and farther behind. Digging my own grave with a teaspoon, and now when I finally feel like I just might be getting somewhere, I'm supposed to pull up stakes and run? To where? Let me guess. Disneyland? You and Manny got together and cooked up all this California talk, didn't you? Well, you can just save it. I told Manny and I'm telling you: I'm not going anywhere!"

Graciela waited until Doc fell silent before turning over and draping a tiny arm over his barrel chest and drawing herself close behind him. "Like spoons," she whispered, and a smile, unseen in the darkness, creased the corners of Doc's eyes. She had learned the expression from him and it had represented a breakthrough in her English lessons, Doc utilizing two real spoons to patiently demonstrate the idiom as he lay behind her one afternoon months ago. Now, their positions reversed, Graciela's anxiety seemed incongruous. "I'm afraid, Doc."

"Afraid? Of what? A priest? Well, forgive me if I'm a little skeptical, but I haven't been farther away from you than I can spit in the better part of a year now and I'd be willing to wager fairly serious money that you're not afraid of any-fucking-thing."

Graciela sat up and threw the sheet back so that Doc couldn't hide. "Is that what you think? That I'm fearless? Why? Because I'm not afraid of the dark? Shadows never hurt nobody, Doc."

"Anybody."

Graciela was out of bed. "Anybody! Nobody! Doesn't matter, Doc! There's nothing out there in the darkness for anyone to be afraid of. But this priest scares me."

"Why? What did he say?"

"It's not what he said. It's the way he feels."

"Goddamn it, Graciela! What kind of sense am I supposed to make of that?"

She crossed the room to the window and surveyed the street below for an instant and then she shook her head. "He just doesn't feel right," she said. "It's like his lips are smiling but his eyes are doing something else. Asking questions or something and no matter how hard I try I can't hide the answers because they're written all over my face."

"But he's a priest, for chrissake! Don't you people tell your priests everything anyway?"

"There are priests and there are priests and I never tell anybody everything and neither should you."

XVI

Father Padraig Killen fidgeted in an impossibly uncomfortable black leather chair in the foyer of the Archdiocese of San Antonio, Texas. He had been waiting for nearly an hour, as he had arrived half an hour early for his two o'clock appointment, and the clock on the wall behind the receptionist's desk now read 2:25.

He was reminded of countless hours spent outside the principal's office when he was a boy. The waiting was always the worst part of the punishment. By the time the ruler or the strap was administered by the presiding nun or priest, any amount of physical pain was usually anticlimactic.

If only Sister Mary-Margaret or Father Cudahy could see him now; she who had assured him on several occasions that he was undoubtedly bound for prison on his way to hell, and he who had never passed up a single opportunity to publicly humiliate him. "If I were you, Paddy Killen, I'd set my sights a little nearer to the ground," Father Cudahy had told him when he inquired in class as to the prerequisites for seminary admission. "You simply haven't the marks."

Well, he showed them. He had entered seminary and been ordained a priest as well. Now he was pastor of his own parish and waiting to be received by a bishop.

Not the archbishop himself, of course, but one of two auxiliaries who, he presumed, presided behind the massive oaken doors that flanked their superior's on either side. The letter summoning Father Killen to the archdiocese had borne the signature of the Most Reverend Thomas Meriwether, auxiliary bishop of San Antonio, whose name also appeared on a brass plate attached to the door on the right. The priest had been pleasantly surprised to receive a response by courier less than a week after he had posted his formal request for an audience. He had labored over his own letter for hours into the long night following his portentous meeting with the Mexican girl, poring over dusty volumes of canonical lore in search of any corroboration, no matter how thin, of his now-incontrovertible belief in her powers. He had seen the Mark on her wrist with his own eyes. She had touched him, and all evidence of his shameful rage had been erased from the back of his hand. It was a sign! It must be! His eyes were trained on the three doors, so he was startled when he was greeted by a voice from behind him.

"Father Killen?" A familiar accent. Irish, but not of the west and not Dublin. Cork, he decided, filtered through a Latin education. "I'm Father Monaghan." The man was a decade older than he, and taller, though slightly built. He wore a dark suit and tunic with a white collar similar to Father Killen's own, but there was no ring to kiss on the hand that he offered, so Father Killen shook it. His host was only a priest, then, and not a bishop at all. He invited the visitor to "Follow me, please." Not "His Excellency will see you now." Confused but obedient, Father Killen trailed a step behind him, down the central corridor to the end, through a door,

200

and down a dozen steps to the basement level. They passed by six or seven open doors on both sides of a narrow hallway in which busy-looking priests manned desks shoehorned into tiny offices and piled high with all manner of clerical flotsam and jetsam. The older priest stopped at the last door on the right and gestured with an open hand. "Please," he insisted.

Father Killen took a seat and then Father Monaghan squeezed into an ancient wooden office chair that creaked loudly as he settled in.

"So." He smiled, folding his hands and leaning across the battered desk between them. "How long since you've seen the Old Sod then?"

"I came over straight out of seminary, Father. Nearly ten years ago."

"That's me as well. Four years in Rome. Two in New Orleans, then Dallas. And not so much as a sight of Ireland in all of these years. But it's a sign of the times, I suppose. Young people leaving, going abroad to make a life somewhere, and there's nothing there to hold them. No jobs. No future." He leaned closer and lowered his voice, but not enough, Father Killen suspected, to prevent anyone who was really listening from hearing. "And now even the Church is gathering in her best and brightest" – he pointed at the younger priest and then tapped his own breast – "and shipping us overseas! So, you've been here in San Antonio all of this time?"

Father Killen suspected that this bureaucrat already knew the answers to most of his questions. "Yes, Father, I served as parochial vicar for the mission under Father Cantu until his death, but – "

"Dear Father Cantu! Yes, I knew him. He was a credit to his people . . . and his calling. What an honor to be blessed with the opportunity to follow in his footsteps."

"Yes, Father. A great honor. He was a good man and a good priest. He will be missed — I mean, he *is* missed. Especially by all of us who were his flock. Uh, Father Monaghan, is it?"

"Yes, Monaghan. Ciaran Monaghan. My mother was from Aran and she had beautiful Irish and she loved the old names! I grew up in Cork myself."

"Beautiful city, Cork. But if you don't mind me coming to the point, Father . . ."

The older priest sat back in his chair as if genuinely surprised. "The point?"

"My letter. My letter to His Excellency."

"Well, of course! That's why you're here. It's just that I read your letter and I noticed the name and peeked at your file and, well, surely you must get homesick from time to time, I know I do, and I just thought — "

"W-wait just a minute. I, I mean, begging your indulgence, Father, but you . . . you read my letter?"

"Well, yes, of course. I am, after all, His Excellency's personal secretary. With the exception of certain high-level correspondence from Rome, I'm the first to open all of his mail. Then I respond — "

"So what you're telling me is the letter I received was from you, and His Excellency never even saw mine."

"Of course not. I mean, I read it first, and then I passed it on, and then I composed the letter you received, but I assure you, His Excellency is well aware of your letter and its contents."

"Oh!" The priest's face brightened and fell in the same breath. "Oh, I see. Then His Excellency isn't interested in what I've . . . observed."

The older priest studied the younger's face in a way that made the moment seem longer than it really was. Not a piercing gaze, but a brief yet all-encompassing inventory of every hint that lay half hidden there. The mask of parochial cordiality vanished and was replaced by a practiced bureaucratic poker face, and the whiskey bottle was already out and the glass charged before Father Killen could refuse, not that Father Monaghan ever asked.

He drained his own glass and held the bottle expectantly until Father Killen emptied his in kind. Only after Father Monaghan had refilled them both did he set the bottle down and reply.

"His Excellency . . . is concerned."

"As well he should be! Something special, something miraculous has occurred —"

Father Monaghan stopped the priest with an open palm before he could gain momentum.

"Miraculous? My dear Father Killen. That is precisely the kind of language that concerns His Excellency." He produced the priest's letter from the top drawer of his desk and thumbed through the seventeen dog-eared typewritten pages. "Words like *miraculous* and *divine* have very specific meaning and gravity in Church doctrine —"

Father Killen pushed away the untouched second shot of whiskey. "I'm well aware of their meaning, Father, having been educated in and by the Church since I was a boy."

"Please do not misunderstand, Father. No one, least of all His Excellency, is questioning either your grasp of language or your theological background. As for myself, as a humble administrator I have nothing but admiration for your dedication to your calling as a preacher and minister to your flock. You are truly doing the Lord's work every day out there in the parish where it counts. But then, well, there it is, isn't it? That's what it's all about. You know these people. You live with them, sharing their every triumph and tragedy. You feel their pain and their joy as well. So when one of them comes to you and tells you that he's witnessed something unusual, that someone, one of their own, after all, possesses certain . . . gifts, then of course, you — "

"No!" Father Killen shook his head emphatically. "Graciela isn't from the neighborhood. She comes from Mexico. Someplace deep in the interior, I should think. She barely even speaks English!" Father Monaghan nodded knowingly but before he could utter any affirmation Killen stopped him. "I know what you're thinking, Father, but with all due respect to yourself and His Excellency" — he indicated his own correspondence on the desk with a wag of a forefinger — "this is no secondhand fairy story that I'm passing along for your entertainment or my own, and this is no ordinary Mexican girl! I have witnessed one miracle after another, Father . . . No, I'm not talking about parlor tricks! I'm talking about lives, Father, real people's lives, not to mention their souls! I have baptized no fewer than four adults in the past six weeks. That's four new Christians, Father. I've confirmed a dozen more who were lost to the streets in their teens, and my catechism classes are bursting at the seams, not to mention the dozens of non-Catholics who turn up at all hours of the day and night. Yes, they're prostitutes and pimps and heroin addicts. Do you have any idea of the scourge of heroin in my parish, Father? There are those who swear that any woman or man who picks up that poison is doomed, and I believed that too, but that was before I watched in awe as one lost soul after another cast off those chains forever. They come to my church and they ask to light candles and they all say the same thing, that they came because Graciela asked them to. And then they're gone."

"Gone?" Father Monaghan asked in a tone somewhere between honest query and exasperation.

"Away! Home! Someplace where they can begin again. Oh, I realize that I can never prove that, Father, but I know in my heart that it's true. As of yet, not one has returned to the streets, I can assure you. As you say, I'm out there every day—"

"Which brings us to another matter, Father Killen. There have been, of late, several . . . complaints from your parishioners . . ."

Father Killen checked the awakening beast within him. *In through your nose, out through your mouth.*

"What parishioners?"

Father Monaghan took notice of his darkening countenance and proceeded cautiously. "I have no knowledge of any name or names, and even if I had—"

"Then you wouldn't be disposed to divulge them. How convenient."

Father Monaghan stiffened. "Father, you forget yourself. I am, after all, His Excellency's representative in this matter. And His Excellency speaks for the Church and the Holy See, and His Excellency is concerned that you may be neglecting your until recently exemplary ministry to the faithful of your parish and have instead immersed yourself in a self-appointed mission to the miscreants of the adjacent red-light district."

"South Presa Street is well within the borders of my parish—"

"Your parish, Father, is your parishioners."

"And Graciela is one of those parishioners, as are all of the fallen who find their way back to the fold! What's more, I have neglected no duty that I'm aware of unless the diocese deems it my responsibility to assimilate every petty prejudice of my constituency. It would seem to me that my vocation would be better served by an example of Christian tolerance and forgiveness. It's not as if I woke up one day and rushed out onto the streets in search of a miracle, Father, and even if I had, South Presa Street would have been the last place on earth I would have looked. These souls, these poor lost souls, by the grace of God found their way into my church. And it was they who led me to Graciela! And not a moment too soon, I might add. Why, it is a miracle in and of itself that the child has survived. Abandoned in a strange country; no family, no friends. Forced to seek shelter in the worst kind of den of iniquity imaginable — "

"A brothel! Then she is a prostitute?"

"No! I have it on the best . . . uh, authority that she is nothing of the kind. And it's a boarding house, Father! A seedy boarding house in a seedy part of town, that's all."

"You've been there?"

"Yes! Well, not inside. Only as far as the front porch. She wouldn't allow me — "

"Then how do you know what does or does not go on inside?"

"There are stories."

"Stories?"

"I meant, accounts . . ."

"Stories, accounts — Father! Do you really expect His Excellency to respond seriously to the frivolous suggestion of the beatification of a — "

"Not beatification, Father. Sainthood."

"All the more outrageous! A cause of canonization brought by a newly minted parish priest and based solely on the idle gossip of harlots and pimps?"

"Not gossip, Father. Granted, without violating the sanctity of the confessional I can only — "

Father Monaghan audibly gasped and crossed himself.

"I can only ask for your indulgence and beg your pardon if I am unable to divulge the identities of my sources, but make no mistake, Father, there are worse than prostitutes residing in the Yellow Rose."

"Father Killen!"

"There are thieves!"

"Father Killen, I must —"

"Lesbians!"

"Father Killen!"

"Even an abortionist! An abortionist, Father! A murderer of the innocent operating under the same roof that shelters the blessed girl . . . yes, Father, *blessed,* at the very least. And I know whereof I speak, for I have witnessed the difference she makes in the lives of everyone she touches!" Father Monaghan flinched as Killen held out his right hand as proof and then withdrew it when he realized that there was nothing there to show. "Oh, I'm so sorry, Father. But you *must* believe me: every word of that letter that you hold in your hand is true, and, as God is my witness, the girl Graciela bears the Mark of our Lord!"

Father Monaghan was out of his seat, around the desk, and to the door in less than an instant. Father Killen's ears popped as the heavy door thudded shut.

"Stigmata," he hissed, "is yet another word that's not to be bandied about!"

"I have seen it!"

The older priest was behind him now, grilling him like a teacher who had caught a student not paying attention in class.

"Where? On what part of her body?"

"Her wrist."

"Aha! Well, as far as I know, every stigmatic recognized by the Church to date has received the Marks in the *palms* of the hands and the tops of the feet. Some even show the wounds of the spear in their sides and the Crown of Thorns on their heads, but unless I misheard you, this girl has only one?"

"I saw no other, Father. I've only met her the one time —"

The older priest leaned over his shoulder like a disapproving teacher. "One time?"

"Yes. But . . . it was weeks before I could even find the girl." He considered recounting his confusion when he left Graciela that day but thought better of it. It was a temptation by the devil, he had decided. His final test. "She wouldn't ask me in, Father, but she came out on the porch and I saw the wound clearly and —"

"And it was on her wrist?"

"It is a fact, Father," Killen recited, "that by all historical accounts, Roman crucifixions were accomplished by driving the nails through the subjects' wrists, the tissue and bones in the palms being far too weak to support —"

"By all historical accounts!" mimicked Father Monaghan. "And this being a matter of theology rather than history or science, historical accounts, no matter how credible in the academic world, are irrelevant. In fact, for the purposes of this discussion, the only versions of events surrounding the Passion of our Lord that matter are the Gospels, Father, which, when they mention any wounds at all, clearly state that they were located on the *palms* of our Savior's hands. That is *hands,* Father. Plural. And His feet. Did you see her feet?"

"Feet? I don't remember," Killen lied. Graciela had been barefoot. "But I saw the wrist clearly enough and it was just like they all said. On her right wrist, and the blood on the bandage was a vivid shade of red and still flowed freely only last week! Graciela received her wound last fall, Father!"

Father Monaghan returned to his side of the desk but re-

208

mained standing, leaning forward to reengage Killen. "According to whom?"

"My parishioners! Good people. The salt of the earth," Killen replied.

"That's right. *Simple* people, Father. Mostly Mexican people. People who speak English as a second language, if at all."

Killen shifted in his chair. "I come from the west country, Father. In my corner of Ireland we still speak Irish every day of our lives."

"And I envy you that, Father. It is indeed a shame that the old tongue was all but dead by the time we drove the English out. But this is America, Father, and the language that's spoken here is English. There are many among your parishioners who have only recently arrived in this country. They are descended, after all, from primitive people. Savages who only a few generations ago ran naked in the jungle and offered up human sacrifices to pagan gods. They bring along with them not only their language but many customs and superstitions that they insist on clinging to even though they can only encumber their transition into their new lives. Imagine, Father, a New York City or a Boston where the Irish kept to themselves in insular communities. Oh, other immigrants have chosen that path. The Italians. The Jews. But the Irish, Father, have always assimilated even when and where we weren't initially welcomed. We worked our way up by doing the jobs that no one else wanted. In the mines. In the streets. As policemen and firemen. Even the priesthood, Father. We've done our bit as well. It took time but we've earned the respect of those that set themselves up as our betters until, well — America may have been discovered by an Italian sailing under a Spanish flag, but the first Catholic president of the United States was an Irishman . . . God rest his soul."

Father Killen blinked as if momentarily dazed before allowing that he had admired the president very much. "I'm just not sure," he ventured, "what all this has to do with my letter."

"Everything, Father. Everything to do with your letter, your parish, and your parishioners. Your *real* parishioners. Not to mention your future. Your calling. Your career."

Killen opened his mouth to react to this latest implication but managed only a pitiful, dry clucking sound as his tongue separated from the roof of his mouth, as impotent as a revolver's hammer falling on an empty chamber. He slid down in his chair.

Father Monaghan stood over him for a meaningful moment before settling into his own seat. He pushed Killen's glass back across the desk and refilled his own. "Have you never wondered why an inexperienced parochial vicar not yet out of his thirties would be handed a parish of his own?"

"I . . . I g-guess," Killen stammered, "I reckoned that there was no one else to fill the post."

"On the contrary, there were any number of more experienced priests around the diocese who qualified. And any of them would have been thrilled to have your post. Such a beautiful little church. One of the original San Antonio missions. Father Alvarez, for instance, wanted the position. From Incarnate Word College. He was born here in San Antonio. Grew up in the neighborhood. He told me that he had always dreamed that one day he would be pastor there. There are others. Father Echeverria, the associate pastor at Our Lady of Sorrows. Father Franco. All scholars. All good priests." He leaned forward and gestured for Killen to do the same, then whispered, "All Mexican."

"I'm not sure I understand . . ."

"Take your predecessor."

"Father Cantu."

"Yes, darlin' Father Cantu. A good priest. A good man. A leader in his community. But there's the rub. His community. His people, Father. Tell me, have you had the opportunity to become acquainted with many of your peers? The other pastors of the diocese, I mean?"

"A few. Father Murray from St. Ann. And I see Monsignor White out at the San Jose mission from time to time . . ."

"And of the parish priests you've met, any Spanish surnames among them?"

"Well, I never gave it much thought."

"Nor should you. Yours is a higher calling, Father. Unfortunately, for we lowly bureaucrats, it is our lot to delve into the worldly, if not the downright unseemly, from time to time in the course of our duty to God and Church. Our function is often more political, for lack of a more savory term, than spiritual. We leave it to our betters to answer the larger questions of doctrine and theology while we dot the i's and cross the t's. Even wash the dishes and take out the trash from time to time . . . figuratively speaking, that is. What's important for the purposes of our discussion here today is that Father Cantu's tenure as pastor of the mission church was an experiment. He was the first Mexican to be elevated to a parish of any size in the modern history of the diocese. Certainly there are a handful of exceptions in small churches along the border. Spanish-speaking congregations, don't you know. But even they are mostly curates rather than full pastors."

The word *experiment* had caught Killen's attention. His mind was beginning to wander, his awareness divided into two platoons: the first was half listening to Father Monaghan; the second, sensing an imminent setback, was formulating an alternative course of action. "Experiment?" he queried.

"Yes," allowed Monaghan and then he paused before elaborating. "A failed experiment." Killen looked no less confused. "Perhaps a more detailed explanation of the political ramifications of the situation is in order."

"Perhaps," Killen agreed, wondering if his response sounded sarcastic. What was this popinjay, this functionary on about? Responding to news of a blessed event, a *miracle*, with politics and protocol!

"Are you aware, Father Killen, of the great events transpiring in Rome?"

"The Second Ecumenical Council."

"Yes. Vatican Two, they're calling it. Sounds very modern when they say it like that. And perhaps that's appropriate when one considers the intended purpose of the council."

"Well!" Father Killen snorted. "Forgive me, Father, but I'm less than certain that I fully understand its purpose myself."

"Oh, I see. A traditionalist. Well, fair play to you. I don't entirely disagree. Tradition is part and parcel of faith. Though I suspect that were we to debate the case in depth, you and I, we would encounter certain . . . differences. Then again, we are fortunate, still in the prime and vigor of our lives and therefore given to flights of fancy and passion; it is the dominion of older and wiser priests to deliberate such weighty matters. But we have our part to play as well, and make no mistake, modernity is precisely what the council is all about. The modernization, where necessary and theologically feasible, of the Holy Roman Church in order to insure its survival in the modern age. The Church is under attack on all fronts, Father! All over the world congregations are shrinking."

"On the contrary, I'm seeing new faces every day."

"An anomaly, Father. You said yourself that most of these new converts disappear after attending Mass a few times. They're only responding to all these stories that they hear –"

"They are not stories . . ." Killen was increasingly preoccupied and had begun to half mumble, staring sullenly at the floor.

"Yes, Father, stories! Rumors. Gossip. These are poor people. Uneducated. Their days are difficult and long. It is only natural that they should welcome any distraction from the tedium of their everyday lives. The world is changing so rapidly that they simply haven't the knowledge or the subtlety to make sense of it all. That is precisely why it is the duty of the Church, of the clergy, *our* duty, Father, to offer them a semblance of stability in the midst of chaos. Some shelter from the storm. What will happen if we, their spiritual leaders, indulge them in every parochial cult and superstition that catches their fancy in an era when the Church is struggling – yes, struggling, Father – to maintain its relevance? When satellites, miniature moons, Father, made by the hands of men, not God, are circling the globe as we speak? If when all is said and done we are not prepared to guide our flock into the modern world, then what kind of shepherds are we?" Father Monaghan opened a drawer and produced a pack of cigarettes, lit one, and then, strictly as an afterthought, offered one to Father Killen. The younger priest never looked up.

Monaghan shrugged and continued. "Father Cantu was a good priest. He served his congregation well for a generation, but during his tenure the world changed profoundly. The diocese would never have considered replacing him, but when he went on to his reward, much care was taken in choosing his successor. You were his assistant, so you knew the parish. You were energetic and intelligent. And, not to put too fine a point on it, Father Killen, your name didn't end in a vowel."

Killen was certain that he must have missed something. "So I got the parish because . . . I'm Irish?"

Monaghan laughed. "You grossly overestimate my influence, Father. But suffice it to say, you weren't Mexican and therefore not culturally predisposed to a soft spot for any of the local folklore. The Church in Latin America has, from time to time, found it necessary to draw rather liberal parallels between Catholic tradition and certain indigenous rites, but this is the United States, Father, not Mexico. It is in the interest of the American Church that at least a veneer of modernity be maintained. Imagine, then, our disappointment when we received your letter, fraught with tales of miraculous transformations and healings by the laying on of hands, not to mention the suggestion of a cause for the sainthood, no less, of a young girl from central Mexico. And to think that dear old Father Cantu drew the attention of the diocese for nothing more than devoting himself to the cult of Our Lady of Guadalupe a little too zealously!"

Father Monaghan rattled on but Killen wasn't listening anymore. He was certain now that no help was forthcoming from the Church; not from this diocese, in any case. It would be up to him and him alone to rescue Graciela from the agents of Satan who held her hostage. He nodded and half smiled and congratulated himself on his mastery of his violent temper. He no longer found it necessary to employ Father Walsh's breathing technique, even though he could clearly visualize his fist crashing down and stanching the incessant verbiage hemorrhaging from the cleric's mouth. Once he had successfully affected defeat, he had to withstand the balance of the lecture while maintaining the appearance of acquiescence for only another quarter of an hour before he found himself shaking hands with Father Monaghan at the front door.

"I knew," the older priest assured him, "that you and I would be able to sort this out, one Irishman to another."

"No doubt," the younger affirmed, and then turned and walked out. He had reached his car and opened the door when Father Monaghan called after him. "What now," he muttered, but he turned and met him on the steps.

"I'm sorry to keep you," Monaghan apologized. "But I nearly forgot! I made a note at some point during our little talk. Perhaps I heard wrong, but I believe that you mentioned something about"—he lowered his voice to the faintest of whispers and leaned close to Killen's ear—"an abortionist?"

Congratulating himself on his ability to remain so calm in the face of such ignorance, Father Killen nodded solemnly and replied, "Yes, Father. In the Yellow Rose boarding house. On South Presa Street. They call him Doc."

The priest didn't go straight home. He needed to think. To pray. He drove downtown to San Fernando Cathedral, parked across the street, and went inside. He had been there once before, when he was newly arrived from Ireland and taking in the local historical landmarks, including, of course, the Alamo. His guide had been dear old Father Cantu, who had pointed out the marble vault just inside the cathedral's front door in which all that remained of the defenders were interred, Crockett's, Bowie's, and Travis's ashes commingled with those of the forgotten. But today he walked past the shrine without a glance and made straight for an alcove in a dark corner of the nave.

The figure of Our Lady of Guadalupe that dominated the tiny shrine was resplendent in its contrast to the limestone wall covered in candle-smoke soot and handwritten prayers for intercession on tiny slips of yellowing paper. The priest took a candle and kindled it from one of the dozens of others, knelt, and began to utter the first words of an unfamiliar prayer, unsure whether he had heard it somewhere before or if he was just making it up as he went along.

"Our Lady of Guadalupe, Mystical Rose, make intercession for the Holy Church, and help all those who invoke thee in their necessities. You are the Woman clothed with the sun who labors to give birth to Christ, while Satan, the Red Dragon, waits to voraciously devour your child. So too did Herod seek to destroy your Son, Our Lord and Savior, Jesus Christ, and massacred many innocent children in the process. O clement, O loving, O sweet Virgin Mary, hear our pleas and accept this cry from our hearts. Our Lady of Guadalupe, Protectress of the Unborn, pray for us! Amen."

Father Paddy Killen strode out of San Fernando Cathedral and crossed West Commerce Street with the confident gait of a man who knew exactly what he had to do.

XVII

"*You* must *tell him!*" the cat spirit spits.

Graciela flinches but gives no ground. "I tell him every day! For weeks now, but he doesn't listen! You know that. You've been begging him for years."

"Ha! He's had years to practice the art of ignoring me. But you had his ear from the day that you walked through the door."

Graciela pads down the stairs, and the cat orbits her in tight semicircular arcs as she moves through the house, sweeping and dusting and tending her altars. Practice and the knowledge that the spirit has no substance in the material world allows her to complete her daily rounds without tripping over her cat-shaped shadow. "Well, he's not listening now," she mutters as she sweeps the last puffs of dust off the porch and props the broom prominently next to the door. Her grandfather taught her that a broom by the door acted as a talisman, a warning to all that the home was clean, purged of any unwholesome medium that might offer comfort and aid to threats from without, spiritual or material. The daily exorcism complete, the sorceress and the great black cat pace the porch like sentries. They begin at opposite ends and cross in the middle, watching, listening, breathing in the air and tasting it. Sifting through for any tang of ill will. The vigil is observed for the hour before sunset and the hour that follows and then repeated around dawn. This was her grandfather's teaching again, that all Powers enter and leave the world through the gap between darkness and light. Nothing can be done to impede their traffic, and only the very arrogant ever try. "It is enough," Grandfather said, "to mark their comings and goings and that they mark ours."

Besides, flesh and bone are what frightens Graciela. She's not afraid of ghosts.

"It's quiet," observes the passing cat.

"It always is," Graciela whispers. "Before it's not."

The screen door creaks . . . Graciela glances back, and Doc is standing there, frozen halfway through the door, as if deciding whether to proceed.

"You two make me nervous!" Doc grumbles. "Looks like the waiting room in a maternity ward out here. Why don't you light somewhere!"

Graciela shrugs. "It will be dark soon."

It's a man-shaped thing that Doc sees, pacing up and down the porch with Graciela, back and forth, back and forth. "What about you, Hank? You a man or a cat?"

"Fuck you, Doc!" the ghost of Hank Williams snaps. "We're just watchin' out for you so maybe you got time to climb out the back window when they kick the door down."

Graciela leans over the rail around the porch to scrutinize the western sky for any remaining blush of color before ducking under Doc's arm and disappearing inside. Doc's still grumbling at Hank.

"When who kicks the door down, Hank? He was a priest, for fuck sake. Not a cop. And it's been damn near a month now and nothing's happened and nothing's going to happen." The ghost rockets across the porch and alights in the rocking chair just as Doc sits down, and the physician very nearly levitates, shivering from the chilling effects of an ectoplasm enema. "Goddamn it, Hank!"

Hank crosses his legs, making himself comfortable in Doc's rocking chair and exposing the intricately tooled top of one cowboy boot. Doc is left to slouch against the opposite rail. "I ain't studyin' on that priest one way or the other, Doc. I'm just sayin' that there ain't no way a feller can keep doin' what you been doin' in one place for as long as you been doin' it without you attract the attention of the law. It was one thing when it was a couple or three girls a month, Doc, but now you're seein' that many in a week. And it ain't just the workin' girls off of the strip anymore, Doc. They're comin' from all over now. Some of 'em bound to have families."

Doc shrugs. "Everybody's got family, Hank."

"I mean family as in good family. Somebody that gives a damn! What if somethin' was to go wrong? One of 'em up and dies on you, like that poor gal Donna."

Doc leans over to wag his finger in the phantom's face. "She was allergic to penicillin, Hank. She had a reaction. Besides, that was before Graciela came along."

"Yeah, that's right, Doc. Before Graciela, who changed everybody and everything around here with a touch of her hand. Without that little gal, there ain't no tellin' where you'd be right now, Doc, and even she says that it's time to go. Time for her and time for you!"

"Excuse, me, Hank, if I'm somewhat suspicious of your sudden

219

conversion to the cult of Graciela! And just exactly where do you suggest we go, if you know so goddamn much?"

"Somewheres else. It don't matter. You've got plenty of cash stashed away in that bag of yours."

"How did you . . . ?"

"You could go anywheres, Doc. Mexico. Or South America. Rio, maybe."

"You need a passport for South America. And what about Marge? She left Graciela and me in charge. She and Dallas won't be back from Padre Island for another week."

Hank shakes his head solemnly. "You ain't got a week, Doc. Can't you feel it?"

"I can't feel anything but a pain in my ass and — "

A car door slammed in the driveway, and the entire porch shook as someone jogged up the steps. Graciela flew through the door primed for battle, but when she got there she found that it was only Manny.

"I just made a pitcher of tea," she offered, and the big man nodded and took his usual seat on the swing.

"You're going to break that thing if you don't lose some weight, Manny," Doc grumbled. "And if you're here to climb up my ass about getting out of town, get in line."

"Damn, Doc. I just got here," Manny complained.

Unseen by Manny, Hank smirks as he surrenders the rocker to Doc and takes his place on the rail.

Doc sat down and flipped the butt of a Camel out into the yard. "Well, I'm just tellin' you before you start. Hell, once Graciela gets going, you'd swear she was a flock of parrots squawking about the same damn thing, over and over. 'Time to go, Doc! Time to go!' Yeah, well, I've already told her and I'm telling you. I'm not going any-fucking-where!"

Graciela appeared with Manny's tea and an unsolicited glass for Doc. Manny winked his thanks as she set it on a table. "But I am, Doc. I just stopped by to say goodbye."

Graciela was instantly in tears. She knew the answer, but she asked anyway. "When?"

"Right now. I'm all loaded up and ready to go."

Manny stood up to catch Graciela as she rushed across the porch. Her cry was muffled as she buried her face in the big man's waist. She couldn't reach her arms around him but she did the best she could. Manny gathered the tiny figure up in the crook of a gigantic brown arm and patted her gently on the top of her head. *"No llores, mija. ¡Por favor, no llores! Todo va bien."*

Hank's still perched on the rail, seething now. "What the hell's the matter with you, Doc? Can't you see the signs? Somethin's comin'. Somethin' bad. Everybody's figured it out but you!"

Doc did his best to ignore the voice and cleared his throat to get Graciela's attention. "You know, you can go if you want to, Graciela. I can get by fine on my own."

Graciela reacted viscerally to the insult. She wrested herself free from Manny and whirled to face Doc, planting her bare feet wide apart and glaring at him, daring him to look her in the eye.

"I'm just sayin'," Doc mumbled, avoiding any further eye-fucking by engaging Manny. "So where you off to, big guy?"

"California, eventually. But first I reckon maybe I'll head south. Mexico. Hell, I'm a Mexican, Doc, and I ain't never been. I got cousins in Saltillo. Reckon I'll look 'em up and get 'em to show

221

me around. See where my people's people come from. Then I'll work my way up through Carlsbad and out to the Grand Canyon. All those places. You know what I heard? I heard they got 'em a motel out there somewhere where you can spend the night in a teepee, Doc! A real teepee like a wild Injun! I got a shoebox full of money out there in the trunk of my Ford, enough that I could bum around for a year or two, if I wanted. All kinds of sights to see up and down the West Coast, Doc. Then, when my money's gone, I'll find me a job drivin' somewhere. You know, Doc, just like we talked about. I hear California's nice this time of year. Hell, California's always nice. At least that's what they say! You sure you don't wanna go?"

The ghost alights noiselessly on the weathered floorboards between Doc and Manny and looks from one man's face to the other as if there is anything left to decide and then . . .

"No, Manny, like I told you, I'm stayin' right here."

. . . twists sideways and spits angrily, any trace of moisture evaporating in thin air along with any vestige of patience or pretense of vigilance. So incensed is the phantom that he doesn't even hear the second vehicle arrive . . .

Graciela spotted the headlights half a mile up the road. She held her breath until the plain white Dodge passed beneath the streetlight at the corner. "Hugo!" She exhaled. The corpulent vice cop presented no threat, she sensed. Manny wasn't taking any chances. He dropped his .38 behind an oleander bush just as Hugo squeezed out of his unmarked car.

"You're all right, Manny." He panted. "I'm still off the clock." He acknowledged Graciela – "Ma'am" – a hint of awe in his tone. "It's Doc I came to see. You got to get out of here, Doc. They're comin'."

"What'd I tell you, goddamn it!" Hank frets, wringing his hands and pacing back and forth behind Doc in a claustrophobic arc.

Doc shook his head in disbelief. "Aw, not you too, Hugo? What is this, some kind of plot y'all cooked up? Who's coming?"

The cop was still bent over pawing at the stitch in his side. "Feds!" he huffed, and then he puffed. "Bureau of narcotics. Big Mike Novak himself!"

Manny whistled. "Time to go, Doc! Graciela!"

The girl was way ahead of him, up the stairs, pattering from room to room, gathering up the meager accumulation of her life with Doc on South Presa Street. Not much. A couple of cotton dresses, a half a dozen pairs of panties, and a brassiere. Even after she'd emptied Doc's chest of drawers into it, the dust-covered suitcase she'd found in the top of Helen-Anne's closet was only a little over half full. Finally, she scooped up Doc's instruments and dropped them in his black bag with a clatter and a snap, and before five minutes had elapsed she was back downstairs handing off the luggage to Manny. Doc had yet to get out of his chair.

"Big Mike who?"

"Michael B. Novak, Doc. The head prosecutor for the western district of Texas."

"But I've been clean for damn near a year now, and Manny –"

Hugo shook his head. "It ain't dope they're after!"

"But you said –"

"I said they got a warrant to search for dope, and search for dope they will, and they'll find some too, by God, if they have to plant it themselves."

"What the hell, Hugo?"

"Look, it's like this, Doc. Yesterday afternoon, just before the end of my shift, I get a call. It's some college-boy junior G-man from the western district. Can I come drop by for a minute on my way home? I try to put him off until tomorrow but he drops Big Mike's name. Says that the prosecutor would consider it a personal favor if I was to show up. What am I supposed to do? I walk across the square and they hustle me up to an office on the fourth floor and, sure enough, Big Mike Novak himself is in there and he sits me down in a cushy chair, a walnut desk the size of a fuckin' aircraft carrier between us. Might as well have been handcuffed to a straight-back chair over in the SAPD. Anyway, Big Mike wants to know did I know anything about a junkie name of Doc. Middle-aged. Well spoken. Some kind of a quack that drifted over from Louisiana way."

Doc was worried now. "And what did you tell him?"

"I lied. Like a rug! To a federal prosecutor! Problem is, I wasn't the only narc that Big Mike talked to and somebody told him plenty. By the time I get to work this morning it's a done deal. Everybody on the squad is invited to a big federal door-bustin'-down party except me. None of this shit makes any kind of sense as far as I can tell, so I call my boy in Judge Fisher's office and he allows how Big Mike's already made the rounds to every judge on the square, state and federal, and been turned down flat by every one of 'em. No probable cause for search and seizure. That is, until he comes across a county judge, *county,* mind you, name of Aguilar, who may or may not have any jurisdiction in a felony case, but Big Mike gets him to sign off on a raid on thirty-four hundred South Presa anyway. Put it together! Big Mike Novak is a bohunk! Catholic! The county judge, Aguilar, is a Meskin! Catholic! Probably Knights of Columbus, the pair of 'em. Somebody's done told them what it is that you do down here, and the self-righteous sons of bitches believe that they've got God on their sides and they're comin'. Maybe tonight, maybe in the morning after it's light, but they're comin', Doc, I guarantee, and you don't want to be here when they do . . . and neither do I!" He excused himself and tipped his hat to Graciela before waddling to his car and backing out of the driveway.

That was Graciela's cue. She stepped forward and took Doc's hand, and the physician snapped out of his torpor. *"¡Vamos!"* she commanded. Doc blinked, well aware that he had lost the battle, but he fired a final volley anyway. "The next girl in trouble who knocks on that door," he offered weakly, "where's she going to go?"

Graciela tugged firmly and Doc knew, despite the slightness of the outstretched arm, that she possessed the strength to guide him to Manny's car if she wanted. "There are girls in trouble everywhere," she said. "You can't help them all."

"I need my hat," Doc grumbled just as Manny appeared behind her, back from loading the Ford. Graciela held on tight.

"Manny, get Doc's hat for him, please. It's hanging on the rack in the kitchen."

When Manny returned, Doc took a last look back through the front door of the Yellow Rose before resolutely accepting his battered Panama from his friend and pulling it down low over his eyes. Just then, yet another car door slammed.

Hank spots him first — a solitary figure unfolding from an unnoticed station wagon parked across School Street. "Priest!" the ghost hisses.

· · ·

Graciela turned to face this new threat, instinctively imposing herself between Doc and the interloper. "Don't let him come near!" she implored Manny, and the big man closed half the distance between himself and the oncoming priest in a couple of loping strides. Then, suddenly, both antagonists stopped, only yards apart.

"H-he's a priest!" Manny stammered, glancing uncertainly over his shoulder at Graciela. "I ain't never hit no priest!"

The devil in Father Killen sensed an opening. "Of course you haven't! Why would you? And what would your mother think if you did?"

"Don't listen to him!" Graciela warned, but the priest already had Manny's attention.

"That's what I thought!" Killen said condescendingly. "You weren't raised to be a miscreant, were you . . . Manny, isn't it?"

"Careful!" the cat coughs, but the Mexican can't hear him. The spirit can only circle the combatants impotently, like a referee without authority.

His own name in the mouth of a priest that he had never seen before was too much for Manny. He glanced over his shoulder again for some sign from Graciela, and the distraction allowed Killen a crucial uncontested step forward. The heel of a hard, heavy black oxford crashed down on Manny's instep, and he collapsed in pain, dropping like a freight elevator until his chin collided with the priest's upthrust head. A second head butt sent the vanquished giant sprawling semiconscious to the ground.

Doc didn't stand a chance. By the time he realized what was happening and stepped protectively in front of Graciela, the intruder was on the porch.

"You must be … Doc!" The priest grunted, putting his full weight into a rib-crushing left hook. Doc dropped instantly but Killen stood him back up with a knee in the groin. "Murderer of innocents!" Uppercut to the chin. "Corrupter of children!" He shunted the helpless physician to one side in a heap. "Well, no more. It all stops here and now!" He snatched Graciela's arm as she rushed to help Doc, but the girl bit him, clamping down hard on the back of his hand. He cursed as he ripped the wounded member free but didn't retaliate. He offered Graciela the other hand instead. "Take it, child! Come with me. I'll take you away from this place. From these people!" Graciela threw herself protectively across Doc's body and muttered a sequence of syllables, low and musical but completely nonsensical to non-Nahuatl speakers: *"Yolistsintlayektli Ooselo, Nekauyo …"* Even Graciela didn't understand what she was saying. She only knew that her grandfather had insisted that she commit the words to memory against a day when every ray of hope had faded. That day had come.

Hank's ghost sputters helplessly over the tangle of humanity. "Get up, Doc!" he screeches, but the physician doesn't respond. He involuntarily shifts between one shape and another, settling into his feline aspect only when the jaguar arrives on the scene to take charge.

Graciela instantly recognizes the newcomer. "Grandfather!" she cries, and the big cat purrs in acknowledgment. Hank follows the older entity's lead, and the two cat-shaped spirits take up defensive positions flanking Graciela and Doc.

Killen saw no shadow or shade of either man or beast. Manny was sprawled behind him and Doc lay crumpled before him and nothing now stood between the priest and the miracle he prized.

His miracle! The priest had eyes only for the Mexican girl, and he never saw Big Tiff coming.

Doc did. He had just managed to struggle up to one knee, but he nearly laughed out loud when he spotted the transvestite pelting up the sidewalk in pedal pushers and an undershirt. Then he recognized the shiny nickel-plated barrel of a Saturday night special, and the hint of a smile vanished. "Gun!" he hollered as Tiff charged the priest like a linebacker zeroing in on a quarterback. The scene unfolding before him was sickeningly familiar. He'd seen it before, beamed in from Dallas, a flickering image on a black-and-white twelve-inch screen. But his was live and in living color and happening right before his eyes, and Doc knew that if he didn't do something, nobody would. "Not this time, you son of a bitch!" he swore. He stepped in front of the priest and turned to face Big Tiff just as the first of eight sharp, rapid pops rang in his ears.

Doc reckoned that none of the bullets had found its mark until he tasted a pungent whiff of gunpowder and seared flesh, stronger than any he had ever known. A halting heartbeat later, a second nauseatingly familiar and even more pungent composite stench pervaded his senses, blood and bile and feces intermingled and spilling from a broken bowel. He felt no pain whatsoever even as his legs betrayed him for the second time in as many minutes, folding beneath him at awkward angles and dumping him to the rough pine boards. Only when Graciela screamed his name did Doc finally understand.

For an instant Big Tiff just stood there, mouth agape, the empty pistol still smoking in his hand. Then he began to wail. "No-o-o-o! I'm sorry, Doc! I didn't mean you! It's that mother-fucker—" but he was cut off by a perfectly executed hook from his blind side, and Father Killen thanked the Lord Jesus, out loud, for delivering him from certain death as he stepped over what he was sure was the last soldier of Satan that stood in the path of the righteous.

The shots had jolted Manny back to consciousness, but it was an eternity of seconds before he was able to gain his feet and climb the steps to the porch. When he finally got there, he found Doc laid low and Graciela covered in blood and being manhandled by the same wild-eyed priest who had knocked him out cold.

"Come, child! It's time for us to go now!" Killen exhorted Graciela, clamping both of his hands around a tiny, doll-like arm and standing her up. When he turned, intent on dragging his captive away to his car, he found a great hulking obstacle in his path.

"She ain't goin' nowhere with you, *pendejo!*"

Nothing that Killen had learned from Father Walsh could have prepared him for the onslaught. The back side of a ham-size hand smashed into the side of his head, wrenching it sideways with such force that his body was forced to follow. Unable to maintain his grip on Graciela any longer, he tried to refocus on his assailant. He had beaten him once. He could do it again. *In through your nose; out through your mouth . . .* But no, the giant hand closed in a semicircle around his throat, and his head slammed into the wall, the clapboard completing the vise and grating at the exposed skin on the backs of his arms as he was hoisted a full foot above the floor. The priest hung there, legs kicking, arms flailing impotently, as Manny effortlessly held him in place. The very life in him was draining away and he tried to scream. He tried to pray. But it was no use. He could only watch his own agony reflected in the eyes of . . .

. . . *a bear! A great brown bear stares back at the priest, dispassionately watching him die. Nothing personal. He is merely prey, a single installment toward a daily quota of caloric intake. This isn't so bad; unexpected, but not bad . . . but where's . . . Jesus? He isn't here, is He? For that matter there is nothing even vaguely human-shaped here, only the bear and a cat . . . no, two cats. One black and one great one, nearly as large as the bear and covered in dark jungle-foliage-shaped spots . . . watching and waiting for whatever the bear leaves behind . . . but listen! Do you hear her? Do you hear her singing? I knew it! I knew she would come! It's an angel! . . .*

"Manny! Stop it!" Graciela shrieked, and when he didn't respond she switched to Spanish and pounded on his back with both of her fists. *"¡Basta, por favor! ¡Dejarlo ir!"*

This time Manny did as he was told and let Killen drop to the floor, where he crawled across the porch on his hands and knees, semiconscious and retching, right into the path of Hugo Ackerman.

Hugo had arrived back on the scene, even more out of breath than before, his ludicrously tiny snub-nosed revolver gripped in one chubby hand, his sweat-soaked handkerchief held in the other. "What the hell is going on around here?" he wondered out loud only half rhetorically as he tried to make some kind of sense of the battleground. Big Tiff was out cold at his feet, still clinging to the gun. Hugo kicked it out of his grasp. Killen made one last halfhearted attempt to slither away down the steps on his belly, but a worn brogan backed up by three hundred pounds held him gently but firmly where he was. "Not so fast, Padre!" the cop warned the priest. "Stay right where you are." Hugo's eyes followed the blood to where Manny and Graciela hovered over a familiar supine figure.

"Doc?" When he was a step closer he realized Doc wasn't going to answer. He waved his pistol at the priest. "Over there where I can see you!" he ordered, and, still crawling on all fours, Killen complied. "Who did this, Manny? How bad is he?"

"Bad enough!" said the big man. "Fuckin' Tiff." He craned his neck, vainly attempting to see around Hugo. "You alone?"

"Not for long! I heard the 'shots fired' call on my radio and I was only a couple of blocks away, but every cop on the south side's gonna be here in ten minutes. Anyway, I guess that doesn't matter now. I better call an ambulance."

"No!" Doc croaked.

Graciela had believed he was dead, and she burst into tears. "Don't try to talk!" she begged. "Help is coming – "

"No! I can't! I won't! They'll patch me up just so they can lock me up."

Graciela looked up at Hugo. The cop nodded sadly. "No doubt. Big Mike means business."

Disembodied amber eyes are suspended in the air over Graciela's left shoulder. A black cat slowly comes into diffuse focus, but it's Hank's voice in Doc's ear.

"Trust me, Doc. If you never listened to me once in your life, hear me when I'm talkin' to you now. They're comin' and this here is the last place on earth that you want to be caught dead or alive. Mark my words. If you die here, your soul will stumble up and down this strip until the end of time. Get up, Doc! If it's the last thing you ever do, get up and run like hell!"

• • •

"I hear you, Hank," Doc affirmed. He took a deep, slow breath. A little pop and a gurgling sound. Not good. At least one hole in his left lung. And he knew he was gut-shot. Crazy fucking Tiff had emptied the pistol. God knew how many little-bitty bullets he had rattling around in him. He was probably fucked in any case, but one thing he knew for sure was that there wasn't a goddamn thing anybody at the Robert B. Green Memorial Hospital emergency room could do for him.

"Hugo, if Manny here was to get me to the car, and we could, uh, well, manage to . . ."

Graciela shook her head and muttered, "No! No! You can't," but Manny had already disappeared into the boarding house once again. With no small amount of effort, Doc raised a bloody finger to his own lips to seal hers.

The cop shrugged. "Doc, I don't think there's any way in hell you'll get a mile down the road, but it won't be me that's standin' in your way. And as for these two . . ." He untangled a pair of handcuffs from his belt and ungently ratcheted one end to Big Tiff's wrist. The hustler regained consciousness as he was being dragged across the porch to where Father Killen cowered.

"Goddamn, Hugo! That shit hurts!"

"They're handcuffs, asshole, they're supposed to hurt." Hugo produced a second pair of cuffs and completed the circle, handcuffing the transvestite and the priest together, wrists to wrists and back to back. Killen, realizing that Hugo was a cop, was suddenly alert and bristling with righteous indignation.

"What is the meaning of this?" he demanded.

"Shut up!" Big Tiff warned the priest in a whisper like a rattlesnake rattling.

Doc was struggling to keep Graciela in focus.

"Listen to me, Graciela. I need you to help me. I need you to get me out of here before the police come."

Graciela's eyes widened with panic, but Doc shook that off.

"You can do this!"

"You're crazy! I can't—"

"Yes, you can! Just get me in that car, and once we're on the road you can say whatever it is you say and do whatever it is you do and I'll be good as new. I know it! I need a miracle, darlin'. It's the only chance I've got. That we've got. Anyway, if we hang around here until the *federales* show up, then you're on a plane back to Mexico and I'm going to the penitentiary. Our one and only hope is to get while the gettin's good and take care of each other the way we always have."

"Now you're talkin'!" agrees Hank's voice in Doc's ear. Only a glance is exchanged between the cat and Graciela.

Killen continued to plead his case to Hugo.

"Officer, isn't it obvious to you by now that you've arrested the wrong man? I am Father Padraig Killen, the pastor of . . . *My God! Aaaagh!"*

Pain that the priest had never imagined in his worst night-mares cut the tirade short. Big Tiff had suddenly raised both of his powerful arms above his head and pulled forward with all of his rage and all of his might and he didn't stop pulling until he heard a pop, louder than the pistol shots, as both of the priest's shoulders separated from their sockets. He gave the handcuffs one last tug for good measure.

"I *said* . . . shut up, bitch!"

Graciela was resolved by the time Manny returned with one of Marge's old army blankets, and not a moment too soon because Doc was fading fast. He continued talking to Graciela and Manny while they bundled him up, but his sentences began to become disconnected and jumbled, and even his own voice sounded dis-tant and thin.

. . .

233

. . . big, powerful arms surround Doc and lift him up and the feeling is familiar and reassuring. His head lolls skyward as he's carried down the steps, and he traces the Big Dipper hanging by its bejeweled handle from an unseen hook on the ceiling of the world. He rolls his eyes back, almost inside of his head, and finds he can only just make out the inverted image of the black cat padding along on Manny's left as they move across the yard. With a supreme effort he forces his chin to his chest and peers the other way to find the jaguar defending their right.

Graciela led the way. She opened the rear passenger door and slid across the seat to the other side to receive Doc's head in her lap. Her ears popped violently as the door slammed shut and Manny settled in behind the wheel.

The V-8 rumbled to life, gears gnashing, crushed limestone crackling beneath vulcanized rubber as the vehicle lurched into reverse and swung around to aim itself south. Doc became aware of the shotgun rider only when he spoke.

"Hang in there, Doc." Hank promises, "Not much longer now." And Doc believes him.

Graciela frantically fished around in Doc's bag. For what? she wondered. She had the contents of the satchel memorized by now. There was no blessed relic there, no alchemist's remedy for man's brutality to man hidden among the tangle of stainless steel and cotton gauze. She ripped long strips of fabric from the hem of her dress and bundled them into pressure bandages the way she'd been taught, but the blood seemed to be coming from everywhere, life seeping out of Doc from so many places at once that she didn't know where to begin. She prayed out loud in three different languages. She admonished Doc, begged and pleaded for him to fight for his own life, but the physician could barely hear her pleadings, lost as they were in crackling sibilance like the fading signal of a radio station left far behind on the highway.

Hank's coming in loud and clear. "Almost there, buddy! Just hang on until we're past the city limits."

"The city limits?"

"Yeah, then we'll be free."

"Free? Free from what?"

"Toil and trouble! This veil of tears! Free to go on to a better place. Or not. Leastways, we won't have to hang around here no more."

Doc looks up at Graciela. Even her face is fading now, but he knows she is crying because he can taste her tears.

"Graciela!" *he calls, or at least he thinks he's talking, but Hank shakes his head.*

"She can't hear you, Doc. You're past that now."

"You hear me well enough."

"I tried to tell you, Doc, must've been a thousand times I tried. You don't have to talk for me to hear you."

"I just want to tell her that it's okay . . . that she can't . . . She can't help me, can she?"

Hank sighs grimly. "She already has, Doc. She wrestled that monkey off your back. I guess it's a one-miracle-to-a-customer kind of deal."

"That makes sense," *Doc agrees.* "Well, I guess that's it then."

"Now, hold your horses there, Doc," *cautions the ghost of Hank Williams, turning to face forward and peering out through the windshield into the thickening darkness.* "We ain't quite there yet. I'll let you know when it's time."

"You do that, Hank. I'll be . . . right here."

Doc can't make out Graciela's features anymore, but he can feel her, her warmth and her unyielding empathy surrounding him as she abandons any pretense of sacrament or procedure and simply cradles his head lovingly in her lap.

Doc silently concurs. "That's right, darlin'. Let me go now. Nobody can help from here on out except Ol' Hank here. He's the only one of us that's been down this road before."

The occupant of the front passenger seat, an impossibly thin, sad young man, turns to acknowledge Graciela with a finger and a thumb on the brim of his Stetson, and for the first time Graciela sees Hank the way Doc does.

The speed limit was forty miles an hour on the last stretch of South Presa Street before it lost itself in the Corpus Christi Highway, and it took every bit of discipline that Manny could muster to rein the big Ford in. The big man prided himself on never having lost a load of contraband to a routine traffic stop and he knew that creeping along was every bit as likely to attract the attention of the police as a heavy foot on the accelerator. He tried his best to keep the needle on the speedometer somewhere between thirty-five and thirty-eight, but from time to time he looked down to find he was pushing fifty. He caught Graciela's eye in the rearview mirror as they passed beneath a streetlight. "How's he doing?" he asked, but he already knew. He'd seen enough cuttings and shootings to know a mortal wound when he saw one, but for Graciela's sake, Manny didn't say so out loud.

Graciela watched helplessly while Doc's face grew wan and tiny glistening drops of sweat, unnaturally cold to the touch, appeared on his forehead. His eyes were closed now but his upper lip twitched, and she thought he was trying to say something, so she bent close to listen. There was only a pitiful wheeze, like a broken accordion, from somewhere deep in his chest.

"'Leaving San Antonio,'" Manny read as they passed the green-and-white reflecting sign on the side of the road. "Now we can make some time."

As the big Ford rumbled into passing gear and bounded ahead down the highway, Doc stirred in Graciela's arms and then mumbled something; she was sure of it this time.

"Manny, the lights!" she commanded, and the big man complied, reaching over his head for the switch and calling over his shoulder, "You okay, Doc?"

The yellowish light revealed that Doc's eyes were wide open but he wasn't looking at Manny or even Graciela.

"Hank?"

"Yeah, Doc," the ghost answers.

"Will it hurt?"

The ghost turns to hang a skeletal elbow draped in appliquéd gabardine over the back of his seat and grins.

"How the hell would I know, Doc? I was drunker than Cooter Brown when I passed."

Graciela only heard the question. Then, as she watched, the corner of Doc's mouth twitched. A grimace? No! It was a smile, curling up one corner of his mouth and then the other before rolling up his face in a wave, erasing every sign of wear and tear except for the laughlines around his eyes.

"Cooter Brown!" Doc chuckled and coughed and then he was gone.

• • •

237

Doc's standing in the middle of the loneliest stretch of highway in the universe but he's not alone. Hank's there too, about ten yards ahead of him, silently watching as Manny's headlights fade into the south Texas night. Or is it West Virginia?

"Where the hell are we, Hank?"

"Nowhere, Doc. We got a little ways to travel yet before we get somewhere."

"Well, I hope it's not far because I'm tired."

"Far? Naw, it ain't far. At least, it don't matter now. Near or far. Short or long. We'll be there directly and that won't be a moment too soon or too late. The only thing that's important is that we're goin' now and nothin' can stand in our way."

"We? You're goin' too?"

"Well, sure, Doc. What'd you reckon I've been waitin' on all these years? I can't go nowhere without you. But it's all over now and I don't have to wait around anymore and neither do you."

Doc ponders that. Now that it's all over, Doc and Hank are headed for someplace neither near nor far and it doesn't matter when or if they get there, only that they're free to go. Makes perfect sense, Doc reckons.

"So which way do we go, Hank?"

"Oh, so you're followin' me around now?"

Doc shrugs and grins.

Hank turns and begins walking down the highway, cocking a thumb behind him in the direction from which they had come.

"Well, not that way."

EPILOGUE

The young girl sat at a table on the narrow walkway in front of a tiny restaurant in Angangueo, Michoacán, Mexico, stirring instant coffee from a jar into a mug of hot milk. She was dark-skinned and diminutive with features more Indian than European and would have blended right in with the local population had it not been for her traveling companion.

When the pair had first arrived, word had spread quickly that there was a giant in town, the biggest man that anyone in the village had ever seen. Most of the gringos that came every winter for the butterflies were taller than any of the locals, but this man dwarfed them all, and what was more, he was Mexican, though he spoke Spanish with a strange accent. *"¡El gigante Norteño!"* the locals whispered as they passed the restaurant by contrived routes to sneak surreptitious peeks at the travelers.

Graciela and Manny had come for the butterflies as well. All of her life, Graciela had heard stories of the migration of the *mariposas monarca,* the beautiful monarch butterflies, and the creatures fascinated her. Each fall a Methuselah generation of the normally short-lived insects emerge from their chrysalises and make the epic journey from Canada down through the central United States until finally they reach the border between the states of Michoacán and Mexico. There they hibernate for the winter, hanging in dense clusters, their wings filling the air with a sound like whispering angels. In the spring they awake and mate and begin the return journey north. It will take four generations for the butterflies to reach home, and then the cycle begins again.

Graciela had come to witness this miracle firsthand. On their first day in town, she and Manny had hired a local guide to take them out to the forest. She had stood barefoot on the cool forest floor and quieted her mind and listened and now she understood that her affinity for the butterflies was perfectly natural. Graciela and the monarchs had the transformative power of a long and arduous journey in common.

When Graciela and Manny had left San Antonio that night, nine months before, they'd run south as hard as they could go until they were certain that they weren't being pursued. Then, just south of Beeville, they left the highway and followed one randomly chosen gravel road until it intersected with another and then continued to a dead end in a dry creek bed. There they laid Doc to rest, burying his body under a cairn of smooth white stones. They held a service of sorts, Graciela covering all the spiritual bases as best she could. Big tears rolled down Manny's cheeks, but Graciela didn't cry, and it was she who prompted a reluctant Manny when it was time to go. She knew that they were leaving behind no part of the man she loved. Her protector. Her teacher. She had learned her lessons and learned them well, better probably than Doc had ever intended. But for better or for worse, Graciela had assimilated no small dose of the best parts of the physician: the dexterity, the courage, and, most important,

240

the compassion at his very core that no amount of shame and degradation could kill.

She had also inherited his instruments. Manny had suggested that they leave them in the creek bed with Doc, but Graciela refused. As they continued on their journey south the black bag was always at her side. During stops along the road, she inventoried and organized its contents, weighing each implement in her hand, assaying it, closing her eyes and listening as it spoke to her in Doc's resonant, reassuring tones. The scalpel counseled steadiness; the hemostats and retractors restraint. Even the curettage revealed its secrets to her, though not without regret, its previous master having specifically forbidden Graciela to even touch it.

They crossed the border at Brownsville unmolested early in the morning of the second day, and by suppertime they were climbing the first march of the Sierra Madre Mountains behind Monterrey. They didn't stop until they reached Saltillo, where they spent the afternoon with Manny's cousins before continuing south.

There was no one left alive in Dolores Hidalgo that Graciela wanted to see but they visited the cemetery on the outskirts of town in the middle of the night and it was there that Graciela saw the jaguar spirit for the last time, standing on her grandfather's grave.

In the old man's voice the spirit speaks a solitary phrase: ¡Siga las mariposas! *Then he turns and pads silently away, melting into the chaparral.*

And Graciela instantly knew what to do. Where to go.

She had been six or seven when the migrating monarch butterflies had passed through Dolores for the first time in her memory. Grandfather had said that they were bound for Michoacán, a place of tall trees on the other side of the mountains, and that they would spend the winter there. She had cried the day that she awoke to find that the *monarcas* were gone, but the old *curandero* had reassured her that in the springtime they would come again on their journey back north.

Within a week of arriving in Angangueo, Manny and Graciela had established a routine that began with coffee and a bite in the little restaurant followed by the morning pilgrimage to the forest. On the drive out they would discuss plans for their own migration back to the border, and Manny would express his misgivings in vain.

"Not San Antonio!" Manny pleaded. "Not South Presa Street!"

Graciela smiled sympathetically but was insistent. "We will go where we are needed. We will stay until it's time to go."

Manny had taken to remaining in the car and reading his paper while Graciela entered the forest alone. He reckoned that only Graciela knew what it was she was listening for and when she heard it she would let him know. When she did he would follow her, or, more accurately, he would drive her wherever she wanted to go and together they would travel from town to town. That was the plan, never staying in any one place for too long, and picking up where Doc had left off.

Or at least Graciela would. She knew the procedure. She'd watched and she'd listened and she knew what to do when a girl was in trouble and no good could come of her bringing an innocent life into an unkind corner of the world.

Graciela never tired of standing beneath the butterflies as they huddled together in living curtains suspended from the towering fir trees, and she was listening and she was watching with every fiber of her being, but truth be told, there was nothing hidden there, no secret signal encrypted in the whispering of the wings. She knew what she was waiting for. Her grandfather had told her.

"Siga las mariposas."

Follow the butterflies.

A single insect drops from a branch far above, and then another, their half-opened wings resembling broken parasols as they plummet to earth. They save themselves only at the very last instant, spiraling upward toward the sunlight filtering through the treetops. Other daredevils follow and soon it's raining butterflies, a deluge of orange and black that never quite reaches the ground.

Manny startled awake as the car door slammed shut and he found Graciela in the passenger seat, her eyes trained straight ahead down the road.

"Time to go," she said softly, and the big Mexican started the car.

ACKNOWLEDGMENTS

Anton Mueller for setting me on the path.

Jenna Johnson for guiding me home.

Jackson Browne and Dianna Cohen for providing a place to start.

Siobhan Kennedy for Catholic insight (forgive her, Lord, for she knew not what she did).

Alice Randall for inventing the very notion of my name on the cover of a book.

Allison and John Henry for thinking I'm cool no matter what.